SHE'S THE ONE

WHO WON'T BEHAVE

S. R. CRONIN

To all the women who know, deep in their hearts, that they can do anything, despite overwhelming evidence to the contrary.

Warning: You Are About to Enter Ilari

Welcome to the thirteenth century in a universe almost identical to your own. The one major difference here is the existence of *Ilari.*

Ilari (el ARE ee) is a small hidden coalition of principalities in far eastern Europe. It has never been conquered thanks to its natural protection and the magic of its people. The lack of outside influence means that much will be new to you. But fear not, you have tools to help.

A map of *Ilari* is located at the front and back of this book. The back also has a description of the twelve nichnas (tiny principalities) that comprise *Ilari.*

Ilarians do not use any variation of the Roman calendar, as Rome never invaded their realm. Each chapter starts with a picture of the Ilarian calendar and the darkened area shows when that chapter takes place. Details about the Ilarian calendar are at the back of the book along with definitions for unique Ilarian words. On the last page, you will find a list of the characters you will meet.

All of this information can be downloaded and printed at https://troublesome7sisters.xyz/.

Ilarians of the 1200s have some contact with the outside even though legend says interaction with others used to be rarer. Ilarian scholars know facts about world history and the current events beyond their borders. What they know matches what you know, of course, because the world outside of Ilari is like the one in which we live.

However, the world inside is filled with surprises.

Enjoy your visit!

The Map of Ilari

The Year of Immense Concern

~ 1 ~

A Different Sort of Spring

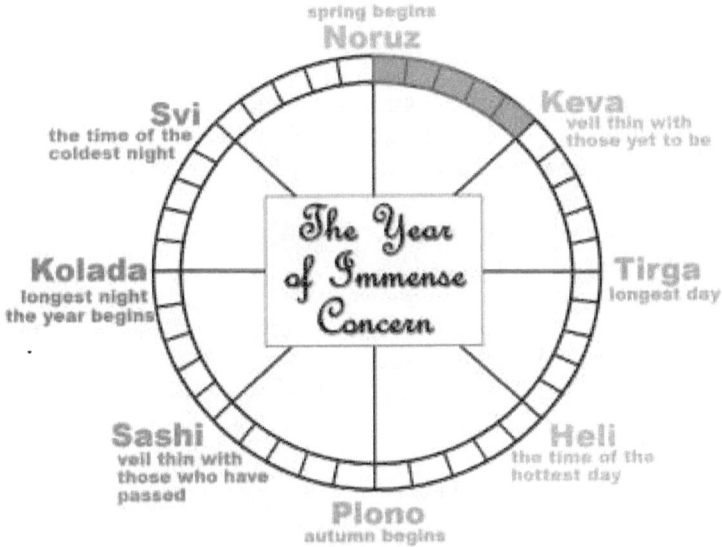

"What's your name?"

I knew every boy who went to my school and the smiling young man asking the question was not one of them. He'd joined our circle of tidzys after the others arrived, standing around the fire with us as we sought partners for the holiday celebration. He'd already introduced himself to several young women. Whatever he murmured incited giggles and a few unmistakable wiggles as well.

When he approached me, these women turned their wide eyes away from his face to give me a narrowed-eye stare of warning. I didn't understand why. His lighter hair and tanned country physique weren't *that* special, although he did have the confidence that makes everyone seem more attractive. And enough indifference to make a young woman willing to do much to impress him.

I didn't play games like that.

My first instinct was to make up a ridiculous name. Duck Piss came to mind. Then I decided the name my family had stuck me with was probably ridiculous enough.

"Gypsum. My name is Gypsum."

"Isn't that some ugly grey rock?" he asked.

"Yup. It was going to be that or Duck Piss, so I guess I lucked out."

I turned away from him and focused my gaze on several attractive men crouching in front of the fire, sharing laughter and ale. As I said, I don't like stupid games or the men who play them.

"My name is Sheep Scump. Nice to meet you."

I turned back. "Well, at least you play along."

"Oh, I play along very well."

Really?

"So, what are you doing here? You got tired of playing with the tidzys over at your school?"

"No. My school got tired of me. Or rather they grew tired of my attempts at humor and asked me to seek education elsewhere. I start classes here after the holiday."

I don't know why I asked the next question.

"Do your parents know?"

He winced.

"They barely knew which school I was at then."

"Oh. What did you do to get kicked out?"

He slipped an arm around my waist and in one slick move he turned the two of us away from the fire.

"I've got a jug of particularly fine red dinner wine waiting in my saddle bag. I hoped I'd find someone worth sharing it with. Would you care to walk over to the stables while I tell you of my horrendous crimes?"

I liked the feel of him. His smell. Okay, I even liked the undercurrent of hurt under his bravado. And I liked the promise of something better to drink than the cheap ale being handed out around the fire.

"Sure. Let's walk, talk, and see where this goes."

He ran his hand up my side and gave my breast a friendly squeeze. I didn't have much to offer in that area, but he didn't seem to care.

I put my hand on his butt and squeezed back.

We both knew exactly where this was going.

We rode together on his horse to another part of Pilk. His old school wasn't far from mine and he took me to the small room he shared with three other students who'd left for the holiday. We drank and had sex the way strangers do -- cautiously, each taking our pleasure while guessing what would please the other. It ended well enough and the rest of the wine tasted even better as we lay together and talked.

Curled up naked beside him on his lumpy bed, I learned of the ill-advised pranks that forced him to change schools. Stupid things. I thought his school overreacted until I learned his closest friend received no punishment at all.

"They decided I had to be the bad influence. Best to get rid of me, you know? Probably shouldn't have let me in to begin with…"

"Because your name is Sheep Scump?" Despite my joke, I sat up, indignant for him.

He sat up as well, scooted next to me, and wrapped a blanket around both of our shoulders.

"No. Because my friend has a father who teaches there. They look out for their own."

Maybe this wasn't the time to tell him my father taught also.

"Your parents weren't inclined to intervene on your behalf?" I saw the displeasure on his face before I finished the sentence. "Wait. I remember. They don't care that you're in school."

"Oh, they care; they just don't care which one. Anything that keeps me from herding goats pisses them off."

I only knew one place in Ilari where goat herding was common. I scooted away from him without thinking.

"*You're* an Edser?"

"Yes." He met my gaze with a look saying *you want to make something of it?*

I didn't. Edsers were known for being cranky, intolerant, and ignorant. So far Sheep Scump had only shown signs of crankiness. I didn't want to encourage it.

3

"So. You're an unusual Edser who wants an education."

"I thought I did. And what are you? The cherished daughter of a ..."

I interrupted him. "Don't go there. I'm not a cherished anything. I'm the sixth daughter of wheat farmers, and I'm the child both parents wish had never been born."

My eyes met his. *Top that* they said.

Spring sauntered into Pilk that year with an abundance of hyacinths. A whole garden of them bloomed outside of Sheep Scump's bedroom and their scent wafted through my dreams when I lay with him. We slept together any night his roommates were gone. They stayed elsewhere often, and I supposed he asked them to.

As we got more comfortable, we teased each other. He enjoyed playfulness and so did I, and our sex got less cautious and more fun. Our time afterward improved too. We often stayed up half the night, laughing at ourselves and everyone else. In between, we shared our worst moments and our deepest hurts and we laughed at them too, all while surrounded by the soft smell of flowers. I'd never had a friend like him, much less one I could pruck.

Yet others hardly noticed the hyacinths. That spring, people avoided looking around, deep in their worries. What was wrong with them?

More Svadlu appeared and more officers strutted around in their yellow capes, filled with self-importance. Sheep Scump saw the changes too, and they baffled him. We both asked others what had happened but our friends at school knew nothing.

Knowing I preferred to study people instead of things, I mostly took classes in Ilari's history and government. I had a history teacher I liked, and one afternoon I visited her office.

"Why is everyone acting so scared lately?" It couldn't hurt to ask. Maybe she knew.

Her eyes widened in surprise and she put a finger to her lips as she gestured me into a chair in her office. She pulled the curtain shut, leaving us in a tiny enclosure lit by a single candle.

"The Svadlu came to us for information," she said in a low voice. "We're not supposed to talk about it, but I'm not going lie to anyone who asks me. Ilari could be invaded soon by those who mean us ill-will."

"What? That's horrible. Why would people do that to us?"

"Come now, you've paid more attention in my class. Elsewhere throughout history others often took over lands that weren't theirs. Ilarians don't understand it, but it appears to have been common."

"Then why has no one done this to us before?"

She smiled and I knew I'd asked the perfect question.

"Well, that's the subject of much discussion in my field. Many propose physical reasons for our safety. Mountains on one side and two large rivers, a lake, and a marsh do make entry difficult. Certainly, that plays a role."

"What else does?"

Another pleased smile.

"The more religious credit the Goddess." Her scrunched face told me she disagreed. "The more sensible think the Velka in the forest once wielded stronger magic and kept all but the occasional traveler or merchant from crossing our borders. Others go as far as believing that only the well-meaning could enter. There could be truth to their theories. The Velka still do unexplainable things."

I didn't know how to respond. My own mother hated these women of the forest, so I hadn't exactly been raised to be unbiased about them. I had trouble believing they could do something as impressive as protecting the entire realm.

My teacher shrugged and gave me a little laugh. "But of course, I study people, so I think people have kept us safe. The people in other lands that is."

She leaned forward in her chair and watched me to see if I understood her. I did.

"You invade places you covet, because you want what they've got," I said.

"Exactly! And others don't know enough about us to come after us."

"So what's changed?"

"There's a mountainous land far to the northeast, with fierce people doing something quite unique. They don't care what you've got. They invade everybody, and we're in their path. The only question is how long it will take them to get here."

Well, that sounded serious.

"Later today, after you've thought about this, I know you'll want to warn everyone you know. But please don't, Gypsum. It won't do any good. You'll sound crazy and I could lose my job for telling a student this information. If you wait, everyone will know soon enough. Okay?"

She stood and pulled back her curtain, her trust in me showing on her face. What could I say?

"Of course. I promise."

She was right about one thing. I didn't need more people thinking I was strange.

I walked back to the room I shared with other students and gathered up thread and supplies to occupy me all day. Then I walked until I found a sunny spot to sit.

Sewing had always calmed me. I'd done most of the mending for my family when I lived at home and it was the one activity that earned me any respect. What a shame this talent wasn't considered worthy of advanced study, like art or music or teaching.

Now I did needlepoint for fun, and crocheted sometimes too, although others usually found my results too disorderly. Tatting was my favorite. The beautiful bits of knotted lace grew in whatever wild patterns suited my mood, and they always came out beautiful to anyone's eye.

Today I took threads in shades of green. Green like the Velka, whom many referred to as green witches because of their talents with plants. We didn't talk about them much at my house, of course, although I got the vague impression my mother's unexplained dislike of them had something to do with me. Maybe I'd work up the nerve to ask her about it. Someday.

I sat cross-legged on the ground in my day dress, cursing the confinement of my clothes. I'd have been far more comfortable in my night shift or even just wearing my breast band and the short breeches I put on under my skirts. I thought of how soothing the sun would feel on my bare skin and wondered why my world denied me such a simple pleasure.

My fingers flew as I made the familiar knots in the thick thread. The voices in my head stopped complaining as I worked, and I felt my shoulders relax. Good. I knew I put myself into each thing I created, and I wanted to infuse this green lace with all the calm I could. Then I'd fasten pieces onto each dress I owned.

Maybe over the next several days, they could wash the image of these horrible invaders from my mind.

I returned late in the day, too late to be fed with the other girls. The older woman who looked after us had put aside bread, cheese, and dried fruit for me so I wouldn't go to bed hungry. She was good about such things. As I chewed on the thick bread, wishing I had ale to wash it down, I studied my afternoon's work. I'd made more leaves than I'd intended.

I nibbled on the hard cheese when a messenger came to the door and asked for me. Most of the women I lived with got frequent messages from their families, but mine wasted no such money. If they paid someone to speak their words, those words had to be important.

"Gypsum Yemi Glonti?" he inquired.

My full name made me cringe. Even as a small child I knew my middle name screamed out to the world that I differed from my sisters and would never be one of them. Not really.

"Yes?"

He moved his left hand up in front of his face to indicate he donned the mask of the person for whom he spoke.

"We don't know your plans, daughter, because you have not shared them with us, but we beseech you to join the rest of your family for the celebration of Keva."

Oh Heli. I'd been looking forward to that celebration with Sheep Scump.

The messenger studied my face, then continued.

"Your oldest sister Ryalgar has chosen to leave the family and join the Velka."

What?! My mother must be horrified. For a heartbeat, I felt sorry for the woman.

"Custom decrees that when your sister enters the forest her family accompanies her, decked out in leaves, flowers, and other symbols of nature. We, we find this difficult enough. Please, come lend your support."

I wondered if my father or my mother had created this message. It was hard to tell. Neither stumbled over their words, usually, and I couldn't recall either of them ever saying "please" to me. And this was more enthusiasm for my presence than I could remember.

"Did they pay you to bring a message back?" They knew I couldn't afford to respond with the little stipend they gave me.

He hastily moved his right hand down in front of his face to indicate he spoke as himself.

"They did. They instructed me not to leave until I had one."

Should I go home for Keva? Ryalgar's decision would move all my sisters up in Mother's expectations for marriage and no one would be happy. Sure, we all loved each other but that didn't mean we understood or even liked each other. Somedays, I didn't like any of them.

I looked at the pile of green lace leaves I'd spent the afternoon making. They oozed serenity. Could I put them all on a single dress?

"I'm to be decked out in leaves and flowers?" I repeated aloud.

He nodded, unsure of the etiquette in responding.

I could cover the tatted leaves with green wood spurge blossoms so they'd look more natural. Maybe I'd made enough to keep everyone calm. I'd go, and I'd put all these leaves on my dress and hope for the best.

~ 2 ~

A Truth, a Disappearance, and a Plan

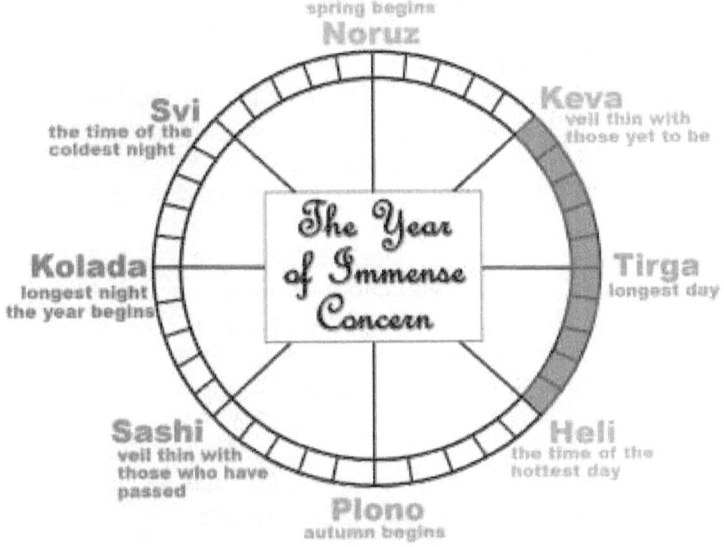

I assumed Ryalgar's decision to join the Velka came from some massive spat with my mother. After all, nothing would piss my mother off more. But no. The evening I arrived at the farm, my sisters told me of Ryalgar's rejection by her lover, a genuine prince from Pilk.

I had trouble believing Ryalgar would run away and live with a bunch of old women because a man dumped her. Prince or not, she had more sense than that. I confronted her the next morning when we met in the kitchen before the others woke.

"The world is full of men," I said as I stoked the fire, encouraging the little flames to warm the chilly room. "They make up half the population." I stopped stoking and looked at her. "What gives?"

She sat sipping breakfast wine, her face half-hidden beneath her uncombed thick dark hair. She smiled at the mention of him.

"This one is special, Gypsum. He understands me. And, well, don't tell anyone, but I'll be able to see him once I'm a Velka."

I gave her a grin of appreciation.

"Well, that's better, at least. You're sure he's worth something this drastic?"

"Yes, but I'm not doing this because of him. The Velka are going to train me. I'll learn their ways."

"Wait. You *want* to be a witch?"

"I want to be a person who lives on her own and does what she wants and knows a surprising number of things, some of which involve magic. Does that sound so bad?"

No, it didn't. But that kind of freedom didn't exist .... not really ...

"What makes you think you can trust these women? What if once you're there they, I don't know, chain you up in their kitchen and make you scrub pots for the rest of your life?"

She laughed, tossing all that dark curly hair out of her face. "I guess that could happen, but I don't think it will. I've got someone on the inside looking out for me. Someone I didn't even know existed."

Panic crossed her face as she finished the sentence. She'd spoken of something she'd meant to keep quiet about.

"Who?"

She exhaled, probably considering a lie and thinking the better of it.

"I guess you're entitled to know," she said. "Perhaps more than anyone." She took another sip of her citrusy breakfast wine as she chose her words. "Our grandmother, mine and yours, didn't die years ago like we were told. She lives with the Velka."

I felt my insides get cold, the way they did when anyone mentioned the odd circumstances that had brought me into this family.

"So my grandmother was alive when I was born?"

"It looks like it," Ryalgar said. "I'm told she joined the Velka a year earlier. Soon after her husband died."

"You're saying that when my mother got pregnant by a man she refused to name, and tended to her needs with only the help of two well-meaning but useless brothers, her own mother wasn't dead? Her mom could have been there helping her, if she hadn't been off playing witch instead?"

"I guess ..."

"So when my mother died and left me crying as an infant, I actually had a grandmother who could have raised me? One who didn't bother?"

I walked away from the fire and straddled a wooden bench, my legs stretched out long as I leaned back on my hands and studied the ceiling. This was too much to take in.

"I don't know," Ryalgar said. "Please. No one gave me the details. Maybe no one talked to Grandmother. Maybe they couldn't get word to her or maybe she couldn't leave the Velka. Maybe Dad begged to take you in when his only sister died. Maybe Mom wanted to raise you with Iolite, like a second set of twins."

"We both know *that* wasn't the case."

My voice had gone as cold as my insides. Mother's resentment at having a seventh child forced upon her had never been a secret. Too many loud arguments between her and my father when we were young had seen to that. To her credit, though, she hadn't mentioned her bitterness aloud for years. She'd chosen to express it in her thinly veiled lack of affection for me instead. Much more civil.

"If what you say is true," I said, my voice growing louder and higher in pitch, "I had another option beyond being raised in this miserable family. And. No. One. Told. Me."

"This family loves you." Coral, the wanted child only a year younger than Ryalgar, spoke as she entered the room holding a finger to her lips. "Shh. Everyone is awake and can hear you talking. Your reaction is understandable, Gypsum, but don't let facts from the past make you forget how much we all love you now."

"Right," I said.

Coral would have hugged another sister at that point and helped wipe away her tears. But I wasn't crying. Rage boiled inside of me – a rage at being lied to, and raised with a myth used to cover up the actions of some despicable grandmother I'd never met.

"And I hate all of you right back!"

I didn't mean it of course, and Ryalgar and Coral knew it as I stomped out of the room and out of the house. I didn't know who had overheard what, so I walked far enough that no one would follow me. Then I kicked small rocks as hard as I could until I calmed down.

When I made it back to the house, everyone had dressed for the big ceremony. Only my mother hadn't changed her clothes. She didn't feel up to the journey.

I pulled on my outfit fast so as not to cause more trouble. I didn't think I could handle a second ugly confrontation. I'd chosen the plainest thing I owned, a grey frock to tone down the ridiculous number of green wood spurge blossoms that covered up the uncanny number of calm-me-down green tatted leaves.

Ryalgar looked regal in her deep burgundy gown sewn for the occasion. She didn't even glance at me after I spoiled her special day. Well, I didn't glance at her either. She shouldn't have picked today to tell me that my whole life was based on a lie.

My other sisters looked like they always looked, except for timid little Iolite. She emerged in a rich purple dress with exceptionally fine stitching. She never wore purple because it called attention to a disease of hers that gave her eyes a lavender hue. But today, she filled her silver hair with purple flowers, too. I found her choice daring, and it raised my spirits a little.

During our uneventful ride, everyone else visited. Anyone who'd heard my outburst with Ryalgar pretended otherwise, except for Coral who kept making sympathetic eyes at me as we rode. I ignored her. Then my breath calmed and my heartbeat slowed as we traveled and as my stitchery did its job.

Once we got to the forest's edge, I learned that the pomp involved all of us waving at Ryalgar as she disappeared into the brush. That was it. A little anticlimactic if you asked me.

When we returned, tired from the ride and sad from the goodbye, my mother gave each of us a warm wet cloth scented with dried rose petals. She saved me for last, waiting until the others had moved on from the cloakroom. The look she gave me as she handed me my cloth puzzled me. It wasn't annoyed, for once.

"Perhaps now you understand why I hate the Velka."

"Yes," I said. I did understand. The Velka had foisted me upon her, one more hungry infant needing desperately to nuzzle at her breasts every time she finished feeding the one she bore. She must have felt like a milk cow, with two babies suckling all day and night and then with year-and-a-half-old twins not yet fully weaned and no doubt crying for their turn as well.

No wonder she hated me. No wonder she hated the Velka.

Well, for the first time in my life, we had something in common. Now I hated the Velka too.

After my history teacher told me of the possible invasion, I had to tell someone, so I told Sheep Scump. I figured it didn't count because I told him everything.

When I returned to school after Keva, I also returned to my worries about this information. I mean, some Ilarians thought we'd die in an unstoppable invasion and kept quiet about it lest they cause a panic. What kind of way was that to face annihilation? I wanted to go out screaming and fighting, not pretending like every tomorrow would be okay until it wasn't.

Added to that, my grandmother's rejection of my birth mother, and of me, stung like nothing in my life had. I was used to feeling unwanted but this was worse, knowing that someone *had* existed who could have been there and chose not to be.

Why had she not cared about me? Most Ilarians took an unwed pregnancy in stride. Any woman could obtain the herbs to end it early on, and those who wanted the child either planned to raise it with the father or, if he wasn't an option, then with another loving male. No one cared.

But a woman who chose motherhood alone, refusing to explain how or why, earned a certain amount of suspicious contempt. I'd been told my birth mother's silence had yielded such, yet she'd refused to waver and had borne me leaving me no clue who my sire was. Did this explain my Grandmother's cold heart?

As I agonized over my situation and Ilari's, my studies suffered. Heli, my attention to everything plummeted. I entered a hole so dark that I never noticed Sheep Scump's despondency, but I should have.

"Stop calling me that stupid name. My *name* is Galen."

"Sorry, Galen. I didn't know it offended you." I took another long swig of ale. My ale consumption had risen dramatically after the Keva holiday. He rolled his eyes in disbelief.

"You can go ahead and call me Duck Piss," I offered. "It won't bother me at all."

"How about I don't call you anything," he said. "Ever." The next thing I knew, he'd walked out my door. I sat and finished my ale, thinking he'd be back later.

By the next morning he hadn't returned, and I decided the problem might be bigger than I thought. So I got really drunk, the way I seldom did, and I stayed that way until two of my teachers sent messengers to my place of lodging to inform me that I would receive no credit for their classes unless I took drastic measures.

It shocked me into better behavior. I got sober, washed up, put on clean clothes, and met with them to learn what needed to be done. I checked in with my other teachers, too, but I was too late for some. They'd already removed me from their rosters.

Then I borrowed a horse and rode to Sheep Scump's quarters. I'd never gone there alone, but I had to fix this. Sheep Scump was the best thing about my life.

Three young men sat playing a card game in their common room and looked up at me when I walked in. I thought I'd met one of them before.

"Galen? He didn't tell you? He went back to Eds."

"To visit his family?" That didn't sound like Sheep Scump.

They exchanged surprised looks over their playing cards.

"No," one said. "He told us school wasn't for him. That classes were useless, Pilk was filled with rantillions and pruskas, sorry no offense, and he might as well go be a prucking goat herder because that would make everyone happy, and it was better than staying here another day."

"He left angry?"

The young man laughed. "You could say that. We thought you probably went with him. You two have a fight?"

"Not that I recall. Uh, maybe."

I had no idea what to do.

I sent a letter to my parents telling them I would finish my classes in a few days and to please send the hired carriage for me. Then I did my best to finish my remaining studies and took my ride home with the emptiest feeling in the pit of my stomach.

One prucking thing in my life had brought me joy, and I'd gone and made a mess of it.

I got home a few days before Tirga and avoided conversation with everyone. Lucky for me, neither my mother nor father wanted to talk with me after the big revelation about my grandmother. Coral discovered she was with child and began plans to marry the father, some bigwig in the Svadlu. The news kept everyone else's focus on her, though it did nothing to keep me from dwelling on the stinging information about my own birth.

Sulphur, Olivine, and Celestine all came and went, occupied with their interests and activities while Iolite and I stayed close to home. We were raised like twins, but we'd never shared the bond Olivine and Celestine did and that summer we seldom spoke. Only once did she say something I remember.

As the late summer sun set, she approached me with the sky's purple reflected in her eyes.

"I was always glad you were there. Growing up. I wanted you to know that."

"Me? Come on, Iolite. I was a pain in the arse when I was little and even I know it. You'd have gotten a lot more attention without me."

She smiled her calm smile. "Exactly."

"Huh?"

"Guess someone would have to be a poor delicate frundle to understand why I wouldn't have wanted *more* attention."

"My shenanigans bought you some freedom?"

"And I remain thankful for every bit of it."

Well, good to know I'd done somebody in the family some good.

I tatted a lot that summer. I mended all the family's clothes, forcing myself to put joyful busy thoughts into every stitch. I figured the more my family went out and did things they liked, the less they'd bother me.

I got to know my horse again. I hadn't brought her to school because I didn't need her in Pilk. Most things were so close I could walk. But I needed her now because she and I were going to take a long ride together.

And I spent time on geography. That's right. I'd never been curious about the distant edges of the realm, places where the river flooded in Faroo, or where the mountains made passage difficult in Tolo. Who cared? But now, they helped disguise my interest in another nichna, one I'd never asked questions about before.

How many people lived in Eds? Did they all know each other? Were most of them on one side of the nichna or were they scattered about? How difficult would it be to find one particular Edser?

After the Heli holiday passed and the days cooled, I intended to ride to Eds and find out.

~ 3 ~

Eds

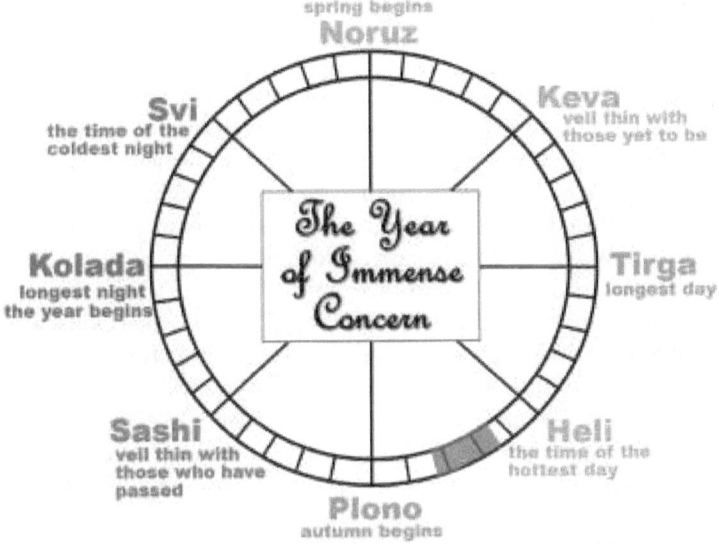

spring begins
Noruz

Svi
the time of the
coldest night

Keva
veil thin with
those yet to be

Kolada
longest night
the year begins

*The Year
of Immense
Concern*

Tirga
longest day

Sashi
veil thin with
those who have
passed

Heli
the time of the
hottest day

Plono
autumn begins

I left a note for my family, promising them I'd be back before school began and assuring them I wasn't doing anything dangerous. I knew they'd be various shades of horrified to learn I'd gone chasing after a man, but this man needed chasing after. I'd driven him away with my selfish moodiness, and I had to fix this.

My horse whinnied when I tiptoed into the barn at dawn, dressed in my riding clothes and carrying full saddlebags. She loved long rides, and the smart thing knew we were leaving. I hushed her.

We started at a slow trot to put some distance between us and my waking family, then we headed north to the corner of Vinx where it touched the desolate nichna of Scrud. I kept on the main road through that barren land, only slowing down as I passed the pitiful hovels the Scrudites called home. I kept an eye out for the wolves famed for their boldness but saw none.

Before noon I passed into the equally desolate nichna of K'ba. No marker welcomed me, but I knew my location by the tents of the reczavy in the distance to my left. Everyone loved to gossip about the reczavy but few knew much about them. Their rumored fondness for nudity and suspected promiscuity made them a subject of embarrassment for many. Some wouldn't even say their name aloud, which I found stupid. I'd always guessed they were misunderstood.

Of all the spots on my route, the one near their tents seemed the safest, so I stopped there for a brief rest before riding on.

Once their tents vanished in the distance, I knew I'd entered Eds. Now I had to make a choice. I could go right, circling Mt. Eds on a path that would take me out to the Canyon River where I could follow the lip of the canyon to the northern border of Ilari and stare out at lands beyond my realm. The idea excited me but I knew this more desolate route reached fewer people. Odds were Sheep Scump and his family didn't live in that direction.

Or I could hug the forest and make my way along its edge to the Little River where I'd been told most Edsers lived. A different sort of danger lurked along this path. Back in the gentle plains of Vinx, Velka inhabited the forest. I now loathed this group, but my hatred didn't mean they were dangerous. I'd never heard of a Velka harming anyone.

Inside the forest next to Eds, however, was Zur. Zurians tried to grab more land at the forest's edge, and the capture of an occasional neighbor could make that happen. I'd keep on the road and not stop until I left the forest behind me and reached the river.

Then, I'd see if I could find anyone who knew of a Rokva family with a son named Galen. If I could find no such people, I had no idea what to do next. If I got the information I sought, I'd ride to wherever the place was. Then, I had no idea what to do next.

Clearly, my plan still had a few gaps.

My dad guessed about three thousand people lived in Eds so I doubted they all knew each other, but I had to start asking questions somewhere. I tethered my tired horse, fetched water for her from the public well, and walked into the first tavern I saw.

"You're a young one to be so far from home," said the barkeep as I sat down. A stout woman with non-descript brown hair, she set an ale and a plate of stew in front of me without my asking. Then she took a look at how skinny I was and added a slice of bread.

"Eat. Does your family know you're here?"

"Oh yes. I, I have a matter to discuss with a friend from school."

Her laugh was more of a snort than anything.

"Not a lot of students in these parts, unless they're little children." She studied me, deciding whether to go on. I passed inspection. "Between you and me, I don't think it'd hurt anyone around here to educate themselves more, but it's not our way. I wanted to go to school in Pilk but my parents just laughed at me."

"I had the opposite problem," I said. "Mine made me go."

She slapped her thigh. "Ain't that the truth? We all want what we can't have. So, who's this boyfriend you're looking for?"

I started to tell her it wasn't a boyfriend, but I stopped myself. Why lie? This woman probably didn't care and if she did, what did it matter?

"His family name is Rokva. Any of those around here?"

She shook her head. "Naw, doesn't sound familiar. Other side of Eds, maybe. There's some out there that got some funny names. Maybe a Rokva."

"You got any idea *where* out there?"

"Naw, not really. I can offer you a room for the night, though. Half price." She smiled. "Student rate."

As she headed off to get me the key, I took a bite of her stew. I hadn't wanted to try it in front of her because I thought it was goat meat and turnips, and I didn't like either one.

I guessed right, but some onions had been added along with herbs and it wasn't bad. I finished it, then soaked up the sauce with the bread.

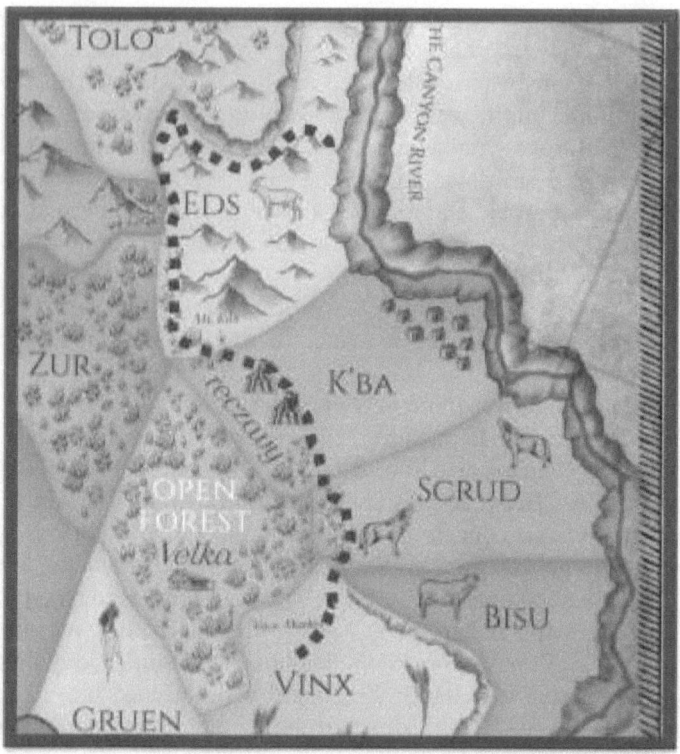

My horse spent the night in the barkeep's family stables, and her happy greeting told me she'd stuffed herself on their hay during the night. We set off together with our full bellies, following the path the woman recommended. I hummed some of Celestine's songs as I rode in the pleasant shade along the bank of the Little River. I followed it almost to the springs where it originated, and I enjoyed its gurgling as I turned and followed the base of the curved cliffs of Tolo, as I'd been told. The rocks must have had little flakes of metal in them because they sparkled in the noontime sun.

I'd seen more of Ilari in the last two days than I had in my life. So much beauty existed in these seldom-visited parts of my realm. Why hadn't I been more curious about them?

When the afternoon sun dipped down to my left above the cliffs, I knew I'd followed their curve for half a circle and now headed north to Ilari's border. I hadn't prepared to spend the night outdoors, yet I hadn't seen a human dwelling in a while.

I'd been told more Edsers lived along the Canyon River than in the hills, which made sense because footpaths down the canyon allowed them to fetch water. I thought I could get to the river before dark. Public lodging didn't exist out here, but most families in desolate areas would take in a traveler for the night.

I left the cliffs behind me, rode around the steeper hills, and finally saw a farmhouse in the distance.

"Let's hope they're nice people," I whispered to my horse.

An older man repaired a pen as I rode up. It held young goats, probably not yet weaned.

"They are adorable," I said by way of greeting.

"They aren't for sale," he replied.

"I don't want to buy one."

"Then what do you want?"

Okay, this was more like what I'd been taught to expect from Edsers.

"I'm trying to find someone. A family called Rokva."

"Yeah. Why?"

"They have a son named Galen?"

"Next farm over. Useless boy. What do you want with him?"

"I don't think he's useless."

"He left his parents so he could go to some fancy school."

"I know. I met him there."

The man laughed.

"You're the varmin girl he's been moping about since he got back?"

Moping because of me?

"His parents wish you'd never been born," the man added.

Pruck.

"Yeah, well, that's a growing crowd."

"You in trouble with the law?"

"No. I just seem to piss people off no matter what I do."

He looked at me before he answered.

"Sounds like you'd make a good Edser. Won't take you long to ride over."

"His parents will let me talk to him?"

"He's grown enough to make his own choices. They won't stop him."

The large stone house sat almost on the edge of the canyon, overlooking the river below. Galen had given me the impression his family toiled to survive. No one who lived in a home this spacious struggled.

Galen walked through the yard as I rode up, carrying buckets of water he'd fetched. He set them both down and stared at me.

I stared back and felt the weirdest sensation. My hands and feet went numb and my heart raced and I got sort of dizzy and tingly everywhere. The next thing I knew I was off my horse, running at him and he was running at me and we kissed and fondled and laughed and hugged and I had no prucking idea anyone could ever want to see anyone as badly as I had wanted to see him.

And, apparently, as badly as he'd wanted to see me.

We calmed down after a bit and looked up. Both of his parents stood on the front porch watching us.

I looked at him for a cue. *Now what?*

"You gonna marry her, seeing as she came all this way to find you?" the older woman said.

"Your mom could use the extra help around the house," the man added, nodding approval.

"We haven't discussed it yet," he replied, punctuating it with a glare at them both.

"Looks like you better," his mom said.

"I'm sorry," he whispered to me. "They have no sense."

"You mind if she puts her horse up, while we go for a walk?" he asked. The dad shrugged, and the mom walked out to take my horse. She turned to me as she did and spoke in a whisper.

"Don't you let him get any from you here, missy. It's not a holiday, not even close, and we follow the rules. Besides, that yearning is what gets them married you know."

Galen and I walked away arm in arm, neither responding to her.

"Are you an only child?" I whispered.

"No. I've got an older sister who lives with her husband's parents. Got an older brother that got out of here by joining the Svadlu and a little sister who's a nuisance. And no, I don't want to spend the next twenty years here tending goats while I watch you learn to cut turnips just the way she likes them ..."

"They won't let me stay in your room tonight, will they?" It wasn't that I didn't want to know more about his family, but I had some immediate needs I had to deal with.

His chuckle was low and throaty.

"There is one way they will. You have any problem telling them we've decided to marry on the next holiday?"

"That's Plono. My sister is getting married then."

"So?" He looked at me baffled. "We're not going to do it. We're just going to say it so we can sleep together and not have to sneak off to the barn."

"Okay. Fine. Tell them that." I'd probably have agreed to tell them anything.

We'd moved behind the barn by then. His mouth found mine and his hands were all over me and honestly we'd never been this passionate when we were back in Pilk. What was the difference?

"I missed you," I said.

"Yeah? I never thought you cared enough about me to do something as crazy as trying to find me here."

"You idiot. I cared about you much more."

After another kiss, I added, "I was just too stupid to let you know."

We made an effort to be quiet that night, together under the covers, and I knew I had to find a way to keep us together.

I rose early to help his mother prepare breakfast, determined to be dutiful. The woman said she needed help so of course I'd do chores while I was here. But I found two other young women working in the kitchen when I got there.

"Meet my hired help," Galen's mother said, gesturing me toward the two young women. "They'll get you going." She walked out.

She wanted me to help her servants?

I noticed Galen's dad giving instructions to three men on the porch as we sat down to eat. Heli, this place had more laborers than my parent's farm. They didn't need Galen's help, and they certainly didn't need me.

Later that morning we took another walk.

"Please. Come back to school. Being there gives us time to sort out what we want, and even if your parents don't like the idea, they can obviously afford it and they won't stop you," I said.

"They won't, but I don't want to go back. You weren't the only problem, you know. I thought I'd like that kind of learning, but …"

"But I know you don't want to herd goats. Not even as part of a comfortable operation like your family has."

"No, I always thought I wanted to live in Pilk with the smart people. Now it turns out I feel as out of place in Pilk as I do here."

I understood. I wasn't all that happy in Vinx *or* Pilk.

"Yet everybody has to be somewhere," I said.

It earned me a laugh.

"Wise arse. So, I want you to take a few deep breaths because I think I've found the place I want to be. Where I hope you'll want to be. I've visited a few times now, and tomorrow I'd like to take you there with me."

"Where?"

"To the reczavy."

Part of me thought it was the most ridiculous thing I'd ever heard. Part of me already thought it made all the sense in the world.

~ 4 ~

Harmony and Camaraderie?
At a Wedding?

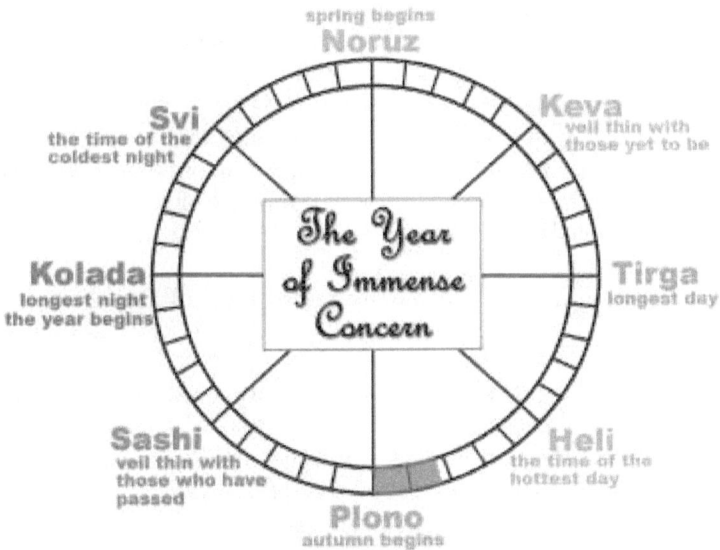

His mother stood in the doorway, hand on her hips, watching us pack to leave.

"So you're going to talk to her parents now?" she said. Galen nodded and grunted.

She looked at me. "Farming people. Better than city folk anyway. What will they think of you marrying an Edser? That you're too good for him? If that's what they say, you send them to me, missy, and I'll let them know that an Edser doesn't stand in anyone's shadow. Do they, Galen?"

Galen made a weird face at me that I interpreted to mean *it's not my fault crazy people spawned me.* However, under the circumstances, it could have meant a lot of other things, too.

His mama didn't seem bothered when I ignored her. I guessed lots of people didn't answer when she talked like that.

"Are we going to have to ride all the way out to Vinx for this varmin wedding?" she asked Galen.

"If you want to be there for it, you will."

"Humph."

"Until today, I've been a man without a home," Galen said as we rode side by side toward the reczavy. I understood. I wanted to find a way out of Vinx, and the people who made me want to leave weren't half as bad as his family.

Then he saw the tents in the distance. The smile on his face confirmed he hoped his home was here.

"They don't let just anyone in," he explained as we approached. "They're divided into tents, and each one is a little different. A tent has to invite you in. We're going to the one I've been visiting, to see the people who decided to let me stay." His eyes pleaded with me. "They could invite you as well."

"I hate having to impress people."

"I know. You'll like them because they all feel that way, too."

A husky young woman with unusually long dark hair came out to take our horses as we rode closer.

"Galen!" she said in a deep and melodic voice. Her eyes lit up when she looked at him and a little flash of jealousy erupted at the familiarity in her tone. I pushed it aside.

"Ksenia!" he answered. He hopped off of his horse and kissed her.

Well, either I could deal with this, or I couldn't. I needed to find out.

The reczavy in the particular tent we visited were all our age or a little older. I counted nine of them, five women and four men, but they kept moving around so it was hard to say. None were nude but most wore little clothing in the summer heat. That was one point in this place's favor.

Galen hugged, kissed, and fondled them all, male and female, as if they were his lovers. Nothing happened beyond that but I got the impression they behaved in front of company.

They made me comfortable in the shade of a breezy lean-to and offered me fruit and wine, then gathered to hear the story of how Galen arrived with the woman he'd been sad about losing during his previous visits. They interrupted his story often to ask me questions and no matter what I said most of them nodded and murmured in understanding.

Let me be clearer. They didn't argue with me. They didn't point out things maybe I hadn't considered. They didn't criticize my choice of words or correct my version of events. They listened with interest. Some of them applauded when I told them of my decision to ride to Eds to find Galen. I don't think I'd ever held center stage to tell a story and faced such a warm reception.

My eyes met Galen's. He smiled but said nothing. He knew how this made me feel, and he knew I knew he knew.

Later, the group left me so I could have time to rest. Many of them went into the large colorful tent that appeared to be where they all lived. There must have been at least thirty such tents that I could see, some far off in the distance.

So, three hundred reczavy? Maybe more? My dad had guessed no more than a hundred people when I pressed him for information.

It gets chilly during summer nights in the dry nichnas and that night they made a fire. As we sat around it and enjoyed a chicken and carrot soup and fresh bread, Ksenia sat next to me. Halfway through eating, she scooted closer. Once she finished her meal, she put her arm around me and held me. It was more affectionate than sexual, but not something a woman would have done elsewhere. I found it odd but pleasant. After a while, she looked me in the eyes.

"We'd like to invite you to come back for another visit," she said. That would have meant nothing in another place, but here I felt her words bestowed an honor upon me not granted to all.

"I'd like that very much."

"Do you think you'll come back soon?"

"I will. I'll only be at school for two anks before my sister gets married on Plono. I'll come on the ank break after that." I looked at Galen. Would he come to visit me in Pilk in between? Did the reczavy leave and visit people? I had no idea.

"Plan to stay for a couple of days next time," a slender, graceful woman with a head full of tight black curls said.

"We all look forward to it," one of the most attractive men in the group added. Okay, I'm pretty sure there *were* sexual undertones in his words. I looked at Galen to see if he'd heard them and if he cared.

Galen looked as happy as I'd ever seen him.

We spent the night together in a small guest tent and did our best to make up for the nights we'd spent apart. By morning I knew I'd be sore for days and desperately needed to wash up before I arrived at the farm. Yet I felt better than I had in anks.

"Hey, Sheep Scump," I said, tousling his hair. "You're staying here for good, aren't you?"

"I am. I brought everything I needed."

"Your parents?"

"I left a note. They won't understand this any more than they understood my wanting an education." He laughed. "Probably less. But they'll be fine. I'll check in on them from time to time."

"So you *can* leave here when you want?"

"Of course. Why wouldn't I?"

"Well, it's just that, I don't know, I've never seen any reczavy anywhere but here ..."

He laughed. "Of course you have. You just didn't know it. We don't wear signs identifying us."

I giggled back. Of course not.

The important word, though, had been "us." He was already one of them in his mind. Any future with him, any future that mattered at all, meant I had to be one of them too.

"I'll see you in Pilk the first ank break after school starts," he promised. "I'll let you know how this is going. We'll talk more then."

Mom and Dad both wanted to know where I'd been, but they approached it differently. Dad asked me to help him out in the barn and then inquired as to whether I had any more geography questions.

"No, not really."

He shrugged and asked me to hand him a mallet.

"Let me know if you do," he said.

That was all the advice on love Dad had to offer.

Mom insisted I help her put up the elderberry jam she'd finished. It was a messy job requiring two people, and I could hardly refuse. She waited until I held my sterile crock under her pot of hot goo, *then* she asked.

"Did you leave here to visit a young man?"

"Yes."

She began pouring out the hot glop.

"That's nice. Why haven't I heard about him?"

"There's too much uncertainty about where we're headed."

She tilted the pot back, slowing the flow with perfect precision.

"I see. Well, don't rush into anything. Unlike your older sisters, *you* have some time left. And as I've always told you girls …"

"Yes, Mom. It's just as easy to fall in love with a prince."

She finished filling the crock to the brim, stopping it right before it ran over onto my hands and leaving exactly enough room for the thin layer of wax we'd melt to the edges to seal the jam.

"Why do you sound so sarcastic when you say it?" she asked as she set the pot down to rest her arms.

"Mom. Did you ever really think I'd marry a prince?"

She looked at me, giving my question a heartbeat of thought before she answered.

"No. I knew long ago my best hope would be to forbid you to marry one, but I couldn't get myself to do it."

We both had to laugh, and I realized that in some weird way, our relationship had improved.

Yet, despite what I'd told her, I wasn't looking for a husband. I'd found the man I wanted and he had no interest in marrying me. So I'd either end up with him or I'd make do without him but either way, I'd probably never marry.

What would I do without him? Maybe find work as a seamstress when I finished school. Or I could make lace, which would be more lucrative. I'd have to live in Pilk for that, though, and in some ways, Pilk was stuffier than Vinx. Everyone always judged everyone else and I didn't like that, but an unmarried woman only had so many options.

Galen arrived at the start of the first ank break as he promised. I'd persuaded my roommates to stay elsewhere so we could enjoy the unrestrained passion I'd fantasized about for days. We tried, but two low clouds hung heavy over us, both brought on by our basic honesty with each other.

I'd been celibate since I'd seen him, as single tidzys were. But over the past three anks, Galen had entered into a marriage of sorts, although one not recognized by most Ilarians. He told me he had taken oaths to care for and be loyal to nine other people I hardly knew. Such a promise was a condition of joining. His tentmates had encouraged him to enjoy his time with me, but they were all, in a sense, his wives. Or his wives and husbands. I wasn't sure what terminology applied but it put me in a funny position.

In a real sense, he'd gone and gotten married without me. What does a woman even say to that? Yes, he fervently hoped I'd marry in as well, but maybe I didn't want to. Maybe they wouldn't want me. Couldn't he have waited? Shouldn't he have waited? I didn't even have a framework with which to process the feelings I had.

The other cloud was external but it hung as heavy and as low. The pending invasion had finally become common knowledge and everywhere we went, people muttered about the Mongols. We heard of how they fought from their horses and conquered realms using small armies no one could defeat. They burned down the lands of those who fought back. These Mongols grew into a monster as people talked, becoming a giant hideous thing lurking in the closet at night.

"Forget it; they'll probably never make it to Ilari." Galen sat on my bed, wanting to turn my mind away from this problem and back to our fun. He couldn't solve the Mongol issue, and he only liked problems he could do something about. But I'd already gotten up to add a bit of wood to the fire and my mind would not be turned.

"How can we think of anything else with such a disaster facing us? I have to do something."

"Look, I'm no great fan of the Svadlu, but isn't that their job?" he asked. "I hardly think anyone in the realm expects a seamstress to defend us."

Then he laughed at me. Not with me, at me, and it hurt.

Sure, we had more sex but it lacked the blazing ardor I'd imagined. Who becomes a flame of passion after being told to stop worrying about something? Not me.

I went to Coral's wedding and did my best to be a good sister. Ryalgar came out of the forest, and Celestine sang a song, and the food was good although the people from the groom's family turned up their noses at it.

Coral's natural plumpness kept her pregnancy from showing much. I made some lace for her to wear and filled it with love and patience, hoping it would help her get through the day. Me, I wore a collar tatted with harmony and camaraderie. I figured you can't have too much of those at your sister's wedding.

As the evening wore on, I danced with a few young men, tried not to drink too much, and looked for people I could actually talk to. I noticed my mother and Celestine having a heated conversation. Odd. Beautiful Celestine had always been mom's favorite child. I think the harmony thing must have kicked in, prompting me to interrupt whatever difficulty had arisen.

As I walked towards them, I heard Mom say, "These feelings pass once you marry. You learn to enjoy being a wife. So say no more of this, please, especially not today."

Had Celestine questioned her role as the family's best bait to catch a prince? Oh my.

Mom saw me and waved me over with unusual enthusiasm. "Come join us, Gypsum." Celestine stood to leave, giving me a frustrated look as I took a seat.

Maybe harmony *wasn't* what the day called for. I tried camaraderie with my sister instead.

"What would you think, Mom, if I told you *I* didn't wish to marry? I'm not sure the traditional role of being a wife is right for me either."

"Gypsum, don't you *dare* start in with me on today of all days."

"I was thinking this might be a good time to talk …"

"What is the matter with you? It's a horrible time to talk."

Whoa. Who'd have thought …

She stood. "If you'll excuse me, I need to go check on Iolite."

If another sister got married, I'd tat an entire dress filled with silence and restraint and wear it instead.

31

S. R. Cronin

~ 5 ~

Other Things a Lacemaker Can Make

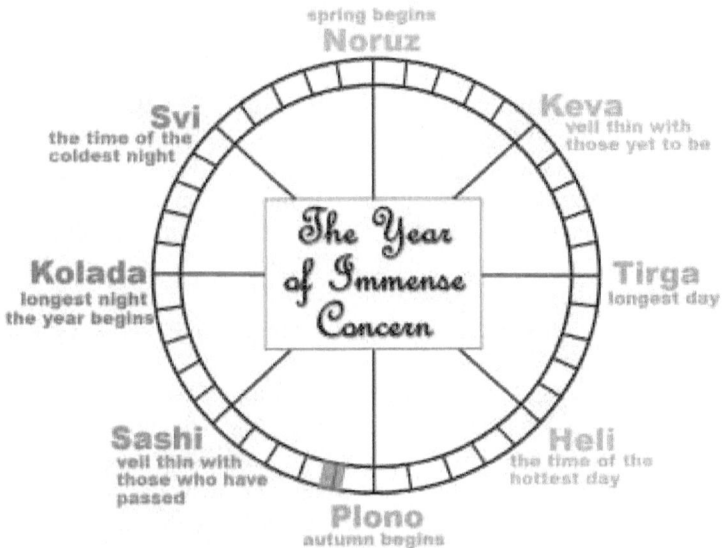

The Year of Immense Concern

- spring begins — **Noruz**
- **Svi** — the time of the coldest night
- **Keva** — veil thin with those yet to be
- **Kolada** — longest night the year begins
- **Tirga** — longest day
- **Sashi** — veil thin with those who have passed
- **Heli** — the time of the hottest day
- **Plono** — autumn begins

I left school on the ank break after Coral's wedding to make the nearly day-long ride to visit with my boyfriend's living companions. Spouses. Family. I still didn't know what to call them in my head but I was pretty sure we were going to do more than visit.

Sheep Scump met me when I arrived in the late afternoon, and I saw the relief in his eyes that I hadn't stayed home. He tended to my tired horse while everyone else hugged me and offered me food and drink and made me comfortable in the same lean-to as last time.

Ksenia sat next to me as the others left.

"My name means 'welcoming,'" she said. "I'd like you to feel welcome here."

"I feel fine, Ksenia. Thanks."

Ksenia smiled. "No, you don't and I don't blame you. Everyone comes here filled with the rumors they've heard. We know some of the stories aren't good. The first thing you have to accept is that nothing will happen here that you don't want. Do you understand?"

"I guess."

Her gaze turned towards Galen as he left the lean-to that housed the animals. I saw her shake her head at him. *No, we're not done talking.* He turned and walked towards the central fire pit instead.

"That's the problem, isn't it?" she said. "Your situation is the kind we'd rather avoid."

"You don't like couples?"

"Oh goodness no, this place is full of them. Many reczavy find a person with whom they share a deep bond. We embrace relationships, as long as they don't prevent those involved from sharing affection with others."

"Okay. That's good to know. So why is my relationship with Galen a problem?"

"Because you care about him so much that you want to make him happy. And for the next few days, we need to learn what makes *you* happy. You, all by yourself. He's well suited to our lifestyle. That's wonderful. But would the way we live please you? Or would you tolerate it so you could be with him? The first works great. The second doesn't."

I understood.

"I'm going to ask you to do the hardest thing in the world, Gypsum. I need you to be honest with yourself. Can you do that?"

I thought honesty had always been one of my strengths but Ksenia had gone to the heart of my dilemma. Would I do anything to be with Galen? And if so, was that a good idea? I had a feeling it wasn't.

"No one wants you to be miserable here."

"You have my word. I'll make an effort to be open-minded and I won't pretend."

"That's all we could ask.

The evening was filled with friendly banter, good food, and excellent wine. Each of the nine people spent time with me, some visiting, others inviting me to join in with songs or games. A voluptuously curvy woman named Varla and I danced while the particularly good-looking man who'd caught my eye last time played the drums. It was fun, maybe a little erotic but nothing I wasn't comfortable with.

Galen kept his distance, and after my conversation with Ksenia, I guessed he'd been asked to. As the group grew sleepy, he came and sat next to me, putting his arm around my shoulders.

"Ready for bed? Would you join me in the big tent tonight?"

The colorful large tent adjoined the open forest, with one side of it nestled under the sheltering trees.

"What exactly …"

"You'll see," he said. "You'll like it."

By the time we went inside, most of the group had retired. He lead me by candlelight to an edge of the tent separated by a thin grey blanket hung almost to the floor as a partition. I noticed two other such private areas, perhaps occupied, perhaps not.

He gestured to the many blankets on the floor. "Join me?"

"I'd love to."

I hadn't intended to have sex with him in the tent, knowing what little real privacy we had, but as soon as he touched me, my skin felt on fire. I couldn't help myself. It had been two anks since we'd been together, and my body craved this more than my sense of propriety objected.

It didn't take long for us both to find satisfaction, and as we lay together in the quiet afterward I heard others. Moans of pleasure were most common but giggles and happy sighs mixed in. One man even hummed a few bars of a song.

I thought most of them were asleep. I guess not.

Did their noises bother me? Not as much as I would have thought. If I was totally honest with myself, I found it kind of charming. I know I fell asleep with a smile on my face.

The next morning Varla asked me to help prepare breakfast. Unlike at Galen's parents' house, she worked with me while everyone else either tended to the animals over in the lean-to or brought the blankets out of the tent for airing. They operated with little conversation, everyone knowing what needed to be done and finding a piece of it to do.

"Your food?" I said once we all sat on the ground around a large low table to eat a morning meal of eggs, strawberry jam, and small cakes made in a pan.

"Yes? We do have food," one of the men agreed.

"I mean, where does it come from?" I pointed at the dense forest on one side and the open desolation on the other.

"We grow gardens as best we can and herd small animals, mostly chickens, but we buy much of what we eat in markets around the realm," Ksenia said.

"That's what I mean. Buy it with what?"

They exchanged a look of amused understanding.

"We don't play all day," Esteri, the woman with all the tight black curls, said.

Another woman gestured to her, pushing down on air with her palm. *Soften your tone.*

"Most of the markets around the realm welcome our products," Esteri added, her tone softer.

"You make things?"

"Lots of things. Toys. Games. Small musical instruments. Joke gifts. Clothing, often erotic. Some places allow us to have market stalls just for adults, others don't. We abide by the rules of each nichna."

I had no idea. People wouldn't speak of the reczavy by name, but they'd buy things from them? Things to enhance their own sexual pleasure? Why did this not surprise me? Then another fact registered.

"Wait. You sell clothes?" I hadn't realized that having a purpose mattered so much to me, but making clothes gave me a way to fit in and contribute.

"We've heard you're a seamstress and a lace maker. We've none such in our tent, but you could meet those from other tents," said Varla, the woman I'd danced with last night.

"I'd love to." This meant I wouldn't have to sit around in the dirt all day, washing dishes as my only way to do my share. I could make things I liked. Perhaps tat lacy things that would be frowned on elsewhere. *That* could be fun.

The others noticed my face light up.

"We'll take you around after breakfast."

During my tour I met reczavy of many ages and styles, noting how they seemed to congregate into groups of commonness. Some tents focused almost exclusively on entertainment, with men and women who danced for money or performed aerobatics. I hadn't known it, but places in K'ba and Pilk provided venues for the reczavy without ever naming them as such. Performances with fire and those with illusions were popular. I learned that it all brought in substantial revenue, which a council of tent leaders portioned out to support the entire reczavy, to provide for the contributors' tent, and to go directly to those who did the work. Between performances and product sales, people here were busy, comfortable, and well fed.

So, one *could* make lace and live somewhere other than Pilk. And the lace products one made here could be much more fun to design and to wear. That alone made this worth considering.

As the sun neared the horizon, the campmates began taking the bedding down from the clotheslines to spread it around on the floor of the tent. Many of the blankets were brought over by the fire instead, as a soft bed begin to take shape.

Ksenia noticed me studying it.

"We're going to invite you to participate in a pleasure ritual tonight. We call it 'cherishing.' There is no problem if you say no, either before we start or at any time during it. Do you understand?"

"I do."

"Do you want me to stop it now?"

Did I?

"No, don't. I'm curious. I, I might stop you once you start though. Okay?"

"Of course. Just be clear."

Raheem, the good-looking man who played the drum while I danced, approached me.

"May I undress you?"

I looked around. Everyone else was clothed, at least by this group's standards, and watching us.

"Just me?"

"Yes. You will be the only one who is completely naked because tonight is about your pleasure, and only yours." He gave me a wink. "We'll all enjoy it though, of course."

Nothing in my life had ever been just about me. Not that I could recall.

I held my arms up over my head and smiled my consent. "Please."

The others all found a comfortable spot to sit and watch. Then all of them, including Galen, made appreciative remarks about my body as my clothes were slowly removed. My undresser fondled me a little as he worked, turning me to give everyone a variety of views as he praised the parts of me that people seldom saw.

Once I stood before them completely naked, they came closer. Some of them touched this or that as I was eased onto my back, laying on the bed they had made for me.

Esteri knelt and gave me a soft kiss on my mouth.

"In our tent, women pleasure the other women. Are you comfortable with that?"

I'd done some fondling with other girls before and found it nice.

"Sure."

She smiled and spread my legs apart, moving in between them and examining that most personal area of all. Then she leaned her face towards it.

Wait, I had not done this. I'd heard men and women sometimes used their mouths to please each other but, well, this was new to me. Should I stop her?

I felt her wet tongue on parts of me never kissed before and decided to wait to object. I felt Raheem's hands on one of my breasts and Ksenia's strong hands on the other. Both caressed my nipples. Hands stroked my inner thighs, and lips kissed my forehead, and for pruck's sake, someone massaged my feet. My body spasmed in pleasure, small waves of it washing over me as I took in all the affection, all the eroticism, all the desires to please me and only me.

The woman stopped at the perfect time, after I'd finished and before I got too tender. The hands became softer everywhere, more supportive, less seeking. I had to give it to them, these people knew what they were doing.

Then the man who seemed to be Galen's closest friend in the group knelt between my legs and dropped his britches. His pizzle was fully erect.

"May I?" he asked.

I didn't think I had any more in me but the idea of his pizzle inside sounded good, so I nodded.

He looked at me, not sure.

"Yes," I said aloud. "Heli, yes,"

He move closer and began. I liked the feel of his movements, but I didn't think it would go anywhere for me. This was too much sensation too fast.

"Consider stopping," Ksenia whispered to him. "She's beyond pleasure for now."

"No. Please don't." I spoke up. "There's joy in feeling a man finish. I'd like you to."

That earned me a smile of appreciation, but I'd been honest, as promised. I did like the sensation, even if I was too tired to enjoy it the same way he would.

I thought we were done when he stopped, but we weren't even close. They brought me water, and more wine, and added more wood to the fire. As the evening turned into night, one man sang to me and three people gave me a back rub, and two of the women danced for me most suggestively and in between their efforts, every one of them found a way to have some sort of sexual interaction with me. Sometimes I had that burst of pleasure and other times I just enjoyed the experience, too tired to get there. But the closeness... the attention... I don't know how to describe it, it was like nothing that had ever happened to me before.

I felt cherished.

Finally, when all but Galen had had a piece of me, they each put their hands somewhere on my body and they held them there in silence. I felt the affection in their warmth.

Then each one kissed me softly on the lips and walked away. All but Galen, who stood nearby with a couple of blankets that he laid over me when they were gone. Then he crawled under the covers with me and wrapped his arms around me.

"How about we sleep out here tonight under the stars?"

"Sure." I cuddled against him, feeling weird but good, and fell asleep before my head could form another thought.

I spent the next day there, touring around and meeting people and helping out with things. The sexual portion of my visit appeared to be over and no one else appeared to be the least bit embarrassed about it.

That night at dinner I finally brought it up.

"Is this, this thing you did last night just something you do with guests?"

Everyone laughed.

"Pruck no," Ksenia said. "It's something we almost never do with guests."

"Oh. You seemed, well, you seemed kind of practiced at it, if you don't mind my saying so."

"We are," Raheem said. "We do it every ank or two."

"Right." I laughed. I don't know why I thought he joked. "Wait, you're serious. This thing you did for me, is that the stuff the rest of the realm makes such snide comments about?"

"Yes," Esteri said. "Well, at least it is for this tent. Others have their own rituals and their own ideas. Here, we take turns, so every so often we all get cherished. Other than that, what people do with their tentmates is their own business."

Wow.

"We've talked about you." Varla, the woman who danced with me, spoke up. "We'd like to have you live with us if you think this is right for you."

For the first time, I thought it might be right for me, not just right for my being with Galen. He watched me with question marks all over his face. I looked him in the eye.

"It feels right. And I'd move in tomorrow to be with you, Sheep Scump, but to do this for me, I need time." I turned to the others. "Is that a problem? Can I come back and visit him while I think?"

That got me looks filled with understanding.

"We've all been through this." "Take your time." "It's a process." "We'd love for you to visit." Sympathy surrounded me. They turned to Ksenia, who had to be their leader even if they didn't call her such.

She nodded. "Unless this causes some unexpected disruption, it's fine. If there is a problem, we'll talk."

A clear blue autumn sky greeted me the next morning as I began the long ride back to my school in Pilk. I left Sheep Scump with his nine other tentmates, knowing I'd miss him but also knowing I needed to try on the idea of being a reczavy while sitting in a classroom and while sleeping in my old room on the farm. I had to make sure that all the parts of me were on board before I did this because it wasn't the sort of thing that would be easily undone. And I wanted to be graceful about leaving my other life behind.

I don't know if I'd ever been so careful with a decision, but then again I'd never made a decision that mattered so much.

~ 6 ~

The Prey the Predator Avoids

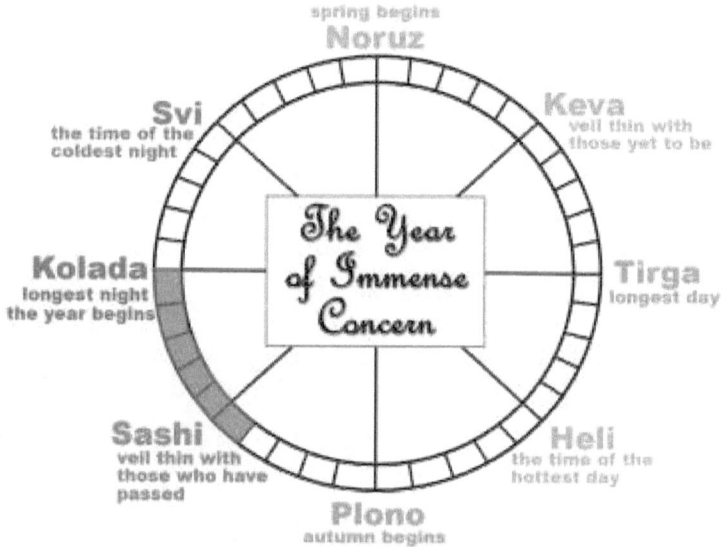

My oldest sister Ryalgar invited me to lunch. At Coral's wedding, she'd said nothing of how I'd spoiled her day, and I'd said nothing to her about my dislike of the Velka. Could we manage lunch the same way? I thought we could, for despite my outburst on the day she left us, and my oath to hate the group of women she lived with, I didn't blame Ryalgar for anything. None of it was her fault.

We drank two jugs of a fantastic pink lunch wine and nibbled on the little things she ordered as we talked of funny stories from the past and anything else that didn't matter. When the fun ended, I left the tavern knowing two things.

One. I'd never seen Ryalgar so happy. She belonged with the Velka, despite having gone there facing resistance from us all. This meant one could leave our family, go somewhere that made no sense to the others, and live a happy life.

It boded well for my joining the reczavy.

Two. My driven and efficient sister didn't wander around Pilk having lunch. Ryalgar always had a purpose, and she'd made the deliberate choice to not tell me hers. Why? I intended to find out.

I'd developed a friendship with the history teacher who'd talked to me about the Mongols, so I started there.

"You want to know about your sister's inquires?" she said. "Why not ask her?"

I noticed she didn't serve the afternoon wine most of us drank. Today as we sat in her cramped office she offered me heated water with tiny white flower petals floating in it.

"They're called jasmine," she said. "They come from the southeast of Ilari. When you steep something in hot water like this, it's called a tea."

I took a sip. It had a lovely sweet flavor and the hot beverage soothed my throat.

"Not everything from the east is bad," she said. "Humans demonize what they don't understand."

I'd come to realize she studied history not because she cared about the past, but because she loved to draw conclusions about people.

"In this land where jasmine grows, do you think they try to protect their younger siblings from unpleasant truths?"

She smiled at me. "Perceptive, aren't you? I suspect this is a human trait. Why?"

"Do you think the younger siblings there want to know what's going on, even if others try to protect them?"

She rolled her eyes. "I'm sure they do. I get your point, and there is no need for secrecy about your sister's inquiries. She came to me for the same reason the Svadlu consulted me last spring. Ryalgar wants to learn everything we know about the Mongols."

"She does? Why?"

"So she can stop them, of course."

I immediately thought of Sheep Scump laughing at the idea of a seamstress stopping an army. It seemed my sister held similar unrealistic illusions.

I took another sip of the warm liquid in my cup. "Could you tell me the things you told her?"

"I don't see why not ..."

I got the names of others Ryalgar had spoken to and as Kolada grew closer and the winds grew colder I made my way to each of them. Without knowing it, without meaning to, Ryalgar had left breadcrumbs with which to trace her planning. The more I followed along, the more obsessed I became. By the time I amassed the facts she had about war, invasions, fighting from horseback, and Mongolia, the world had become scarier than I imagined.

We weren't lucky people hidden in a safe cocoon. We told that story to our children and maybe our little sisters. We were ignorant people about to be eaten alive by a predator who devoured creatures like us to survive.

We were in his path. He was hungry. We were doomed.

But wait...

No predator ate every creature in its path. We had to find a way to become the small animal or plant that survives. We couldn't run like deer, so we needed to be the cactus, or the skunk, or the prey that tastes bad or has a tiny body with a deadly sting.

We needed to be ugly, deceptive, poisonous, and stinky, with the hard outer shell of a clam hiding our soft and tasty insides.

We weren't that way now. How did one get to be the sort of creature that a predator avoids?

Well ...

I'd been invited to join a group that thrived on the fringes of society. Much of their behavior offended and even antagonized other Ilarians who outnumbered the reczavy over a hundred to one. Yet the reczavy crafted a comfortable life and were left alone.

They did it by being more amusing than threatening. By providing goods and services their detractors sought. By staying out of sight and appearing smaller and more harmless than they were.

Who would be better qualified than they to turn Ilari into a moth hidden on a branch or a porcupine ready to strike?

This could work.

Over the upcoming anks, I'd learn everything of use from all the smart educators here. Then over Kolada, I'd spend the biggest holiday of the year at home with my family, being the good daughter and sister I'd seldom been. I wanted them to realize how much I cared for them and to remember it when they became horrified by the choice I made.

Then, during the winter break in Svi, after I finished my classes, I'd run away to join the reczavy. Once there, I'd learn details about being the prey the predator avoids.

My parents hired a coach to bring Iolite and me home for the holiday. Our driver fetched her first at her exclusive little school in the difficult-to-reach spot tucked up inside of a branch of the Little River.

Iolite had been born a frundle, and she exhibited the physical signs of her condition. Those who looked noticed her silver hair and a height slightly below that of a woman on the short side. Everyone could pick out her purple eyes from across a room. She stayed in the carriage when it arrived at my school as she didn't like the attention she often received.

I climbed in and made myself comfortable next to her. We'd barely begun our journey when she updated me about the family. As usual, she knew more about what was going on.

Celestine's musical career had taken off, and she'd be performing elsewhere during the holiday. Ryalgar had wanted to come home but couldn't because Coral had come into the forest to give birth.

"Now? She's not due for another eighth."

"True but her Svadlu husband wants her to be safe if the baby comes early."

"So, Celestine, Ryalgar, and Coral all won't be part of this year's celebration?"

"It's worse. You heard about Sulphur joining the Svadlu?"

"Ryalgar told me. I don't know why everyone was so surprised."

"I agree." Iolite nodded with a raised eyebrow. We shared a common belief that only the two of us saw our other sisters clearly.

"Wait, Sulphur's coming home, isn't she?"

"I wish. She's escorting Coral into the forest."

"And Olivine?"

"She's visiting Ryalgar now. Mom thinks she'll be home before Kolada, but maybe not. What I'm saying is it could be just you and me this year."

Iolite looked as unhappy as I felt.

"I'm sorry," I said. "I know I'm not the best sister for a family celebration. You okay?"

"Probably. I haven't been sleeping well. Weird dreams."

That was cause for concern. The biggest liability of Iolite's condition was the emotional and mental instability that frundles sometimes experienced.

"Weird like how?"

"It's okay. *I'm* okay. Don't make a big deal out of it. Please."

"Sure. Whatever you want." I squeezed her arm to affirm my loyalty but she was already staring out of the window, lost in her thoughts.

All the Kolada delicacies we'd had as children filled our kitchen when we arrived. I knew Mom had little help these days and making this stuff took a lot of work. It warmed my heart that she'd done it for only Iolite and me.

"Thanks for cooking this! I love these little things." I picked up a tiny raisin cake.

She looked at me. "I expected more daughters when I made those."

Don't react. Don't take it personally.

"Of course you did. I'm sad more of my sisters aren't here, too."

And so it went.

I tried, I really tried, but when people are used to you being a little snotty they don't know how to take it when you aren't. But of course, none of the three knew I was saying goodbye as best I could.

On the afternoon of Kolada eve, when Olivine still hadn't arrived, my mother resigned herself to spending the holiday with only two daughters.

"So, tell me about this young man you mentioned last summer? Do you still see him?" She tried for a cheery conspiratorial smile.

Dad worked in the barn while Iolite rested. Mom and I stood in the kitchen, fetching plates for the evening feast. I'd started drinking full-strength dinner wine, and I didn't want to talk about Galen. I'd pretty much used up all the niceness inside of me and felt I'd gotten nothing back for it. But none of that excused what I did next.

"I'd rather talk about my mother."

She looked at me puzzled, then her eyes filled with tears.

"I *am* your mother."

"You are. You are." I hadn't meant to make her cry, for pruck's sake. I'd meant to shock her into giving me some facts. "I mean, I'd like to know more about the woman who gave birth to me."

"Tonight? What's to know? Liya was your father's only sister and she died when you were two months old."

I'd brought her up because I had to know this one thing before I left for good.

"Did she? You see, you told me my grandmother died, and it turns out you lied to me. I want to be sure I have the truth about my birth."

"You are such a frustrating child. Why couldn't you have been the grateful and cooperative type?"

"Maybe I tried to be but nothing I did was good enough."

We stared at each other, both realizing we were headed into the most honest conversation we'd had since she'd screamed at me as a child and I'd sometimes dared to scream back.

"I wanted to be *your* daughter but you wouldn't let me. You let me know from the beginning that I didn't belong here. You even saddled me with *her* middle name. Gypsum Yemi Glonti. No, I couldn't be Gypsum Renata Glonti like your real daughters. Why? Did you hate me that much even as a baby?"

"That was your dad's doing." The tears had stopped. Her voice went cold. "He thought it insulted the memory of his sister and his precious mother, for you not to carry *their* middle name as a proper girl in his family would. I told him it was a mistake, but he wouldn't listen to me."

And I'd always assumed she didn't think I was good enough to carry her name.

Given I'd made a mess of the evening already, I went for an answer to my other burning question.

"What do you know about my dad?"

She raised an eyebrow.

"I mean the man who got her, got Liya, pregnant. Dad told me she wouldn't identify him but you all must have known more. Was he married?"

I could see the resignation on mom's face. This was going to happen tonight whether she liked it or not.

"No. He wasn't even an Ilarian. She told us he'd gotten in trouble with the law in his own country and swam here across the Wide River."

"A murderer?"

"No, nothing that bad. A con artist who cheated people, she said. I guess he was good at it. He promised her he'd reformed but fell into his old ways again. Fled with the Svadlu on his heels after she got pregnant. She felt embarrassed she'd fallen for such a low life." My mother drew in a long breath. "Rightfully so."

I suppose that did nothing to make mom eager to raise me…

"And you never told me this because …"

"Because I promised your father I wouldn't. He feared you'd think less of yourself if you knew. I saw his point but decided long ago that I'd give you the full story if you ever asked for it."

"Thanks, Mom."

"For?"

"For the truth."

"You're welcome."

I gave her a half smile. "And for raising me. It can't have been easy."

"It wasn't."

She said no more, but as she left the room she gave a me soft wink along with a smile.

The Year of
Extreme
Distress

~ 7 ~

Wind and Fire

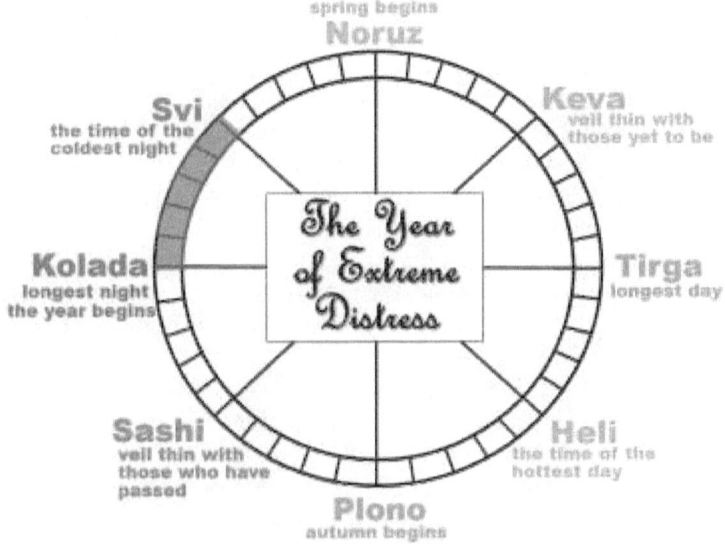

Noruz
spring begins

Keva
veil thin with
those yet to be

Svi
the time of the
coldest night

The Year
of Extreme
Distress

Kolada
longest night
the year begins

Tirga
longest day

Sashi
veil thin with
those who have
passed

Heli
the time of the
hottest day

Piono
autumn begins

Dad asked me to join him in the barn the next morning. He often spoke with my sisters out there, but seldom invited me. I supposed Mom had told him of our talk, and he wished to add something.

"Jepsa," he said as we walked out the door into a windy morning with an angry grey sky.

I pulled my cloak tighter around me. "What?"

"Jepsa," he said it louder, forcing his quiet voice to carry over the wind. "It's the name my sister gave you when you were born."

51

"It's pretty." We hurried towards the barn, stepping around the mud puddles left by the half-melted snow.

"I thought so. She told me it meant 'birdlike.' I hated to change it but, well, all your sisters were named for rocks, and I didn't want you to be different."

"Then why not name me Diamond?" Then I realized why. He wanted to give me a name that sounded as much like Jepsa as possible.

"She only lived for two more months?"

He nodded. We'd reached the barn, and he opened the door. The drafty building felt comfortable after the bluster outdoors.

"Liya seemed fine when you were born," He lowered his voice to its normal pitch. "Happy. She loved you. We should have checked in on her more, I know, but the twins were barely a year old and they ran us ragged and Marketa was already eight months pregnant with Iolite. We'd hired a neighbor girl to help and to check on Liya, too, but we learned later that she often snuck off with her boyfriend instead. And, well, I *was* gone a lot, teaching then, and I had no idea things had gotten so bad."

It never occurred to me my father blamed himself for his sister's death, but the way he averted his eyes now told me he did. Then again, how would I have known? We never spoke of these things.

"Why the lie? About Grandma?"

I felt the guilt and sorrow in his shrug. "There was almost nothing I could do for your mother after I asked this of her. I needed the farmhands, but I offered to spend coins instead to hire as many girls for her as she needed. She told me not to bother, three inept helpers would be worse than one."

A strong gust of wind rattled the shutters. We both shivered as his eyes met mine, begging for understanding.

"Your mother had one request of me. She said she never wanted you to know you were rejected by your own kin. She didn't want to face childish tantrums when you screamed you wished your grandmother had taken you in. She didn't want to tolerate threats to run away and live with your grandmother every time she said no to you. She promised me she'd do her best but *only* if I took my mother out of the picture. Completely."

"You don't think she did this to punish you, or punish Grandma?" I couldn't help asking.

"Well, it hurt me and my mother, it's true, but I don't think your mother intended that. Her arguments made sense. If she had all the work of raising you, she wanted a clear claim to you as well. I gave her that. It helped."

"Yet you wouldn't give me her name."

The barn door blew wide open as I said it; he pulled it closed and secured it better.

"That's why we walked out here in this mess. Your mother told me how you felt. She was touched, I think, to learn you wanted the Renata name that her women carry."

"I am of her, Dad, even if I'm not of her womb. She is the female who shaped me. No woman in your family did that."

He gave a sad nod of his head. "I understand that now, but then I felt guilty erasing the lovely name my sister gave you. Yet I wanted you to fit in here."

"So you thought you'd make up for it by leaving me with the female middle name from your side."

"Exactly. And now, well, I'd like to undo that mistake. Your name can be changed. I'll handle the petition to the Royals, you won't have to do anything. You will become Gypsum Renata Glonti. Will that make you happy?"

Happy? It would once have made me ecstatic. Yet all I could think of now was how upset mom would be when someone with the Renata name joined the reczavy.

"Let's wait, Dad. I'd like to think about it."

He took a step back from me, puzzled. Once Dad decided on a solution, he wished to fix things and move on. "I guess we can wait but I don't understand why."

"I've learned a lot on this visit. I need some time to sort it out. Please."

The wooden door rattled as though it had a mind of its own, one determined to thwart us and fly open again.

He pointed to the house. Our conversation had ended. We sprinted back into our cozy stone home and said no more about it.

Two anks after I returned to school, sunshine overtook the winter storms. Ilarians used mild winter days to go to the market and travel, so I wasn't surprised when Galen showed up at my place of lodging. The women I boarded with knew he'd left school and they knew I missed him although I'd seen no point in telling them he'd joined the reczavy. They didn't take long to find places they needed to go. We all looked out for each other like that, even if we didn't confide much.

"I was hoping you'd come here …" I said, running my hands through his hair. We began by kissing. We finished much later lying on my bed, laughing and happy.

I knew he wanted to know my plans almost as much as he'd wanted what he'd just gotten. Maybe more …

"I'll be joining you," I said. His face glowed as if a sunbeam had hit it.

"Thank you," he replied, more to the sky than to me. I wondered who he thought he spoke to.

"But not until classes break in late Svi."

"Why? Your classes here don't matter. No one out in K'ba gives a rat's arse about what you study in Pilk. Why not come with me tomorrow?"

"I don't *want* to come with you tomorrow. I want to finish my classes. They matter to *me*. Besides, I'm doing other things here. Learning about more, more serious issues. I have to be honest with you, Sheep Scump."

He winced. I think he'd figured out I used that nickname when I wanted something from him.

"What?"

"I've added another reason for joining the reczavy. You may not like it, but I've got to get you on my side. Listen with an open mind."

"Okay?" Caution had replaced the sunbeam.

"I know you think I shouldn't worry about this invasion and it's the job of the Svadlu and all that. But I know things you don't."

I saw the beginning of a smile.

"Don't you dare be condescending."

"I wouldn't dream of it. Well, maybe I would. But one of the reasons I came to Pilk, besides the obvious, is I need to talk to you about this Mongol thing. How do you know what you know?" he asked.

"Why do you care?"

"Why do you care why I care?"

He reached for the jug of wine he'd brought and poured us both a cup.

"I'll go first," he said. "We're trusting each other here, right, Duck Piss?" He only used that name when he wanted to get me on his side.

"To the death, Sheep Scump."

"Yeah. That may be the problem. Look, I told you my brother is in the Svadlu. Well, he's more than in the Svadlu, he's like important with them. He's nine years older so we're not that close but I visited him before I came here." He laughed. "I admit, I wanted a good free dinner."

"Okay. So you came to my doorstep well fed. That was smart."

"Yeah, well, he and I spent more time talking than we have in years."

"He knows you're in the reczavy?"

"He does now. He thought it was funny. My parents were so pissed when he joined the military. He congratulated me on finding a way to piss them off even more."

"I kind of like him. For a Svadlu."

"Yeah. He's probably one of their better ones. Anyway, he talked about this invasion thing, and pruck, this is serious. He says there's no way in Heli the Svadlu can defend us from what's coming and yet most people won't admit it. He was glad I'd joined the reczavy because he thought I could crawl into the forest and hide with the Velka and survive."

"Giant pucks of cow scump. The *Svadlu* think this is hopeless?"

"The thinking ones do. Another group just wants to train, recruit, and pretend."

"That's what I want to talk to you about."

"That's what I want to talk to you about."

We said it at the same time and both laughed.

"We have to get ready to hide," he added.

"We have to get ready to fight," I spoke my words as he said his.

"Huh?"

I don't know which of us was more puzzled.

"Galan, hiding is a fine last choice but everyone else dies if we do that. We need to find a way to *do* something."

"Do what? I'm *not* being condescending here; I'm being realistic. If our army can't fight these people off what in Heli do you think you can do?"

"I can go join a group of people known for their tricks and their illusions and persuade them to help me."

"Wait. You're joining the reczavy to *recruit* them? To get them to help you fight a hopeless war?"

He started to laugh. "I've got to hand it to you, Duck Piss… That is the most original reason for joining a camp full of free-sex nudists that anyone has ever come up with."

"Thanks. I pride myself on being unique."

I could tell he was more pleased than he let on as he gave my idea thought.

"What if they say no?"

"I don't think they will. Not all of them anyway. Not when they hear what I have to say. But I'll join them even if they do and I'll work on this on my own because I don't think they'll stop me as long as I do the other things I'm supposed to. Then I'll keep trying to win them over, one by one, because what else can I do?"

"Prepare to hide in the forest with me when the time comes?"

"Oh, I'll do that too."

"Okay then. My idea is our backup plan and I'm your first recruit."

Galen and I parted two days later as the best of friends and lovers. He accepted my staying in Pilk for five more anks. He'd share news of my decision with the camp and come back to visit me when weather permitted. He'd leave it to me to convince our campmates once I arrived.

Then, shortly after the Svi holiday, I found out what Ryalgar intended.

Not that she told me directly. Or even indirectly.

Rather, I happened to look for Celestine at the inn where the musicians all stayed. She wasn't around; she never was. But her friends told me about how Celestine was now part of Ryalgar's growing plan to save the realm. *Really?*

I knew my sister Celestine had been in the forest when Coral gave birth. But I didn't know there had been another exciting development in which Coral and Celestine discovered some weird power with their combined voices, a power that made animals obey them.

This seemed particularly odd because Celestine had no skill with farm animals. But Ryalgar thought her two sisters, assisted by others, could make the Mongols' horses throw their riders to the ground, thus stopping the invasion. Problem solved.

Well. It sounded like they wouldn't need the reczavy. I confess to feeling a little disappointed before I decided having my life saved was better than getting to participate. Good thing others had pursued creative solutions too and found one.

But, just to be sure, I asked more questions.

I learned that two anks after the Svi holiday, my father would bring horses and straw to a large farm in Vinx where Ryalgar would hold her first practice session. Many singers in Pilk planned to attend, to sing with Celestine to amplify her voice. Ryalgar sought other ideas for inciting fear in horses and had considered using smoke but felt it was too risky. She feared burning Ilari down to save it.

But fire wasn't risky when *my* group used it. Maybe the reczavy had a part to play after all.

The next day I went to the market. The Velka's tent stood out, decorated in winter greenery. I waited until one of the two women had time to talk.

Yes, I did hate these people for taking my grandmother away from me. But today, I needed them to deliver a message.

"You're another one of Ryalgar's sisters?" the woman said. "There certainly are a lot of you, aren't there?"

"I suppose so. Listen. I need you to tell her about fire. Tell her I'll have people at the practice two anks after Svi, people who can handle it safely."

"Oh, she'll be happy to hear that. Who do you know works with fire?"

"Um, some entertainers. Just let her know."

"Entertainers, hmmm. I'll make sure she hears of this."

Now I just had to find those entertainers and convince them to go.

~ 8 ~

A Fast Exit From Pilk

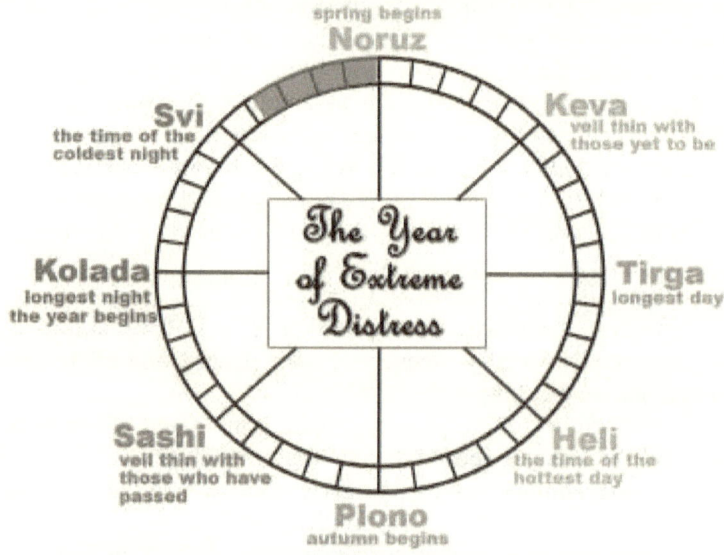

spring begins
Noruz

Svi
the time of the
coldest night

Keva
veil thin with
those yet to be

The Year of Extreme Distress

Kolada
longest night
the year begins

Tirga
longest day

Sashi
veil thin with
those who have
passed

Heli
the time of the
hottest day

Plono
autumn begins

My feet hurt and my throat was dry by the time I arrived in the part of town where the reczavy performed. I'd already discovered three thousand Edsers didn't all know each other. How well would three hundred reczavy know their neighbors?

I walked up to two men. Each twirled a metal stick as long as his arm as he danced around. Then at the same time they both threw their sticks into the air, each catching the other's stick as it fell. If the ends had been on fire, which I'm guessing they would be during a performance, it would have been quite impressive.

"Hi."

They both turned to me.

"We're closed now. Performances start at dusk."

"I'm not here to watch you."

"We're not hiring."

"I'm not looking for a job."

They both stopped and stared at me.

"What *do* you want?"

"I'm, I'm in the process of moving. To where the forest meets the desert in K'ba." That was the politest way of referring to the reczavy, and I figured politeness wouldn't hurt if I'd been misinformed.

"So?"

"I'm in Pilk without a horse. I need to get a message to my new tentmates and, well, I know I'm taking a big chance here but I hoped you could help."

"Which tent?"

"Uh…" *Pruck, did the various tents have names? Why hadn't I asked?*

"The tent is painted in lots of colors. It sits almost in the trees."

They didn't look impressed with my description.

"The people in it all are young, like me. School-age still, pretty much, and new. There are ten of us. I'll make eleven."

They looked at each other. I'd perhaps narrowed it down.

"You're not talking about the tent that just let an Edser move in, are you?"

"Yeah. Galen. He's my boyfriend."

They gave each other a weird look.

"Ksenia said that was okay. He can still be my boyfriend."

They both laughed. "He can be anything you want, honey," one said. "We're just amazed Ksenia invited an Edser to join us."

"One *should* keep an open mind," his partner said, more to the other guy than to me. "So. What is this urgent message?"

I launched into a spiel about my desperate need to find people who could handle fire and would attend something two anks after Svi.

"You're smarter than you let on, aren't you? Okay, you've obviously found two people who perform with fire. Tell us why you need us."

I told them everything I knew, down to the details of how our Svadlu needed help even if they would never admit it.

S. R. Cronin

"So here I am, in Pilk, trying to …"

The two men exchanged a meaningful look.

"We get it," one of them said. "Can you come back here the day before this gathering?"

"Sure …"

"Good. You can ride there with us. We'll bring friends." He gave me a wink. "It'll be fun to surprise these people with what we can do."

On the day I led them to Ryalgar's practice, I watched from a safe distance, hidden in the trees so neither my father nor my sisters would know I was there. Five fire-capable reczavy worked their magic to add to the horses' agitation, and they did well. Everyone could tell my sister Coral's voice, when joined with adept singers, had a strong effect on the horses. But, everyone could also tell we couldn't possibly count on the horses to respond as we'd hoped.

The entire Mongol horde would not be stopped by this. Maybe slowed down or reduced, but we needed more ideas. I still thought the reczavy could provide them.

Then, it was the middle of Svi and I was done with my classes. I'd never do the fourth and last group done by most Ilarians but at least I'd made it this far.

Ready to go, I looked around the room and a problem stared back.

I had no horse. When I left for school, my parents suggested my horse would be happier in Vinx given that everything I needed was within walking distance from the school I'd picked. I figured they hadn't wanted the expense of renting stable space. Older sisters had needed horses to get to and from school but I had a same-aged sister who required a carriage ride. However, going to school in a carriage allowed me to bring more crap with me than most.

Now, I'd leave for good, riding behind Galen on his horse. I could bring precious little. What about my things?

Well, everyone expected me back and my share of the room had been paid for. I could simply leave my stuff. I'd been gone so often that no one would worry for a while.

Eventually my parents would look for me. I felt a little nauseous at the thought, and I wished I had a way of preventing the anguish this would cause. They'd ask my roommates where I was, and none of my roommates would know. Or would they?

Galen had been less closed-mouthed when he was in Pilk. Some of his friends probably figured out where he'd gone, and they knew people I knew. My friends would hear. Would that be before or after my parents showed up?

Thanks to the dense forest in the middle of our realm, there was no easy way to get from Pilk to the reczavy. The shorter distance involved following the banks of the Little River through the eastern edges of Kir and Lev into the lower reaches of Tolo where a horse could cross the small stream. That ride took half a day. Then one had to ride through Eds, tracing the edge of the forest while avoiding trouble from the Zurians.

The other way to get to the reczavy involved circling the long way around the forest through much of Ilari's open farmlands. This easier route allowed one to ride faster, but it went through Vinx, and Vinx was the last place I wanted to be seen as I made this journey.

So Galen and I picked our way along the river bank, then rode hard along the contentious border between Eds and Zur.

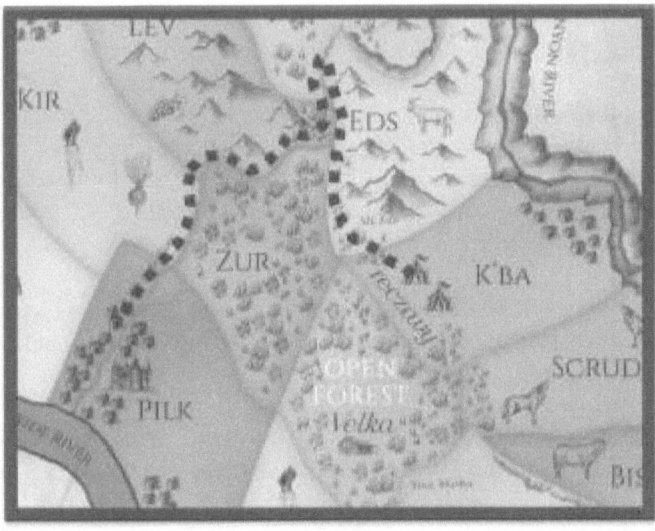

The first night back in the big tent made me nervous, but I needn't have worried. They greeted me like I belonged there, gave me plenty of space, and gave Galen and me time alone. I slept better next to him, surrounded by the snoring and muffled sex sounds of others, than I had in my crowded room of strangers back at school.

Ksenia told me it would be several nights before the group picked a member to cherish. I'd be free to participate or to wait until I felt more settled. Everyone adjusted in their own way, she said. In their own time. There was no rush.

I felt relieved. New tidzys need time to warm to sexual activity, after all, and some more than others. My tentmates wanted to give me the same sort of time and I appreciated it.

A few nights later, the group gathered to cherish Varla, the voluptuous woman I'd once danced with while Raheem played drums. We'd formed a friendly bond from that, and I wondered if her selection was deliberate.

As the sun dropped towards the horizon, bits of blue peeked through the clouds that had covered the sky, creating a sunset filled with pinks, oranges, and purples. We placed Varla close to the fire to keep her warm. I mostly massaged her feet while I enjoyed watching the eroticism of her repeated satisfaction. She had learned how to make the most of such a night, and she inspired me to enjoy my second cherishing more.

Near the end I joined Raheem in a two-person massage of her private parts. I followed his lead, recognizing that he was instructing me as well as pleasing her. Despite being female I learned a few things.

The next day Varla gave me an affectionate hug.

"I'm glad you chose to be part of this." She bumped her hip against mine, the way she'd done when we danced. "You're going to make this whole tent more fun."

I often spoke of the possessions I'd left behind, so I shouldn't have been surprised when a few days before Noruz, entertainers from another tent found me

"We're riding to Pilk tomorrow to perform for the Noruz holiday. We hear you have things you need. Come! Share a horse with one of us, gather your stuff, and make peace with those you left behind. When we're done performing, we'll bring your things back here."

It seemed like the perfect offer. What problems could possibly arise in Pilk over Noruz?

When I arrived at my old place of lodging, three of the four women had gone home for the holiday, and the fourth gathered her things to celebrate with the boyfriend she planned to marry.

"There you are! We'd started to worry about you. Everything okay?"

"Never better. Um … Things have gotten more serious with Galen. You remember …"

"Of course. The one who went back to Eds." Her eyes widened. "Are you really going to live in Eds with him?"

"We're exploring other options."

She gave me a smile of understanding. "That's good. Maybe you can live in Vinx with your parents."

"Can I ask a favor?" The caravan wouldn't leave until two days after Noruz and that meant I had four days alone here to do nothing but pack. "Are you riding your horse today?"

"No. Ride her if you want while I'm gone. She's at the same stable, and she can use the exercise. Just make sure and wipe her down well when you're done."

"Of course." I'd borrowed her horse before and maybe hadn't cared for her so well.

I heard her boyfriend yell from the street.

"Gotta run!" she said. "He's got a coach outside waiting." She giggled at the extravagance. "See you after the holiday."

I hadn't gotten far with my packing when a messenger knocked on the door.

"Everyone is gone," I told her.

"I seek Gypsum Renata Glonti," she said.

"Oh. That's me."

My father must have changed my name. I felt a small surge of happiness at hearing it spoken, though I knew it would add to my mother's heartbreak once she learned where I'd gone.

She moved her left hand in front of her face, donning the mask of my father.

"Dear daughter. Your mother's joy at the prospect of changing your name was so strong that I was compelled to move forward. Forgive me for rushing you."

Well, that was the first time I'd heard "forgive me" from my father's lips.

The messenger continued.

"Good news. Your mother and I will be in Pilk for Noruz, to celebrate an achievement of your sister Sulphur. She is being granted the status of Mozdol in our army. Isn't that remarkable? We are proud of her and wish for you to join us in her celebration. The messenger has details of where and when to meet us. We trust we will see you there."

The messenger removed her imagined mask and began to tell me of the tavern I was to meet them at. I listened, too numb to stop her.

Don't misunderstand. I wanted Sulphur to be successful and happy. But if ever two sisters differed on everything, it was her and me. I couldn't possibly sit through a ceremony involving her achieving rank in a pompous organization like the Svadlu and appear happy about it.

And I certainly couldn't do it and then announce to the family I'd joined the reczavy. Sulphur would be shocked. She hated these people, though she'd never met one as far as I knew. I'd spoil her special day and I'd already done that to Ryalgar.

Yet, I also couldn't sit there and cheer, then disappear. No, that would be worse. They'd be angry about my deception as well as my choice.

So what could I do? My father knew where I lodged and he'd come to find me if I didn't show up. If I wasn't here, he'd ask around and people would try to help him find me.

I had to leave Pilk. I had to be somewhere else by tomorrow.

Fortunately, I had access to a horse. If I left now, I could ride along the banks of the Little River and take one of the trails up into Lev. I'd be safe in the hills by nightfall and I could ride back the day after Noruz when all had settled down. My family would assume I'd ignored their message and gone off to celebrate the holiday with friends. They'd be frustrated with me, but not surprised.

I reached into my pockets. I didn't have many coins left but cheap lodging existed in Lev. My roommate hadn't exactly given me permission to take her horse on a four-day journey, but this was an emergency.

I grabbed all the food, drink, and warm clothing I could carry and headed to the stables.

~ 9 ~

Ten Strangers in Lev

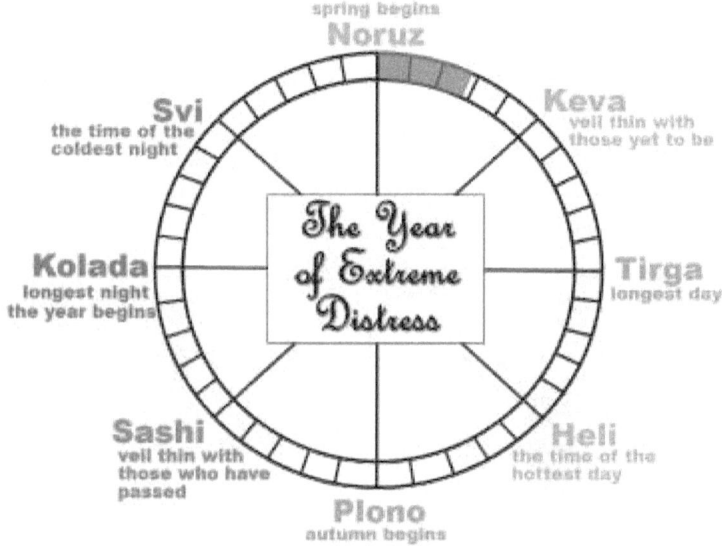

I became just another young woman sauntering off to enjoy her holiday as I rode through Pilk Central with the hood of my cloak low over my head. Once I crossed into Kir, the crowds thinned. I picked up my pace and by late afternoon the growing hills told me I'd made it to Lev. The first vineyard tempted me with the smell of food and the sounds of laughter beaconing from the courtyard. But I turned my horse towards a less traveled trail leading away from the river, hoping to find a cheaper and more secluded place.

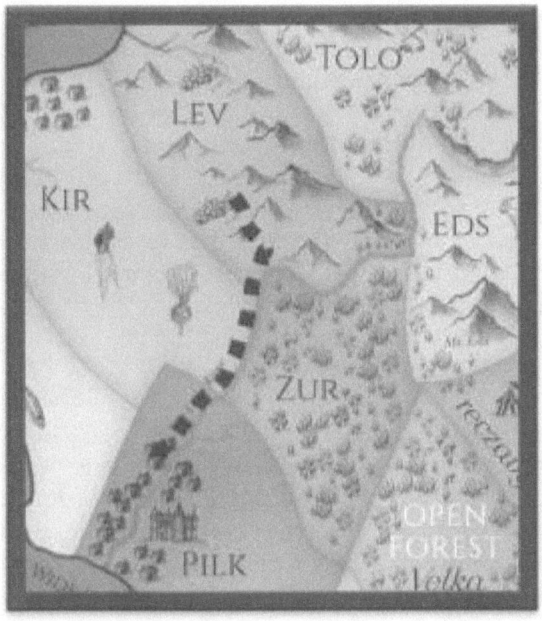

I rode further than I intended, lulled into my own thoughts, so when the lanterns from a small place in the distance caught my eye, I realized darkness had almost come and I needed to stop.

I tended to my horse first, watering him from the well in the courtyard then leading him to their stables. He gave me a grateful look as I held out a rare winter carrot from my pack. Above the sounds of his chomping, I heard boisterous voices.

A group of men sampled the wines, and had for a while, judging from their voices. I tried to catch their words but I couldn't. The cadence of their speech didn't sound like Ilarian. I'd heard other languages before but not this one.

Ten men, all with the shiny straight black hair of a Faroojer, drank and talked. The resemblance ended there, though, although these men did look like other Ilarians who showed traces of different wanderers and traders who had settled here over the years. I wondered where they came from. They seemed pleasant enough, and it was too late in the day to be choosy, so I went inside. I'd heard that a lone woman traveler had more to fear in other realms, so I averted my eyes when I entered. I didn't need any misunderstanding.

The proprietor greeted me.

"They've caused no trouble since they got here at midday," she told me. "They've been nothing but respectful."

"Where are they from?"

She turned her palms upward. "How would I know? Can't understand a thing they say. They point to what they want, and I point to coins to get paid. They seem to have a pretty good tolerance for alcohol, but I showed them their rooms just in case."

I looked over at them. They paid no attention to me, caught up in some story two or three of them told.

"Come. I'll put you in the room next to mine and bring you your dinner, so you can get some rest."

I expected to sleep soundly but I didn't. The bed had lumps. I worried about my borrowed horse alone in a strange stable and about having enough coins to last me. I needed to get back to tatting. I worried about my parents looking for me at school. They'd be worried when they couldn't find me. Yes, I worried about their worrying.

And, of course, the specter of these evil invaders loomed over it all. These fierce and horrible Mongols were coming to devour us. How could anyone possibly sleep?

When I did finally doze, I had the dream, the one that had haunted me since I was five.

In it, our whole family celebrates a holiday. Perhaps Noruz. Mom holds the hands of the twins, while Dad holds my hand and carries Iolite. The older ones get to play, free from such parental constraints.

A tall thin man with pale blond hair trips and falls in front of us. Embarrassed, he calls Mom a pruska, pretending she made him stumble. Dad helps him up and speaks to him with kindness, which annoys Mom.

I'm fairly sure those things did happen because I have a memory of them, although to be honest it's hard to separate the memory from the dream.

I know the next part never happened, although it does every time I dream about it.

Dad helps the man up and says, "Would you like a daughter?" He waves his hand at all of us. "I've got plenty to spare."

They both laugh because having lots of daughters is some inside joke only men understand.

Then the drunk man looks at each of us and he locks eyes with me. Our eyes are exactly the same color of grey.

"I'll take that one," he says pointing to me. And then the dream ends.

Early the next morning I woke to the sound of the ten guests talking in serious tones in their strange language and heard my hosts scurrying to make them breakfast. It sounded like they had decisions to make and places to be.

Me, I did not. Today was Noruz Eve. I needed to lie low through tomorrow, and then get back to Pilk and find the caravan that would take me and my things home.

Perhaps the owners of this inn had mending they needed to be done? Everyone did. I'd see what I could exchange for room and board.

By the following evening I'd fixed the torn curtains at the inn, and mended their sheets and tablecloths. She'd freshened my mattress, fed me well, and sent me off with almost as many coins as I'd arrived with.

My horse and I took it easy on the way back. Once we reached the Little River, most of the traffic went the other way as revelers returned to their homes. I kept the hood of my cloak low and spoke to no one, but I noticed reoccurring comments around me.

"Can you believe they rode right up to the palace in Pilk, bold as can be?"

"I hear there were at least a hundred of them."

"Oh no. Who told you that? There were only ten."

"We should have killed them right there. What's wrong with our Svadlu? Letting people ride in and make demands like that. How did they even get in?"

"Surely you don't believe that old myth about no more than three outsiders being able to enter Ilari together?"

"Not anymore I don't."

"We won't pay them their tribute, will we?"

"Of course not. The Royals were just getting them out of our realm so we can start our plans to slaughter them later."

69

The Royals were just getting them out of our realm so we can start our plans to slaughter them later?? Something important happened while I was in Lev.

Ten people had ridden into Pilk and demanded tribute. Where had they come from?

The sounds of my ten fellow guests leaving the inn two days ago came back to me. They had undoubtedly been ten foreigners on a serious mission.

How many of those did I think rode around Pilk that morning?

Oh, surely not. My ten guys seemed kind of sweet. They couldn't have been ... wouldn't have been... I'd have known if our enemy shared the same roof with me, wouldn't I?

I got my roommate's horse settled back in the stable, then I faced a quandary. I could go back to my old room but my roommates would have returned, and I'd face their questions. Where had I been? Why had I left? Where was I going?

Or I could walk over to the part of town with the theaters. I could make it by dark, and I could spend the night wherever the reczavy caravan slept. I knew they'd welcome me.

The choice was easy.

Few lights and no sounds came from inside the theaters. I wandered into a tavern where a few customers sat around a large table, drinking ale, having the same conversations I'd heard earlier in the day.

"Where is everyone?" I asked.

"Many fled when they heard we'd been attacked. They canceled all the holiday shows."

"That's a shame," I said. "Any idea where the entertainers went?"

That earned me a snort of a laugh.

"If rumors are true, they ran back to where the forest meets the desert in K'ba, if you know what I mean."

Yeah, I did know.

"Why?" I asked.

"Oh a couple of rantillions heard about these envoys and thought it would be funny to tell the reczavy, no offense, that the Mongols had targeted them for death," one said.

"Dumb-arse joke got out of hand," the woman next to him added. "Next thing we knew, poof. Our shows vanished."

"Poof, huh?"

Now I had a problem. I was too exhausted to walk back to school and the coins in my pocket wouldn't last long in expensive Pilk. Yet my transportation home had evaporated.

"Miss?" The girl behind the bar spoke to me. "What's your name?"

"Gypsum. Why?"

"Well, you look like the one they described. Tall, thin, pale blonde. The people who left said you'd be looking for them and to tell you they'd send somebody for you tomorrow."

So I only had a problem until the morning.

I did know someone who often stayed nearby at the inn known for housing musicians. Would she let me have a spot on her floor? I thought she would. Sisters did that for each other.

She seemed startled to find me at her door.

"Are you hurt?" she asked.

"No, I'm fine. I dropped out of school, and I don't want Mom and Dad to know, and I've nowhere to sleep for the night. Can you help me?"

She looked perplexed. She wore her night shift and glanced at her bed.

"You don't have to listen to a long explanation," I said. "Just let me sleep here tonight. Tomorrow someone will get me to where I need to go."

"Should I ask you where you're going?"

"Only if you want to stay up for a while."

She laughed and, despite our fatigue, we shared our biggest secrets before we retired. I learned she'd fallen in love with a woman. It didn't surprise me. Celestine's interests had always tended that way though the rest of the family ignored it.

I told her I'd joined the reczavy, and she put on her best face to tell me she thought it was great. I knew she didn't mean it, but I appreciated the effort, and there was some comfort in the fact that at least one of my sisters knew.

I woke to a knock the next morning. The sun shone high in the sky and Celestine had left. Galen stood in the doorway with three of my tentmates. I don't know how they found me, but they'd come to take me home.

Settling into my new life felt so natural that I didn't think much about it. I began tatting again. Working with threads soothed me, but now I had the added fun of designing sexy little garments that would be a pleasure to wear and to see.

Did I infuse these fun items with playfulness? Of course I did.

My creations brought squeals of delight from my tentmates, so I tatted a special something for each as a gift of appreciation for them and their bodies. I think that cemented my acceptance, if any further cement was needed.

Those who sold our goods took my creations, and soon I had coins in my pocket and clients asking for more. Ilari did offer the perfect life for me and against all odds I had found it.

Then I learned that not one, but two sets of people wanted to destroy it.

We all knew about the first threat, and the ultimatum which had, in effect, told us they wouldn't be a problem until the coming winter.

The second group determined to destroy my happiness surprised me. I learned of them when I found Galen out by the cooking fire shouting at three others.

"You can't judge an entire nichna by the rantillions who run it!" he yelled at Ksenia. "Look at the scoundrels who run the other places. Do you trust them? Of course you don't!"

"The Eds Royals wouldn't dare try something like this if they didn't have the support of many Edsers and you know it," she yelled back. They both leaned forward with hands on their hips, glaring at each other. I'd never seen either of them that angry.

"We got a good deal of grief for letting an Edser join us," one of the men added, giving Galen the first unfriendly look I'd seen from any of them.

"Yeah! And to your credit you ignored them," Galen said. "So now what? You want to kick me out because of where I grew up? How many of you come from places that are supportive of us? Huh?"

"Wait. Stop." I walked right into the middle of it without thinking. "Galen's right. We don't kick people out because of what their relatives do. Yes, I'm new here but even I know that."

I turned to Galen.

"What's going on?"

Ksenia answered before he could open his mouth.

"We had a meeting with all the tents this morning One tent leader has a cousin who tends to the Royals in Pilk, and he overheard a conversation about Eds annexing K'ba."

"You mean taking it over?" I said. "That's ridiculous. Eds has no army. How would they even do such a thing?"

"He heard the ruling prince of Eds made an agreement with the ruler of K'ba. No army needed."

"Surely the Svadlu would stop them?"

"Perhaps, but they're focused on training for this invasion now. I think the Edsers count on that."

I knew nobody here liked the Eds Royals. Few Ilarians cared for them.

Jofim, the man who'd complained about admitting an Edser, added, "We hardly know anything about the K'basta Royals except that they've always left us alone. Who knows what sort of deal they've made. Friends in the settlements tell me no one has seen the Ruling Prince of K'ba in over a year."

"So why do we care if Eds runs K'ba?" I looked into the eyes of all four of them and saw fear.

"Because the ruling prince of Eds brags to his people that he'll eliminate the reczavy once he's in charge. We'd never have guessed how much the Edsers like that idea."

"What's it to them ...," Esteri, the young slender woman with curly dark hair, spoke up. I'd once thought of her only as the person who introduced me to oral sex, but she'd become Esteri instead. "We don't bother them. Why would they go to such trouble?"

Ksenia answered, "It appears we've underestimated how much our lifestyle infuriates part of the population."

"So we'll just retreat into the trees," Galen said. "No one has jurisdiction in the forest."

Ksenia shook her head. "We'd have to go in deep before they'd leave us alone. Most of our tents won't fit, we couldn't grow a thing, and we don't have paths like the Velka do."

"That settles it then," Galen said. "I'll go home and see what I can learn."

No one said, "Don't go!" Not even me, although I thought it.

~ 10 ~

Mom Sends Her Love

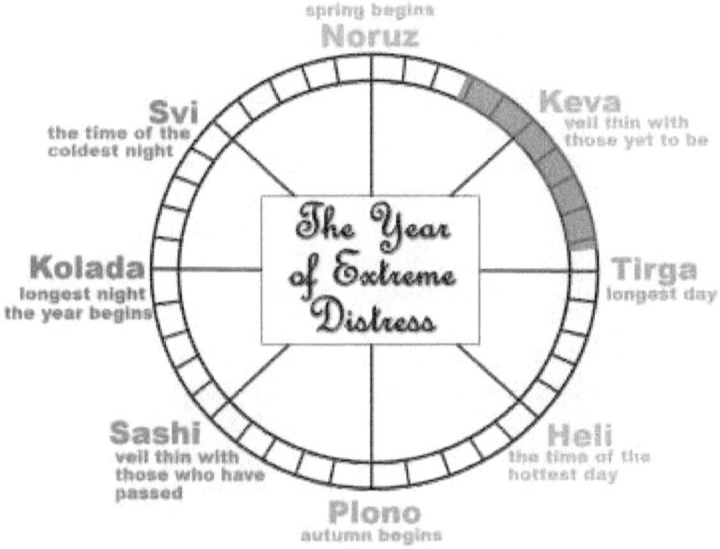

The afternoon before Galen's departure, an unexpected guest arrived.

"Do you want to see your sister?" Varla yelled to me as I rested in the tent. I grabbed the nearest robe. I'd known that sooner or later someone from my family would check on me. Which sister had drawn the short straw?

Her thick dark brown hair above a curvy frame was unmistakable from a distance.

"Ryalgar?!"

She lived closer than the others, but I thought planning Ilari's resistance kept her too busy for family problems. I admit I was

75

flattered, although I had no intention of returning to my former life.

"I don't care what you say. I'm not leaving," I said as I walked toward her.

"That's fine. Mom doesn't know you're here. Yet. Dad was too shy to come. He sent me to make sure you're okay."

"Of course I'm okay. I belong here."

I watched her eyes take in our beautiful colorful tents and my happy campmates and I wondered if she envied us and our freedom.

"Then I'll send word back to Dad that you're well. He'll be glad to hear it."

We looked at each other for several more heartbeats while I searched for the right thing to say.

"You three want some dinner?" Suloom, Galen's closest friend, broke the awkward silence.

I felt sure she wouldn't accept, but she surprised everyone, including the two women who accompanied her.

"That'd be great. We'd love to. While we eat, can I tell you about this other thing I'm working on?"

"Is it of interest to us?" Galen asked.

She laughed. "I hope so."

As we ate, Ryalgar gave the details of her analysis of the Mongols and Ilari's limited options for survival. I had to give my campmates credit. They listened politely, although perhaps the high quality of Ksenia's chicken stew contributed to their silence.

Finally, Esteri said, "We've already heard a lot of this."

Ryalgar pulled her head back in surprise. "From whom?"

Esteri pointed her thumb at me.

I watched the realization work its way down her face. Little sister was as keen to save Ilari as she was.

"I'm sorry, Gypsum. I had no idea you'd given this much thought or I'd have included you sooner."

Had that been another *apology from my family?*

"It's okay."

Galen found this juggling stick he planned to take to Eds as a weapon and it must have brought him comfort because he'd hardly put the thing down. He'd been pounding it nervously against his palm since Ryalgar arrived.

"We know we don't get to live this life under Mongol rule," he said. "So, you don't have to convince me to help you. Many of us are already convinced. What do you need?"

"What can you do?" she answered.

"Tricks. Illusions. Carnival acts. Pranks."

"You work with fire, right?"

I interrupted. "I got our entertainers working with your horse people on that one already."

"Oh. Okay. Well, I am looking for a third way to reduce the number of invaders. I've got, I hope, six out of ten of them still on horseback and headed to Pilk, thinking they're going to win this thing easily despite my first two setbacks. I need one more way to slow them down, spook them, and capture more of them."

"Why don't you start by sending them somewhere other than Pilk?" Ksenia asked. "I mean, make it look like they're heading there, but route 'em south to the river instead."

"Yeah. Then we can throw eggs at them!" Rakhim had already agreed to help, though his tendency to think of this as more of a prank than a battle bothered me.

"Eggs filled with itching powder!" Another yelled.

"Thrown with catapults," said a third.

They all laughed, and I worried Ryalgar wouldn't think we took this seriously.

Instead she said, "Is that possible?"

"Which part?" Galen grinned at me.

"Any part."

"It's all possible, big sister," Galen said. "How about we make Gypsum here your official liaison. You two work out the specs. We'll deliver."

She gave me a quick look to see if I objected. I couldn't have been more delighted.

"Does this mean you'll visit me again?" I asked.

"It means I'll come here often."

This was more acceptance than I hoped for. But why not push for one more thing?

"And you'll handle things with Mom and Dad?" I asked.

She hesitated, but not for long.

"Sure."

We had a deal.

Now all I needed to do was to persuade my tentmates to have an appropriate sense of urgency, eliminate the threat of this crazy takeover by Eds, and coax three hundred free-spirits into becoming life-saving warriors.

I could do this.

Suloom rode half a day with Galen to keep him company and brought news when he arrived back that evening. Ksenia scooted over to make room for him around the fire, as the last of the light faded from the sky.

"So what did you learn?"

"Two talkative herders offered us a midday meal when we stopped to rest our horses. We found out they like their Ruling Prince because of the deal he struck with the Royals in K'ba. Did you know that in both nichnas the cousins, uncles, and nephews cannot assume the throne? It has to be a direct descendant of the Ruler. No one else qualifies."

We all talked at once.

"Some of these succession policies are so squirrely. Ilari ought to think about standardizing them."

"That will never happen. Every nichna values its uniqueness too much."

"Yeah but this policy invites disaster."

"But it keeps power close to the Ruling Prince, which I think is the point."

"Why type of deal did the two nichnas make?" Ksenia asked.

We stopped talking.

"The herders only knew that the K'basta Royals don't have a qualifying heir," Suloom said, "and the Eds Ruling Prince proposed some clever loophole. The K'basta Royals took the deal even though it includes a scenario in which Eds gets to annex K'ba. Looks like that scenario will happen."

"Why would K'ba agree to such a horrible pact?"

"Maybe it was their only choice," Suloom said.

"Let's hope Galen finds out more."

On the next sunny day, I took one of the chairs common amongst the reczavy, a large cloth bag stuffed with straw and dead leaves, and I pulled it out into a quiet spot in the sun. A soft breeze blew the warm air around an entirely blue sky. I stripped down to my britches and breast band, enjoying the sunshine on my skin and cursing those who'd take this pleasure from me.

I'd brought parchment and ink so I could organize my ideas for confusing our invaders. As I sketched what I knew of the realm, I liked the possibility of diverting our attackers to the Wide River. It curved inward at the point where Pilk and Gruen met, providing a perfect location.

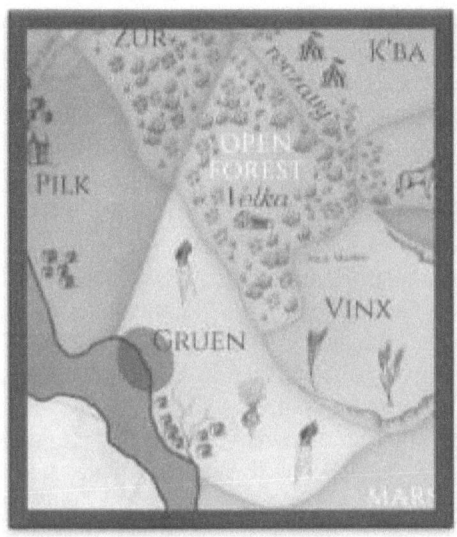

Ksenia grew up in Gruen and remained close to her brother. Maybe he'd talk to people about working with us. Some would refuse, but the farming folk of Gruen resembled the grain growers of Vinx. Plenty were practical enough to remain silent about their opinions if it meant they could save their homes.

The river could help us capture our attackers but we'd need adept swimmers. Few Ilarians ventured into water over their heads, except for the Faroojers. These fisherfolk prided themselves on their prowess in the water. Many Ilarians considered them untrustworthy, and some probably were, but I'd find ones who weren't.

"Meet good Faroojers," I wrote at the top of my list.

I also needed someone who could build a second road leading to the river. I couldn't imagine who could do that.

And what would I do with these Mongols once I diverted them? I closed my eyes and remembered the jolly men drinking at the inn in Lev. Under other circumstances I'd have joined their table and drunk with them. Yet, I didn't doubt these men could fight and kill. All the humans I knew managed to be fierce at times and friendly at others.

The sight of a horse heading towards our tent interrupted my thoughts. By now I knew the people in the surrounding tents, and this rider wasn't one of them. As he came closer, I saw the identifying sash worn by messengers riding into areas where they didn't feel safe. He had no cause to worry here, but he didn't know that. I'd heard most messengers wouldn't enter our camps, making him one of their braver ones.

He rode over to my chair and stopped, carefully keeping his eyes on my face while ignoring my inadequate clothing.

"Gypsum Renata Glonti?" he inquired.

"Uh, yes. But who would send me a message here?"

He smiled without lowering his eyes. "Your mother would."

He reached inside his jacket and took out a letter. "She informed me she preferred you read this in her own hand and she asked me to wait for a return message."

I stood. He studied the blue sky as I took the paper he offered. Mom had double sealed it with wax. My hands shook as I opened it.

"My dear daughter," it said. "Ryalgar has informed me of your current location. I have searched my heart and mind for why you would do this after the peace I thought we made with each other, and after the joy I felt by including you with the Renata women."

I felt a little squeeze of sorrow in my chest. Yes, my timing had been poor.

I read on.

"Ryalgar says you are safe, and I am grateful for that. She thinks you may even be happy there. This I do not understand. I considered taking back the Renata name when I learned of your whereabouts, but decided that would not only be petty, it would be wrong. You belong with the Renata women no matter what you do.

"She tells me you and your new people will aid her in her plans to defend Ilari. Know that I am proud of her and proud of you, too. The Renata women have a colorful history, much of which I put aside when my mother died. I should have shared more of it with you girls. Then perhaps you'd understand me, and each other, better.

"So go be whoever Gypsum Renata Glonti needs to be and know that I will always love you."

She signed it with her flourish of a signature, and I could tell by the smudging that she'd closed the letter before the ink had fully dried.

The messenger hadn't taken his eyes off the horizon while I read.

"Well?" he said. "She's paid for your answer."

"Tell her …. tell her I want to hear all her stories about the Renata women someday and that I love her, too."

Blue skies and soft winds filled the next two anks of Keva. I missed Galen, but hoped his absence meant he gathered much information. Every day I watched for his return. Every night I went to bed longing for him.

I participated in two group cherish ceremonies, recognizing that while I was free to refuse, to do so would feel hurtful to the others. I'd no desire to put distance between me and them – I relied on their friendship and support and even our physical closeness to keep me going. However, when various tentmates made overtures to provide me with sexual pleasure one on one in Galen's absence, I turned them down with the truth. I wasn't in the mood. They understood, or if they didn't they were kind enough to pretend they did.

By the second half of Keva, Galen's long absence worried me. I spent too much time inventing scenarios in which everything was okay and yet he couldn't get word to us. As more days passed, those scenarios became harder to believe.

Every time I started a chore, Varla appeared to help me. She seldom mentioned Galen, but talked through my plans to help Ryalgar as we worked.

I noticed Suloom looked as worried as me, and by the third ank he and I took to sitting together each day at sunset, sharing a blanket as we stared north, hoping to see a horse riding our way.

After a few nights of that, Esteri began meeting us when we came back to camp in the near dark. She led us to two bowls of warm water scented with dried rose petals and followed our foot soak with a short massage.

Raheem had always flirted with me more than the other men, and I enjoyed flirting back. To be honest, he attracted me almost as much as Galen. After I turned him down, he began doing little fun physical things with me. A kiss on the hand. A slap in the butt. A peek down my shirt. All playful and given with his assurances that he'd gotten my message but wanted to keep my wheels greased so I wouldn't be totally rusty when Galen got home.

I took his antics for the affection they were. These were my people. We took care of each other, each in our own odd way. I don't know what I'd have done without them.

As Tirga neared, the spring warmth turned into unseasonable heat. Already sweating as we finished a midday meal, we watched a woman wearing men's pants walked out of the forest towards our tent. I'd been told the Velka scouts dressed in such a fashion.

"I come with a message," she called out, perhaps too nervous to come closer. "Your sister will send two women six days after Tirga. Be prepared to go with them to the Velka lodge where Ryalgar will acquaint you with the plans that have been made and prepare you for your role."

What? Ryalgar expected *me* to go into the forest and stay with the women who'd taken my grandmother from me? Did she not understand my anger? Had she not listened to me at all?

"I can't go there!"

"Why not?" the woman yelled back

"Because ... I don't wish to spend time with the Velka."

It's hard to explain a complex subject when you have to call out the words to someone twenty paces away.

"You must," the messenger hollered. "Your sister has filled her walls with a map of Ilari, and it has information you must see. There is no other way."

No other way. Great. Well, I could go and speak only to Ryalgar. Get in there, learn what I needed to know, and get out.

"Tell my sister I wish to keep my visit as short as possible but I will be ready when you say."

~ 11 ~

In the Forest

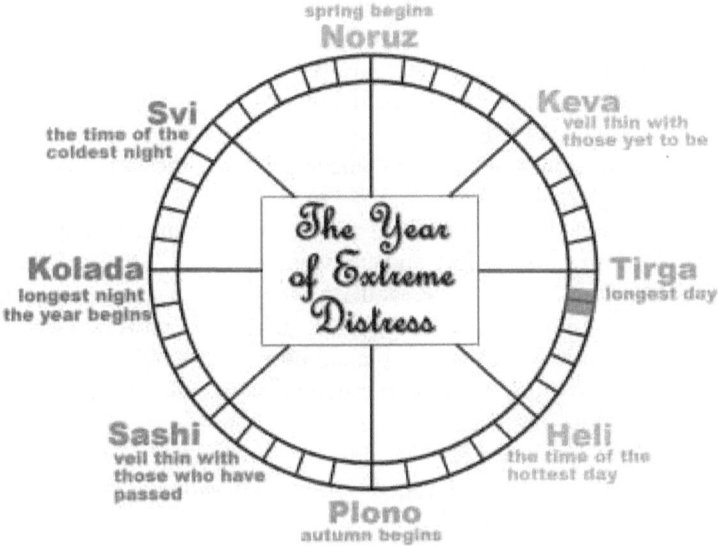

I did my best to be nice, I really did. Okay, maybe my best wasn't that impressive but I tried.

The stout woman in men's pants who led me into the thicket of trees paid no attention to my sulky behavior. Her job was to get me to the Velka lodge and if I didn't particularly want to go there, she didn't much care.

She explained that the Velka allowed the underbrush here to grow thin as a courtesy to the reczavy. We were neighbors after all, and they wished for us to be able to move freely along the forest's edge.

"Deeper in the woods the plants will form a barrier. You'll need to follow me closely to get through," she said. "Donkeys wait for us on the other side. We'll ride the rest of the way."

Her attitude contrasted with that of the skinny younger woman with a long stringy ponytail who met us and welcomed me to the Velka's home. I could tell she *wanted* me to like her, and my lack of warmth baffled her.

Well, I hardly wanted to tell this stranger my life story. I had reasons for feeling the way I did, and she didn't need to know them.

The massive stone lodge in the middle of the clearing dwarfed the castles of Ilari. In contrast to security-conscious castles, however, craftswomen had built the lodge to let in maximum light and accommodate as many plant-filled porches and balconies as possible. Heli, if living here hadn't meant being without men, I'd consider applying.

And, of course, if it hadn't been home to the hated woman who was my grandmother.

Ryalgar stood on the front porch to greet me. Perhaps she understood my discomfort and perhaps she cared. Or maybe my efficient sister knew she needed my cooperation and wanted to make me as comfortable as possible. Either way, I took the deal.

I greeted her with a hug, picked up my rucksack, and let her lead me to her room without so much as an introduction to all the curious women who watched us go.

At least the Velka scout hadn't lied. A massive, detailed map of Ilari filled one wall in Ryalgar's room, with notes inked in amid arrows and question marks. Windows took up two other walls, letting in ample light for examining her work.

"We're going to go over this?" I asked.

"This and more." She turned to the skinny woman who wanted me to like her and followed us in.

"This is Idris. The two of you will work together to formulate our plans."

I saw the hopeful look in the woman's eyes.

"I'm sorry, but only work with you, Ryalgar. And I formulate the plans involving the reczavy by myself."

Ryalgar didn't seem surprised or annoyed by my response. She turned to Idris.

"Give us some time alone, okay?"

The girl shrugged and left.

"Could you have been less rude?" Ryalgar hissed after the door had closed.

"Hey, I'm being nice just by *being* here."

Ryalgar stared at her wall for a few heartbeats.

"Look. This is getting complicated fast. I've got three fronts going on at once, and I can't possibly be as involved as I'd like in each one. You need to let me have some help. What do you have against Idris?"

"Nothing except that she is a Velka."

"Well, she's not much of one. I mean, she's only here because she ran any from home when she was barely a woman. I don't what she ran from in Eds but we offered safety."

"In *where*?" My voice went up several tones on the second word.

"Oh, that's right. I forgot. You reczavy dislike the Edsers. Bat scump."

"No, I don't share that prejudice. I mean, uh, the man I'm with, well, he's an Edser too."

Both of her eyebrows lifted.

"You're involved in a courtship?"

"Yes. Sort of. I guess."

"He's an Edser??"

"Worse than that. He's an Edser who's joined the reczavy. You might not know it from that description, but he's a good guy."

"Ohhh kaay." She spread the word out as though she needed the time to consider the information. "Any chance your situation would make you *more* willing to work with Idris?"

"It might. I need to learn more about Eds. Maybe she can answer questions as we get to know each other."

Ryalgar brought Idris back in, and I gave her my warmest smile.

"Sorry. I didn't fully understand the situation. I'm, uh, I'm looking forward to working with you."

She beamed. This one needed acceptance. What a shame she hadn't run away to the reczavy instead of the Velka. Many of our tents could have filled the yawning gap in her young heart.

Over the next few days I met more women close to Ryalgar. The Velka spanned a surprising age range, as well as styles and interests. I forgot about them being Velka as we talked.

"I haven't had the chance to tell you, but our goal is to not kill a single Mongol. We've learned their Khan puts a high value on the lives of his soldiers, and we hope he'll approve a peace treaty with us if we resist their takeover without bloodshed," Ryalgar told me at one such gathering.

"That works well with our plans."

"What exactly are you planning?" The only woman in the group who carried herself as if she was more important than Ryalgar asked the question politely enough.

"Right now I'm concentrating on a combination of throwing eggs, needlework, and circus acts," I said.

"I see." She exchanged a look with one of the other women. I noted their faces. Ryalgar needed to be careful around these two.

"My biggest concern …" I stood to give my butt a welcome rest from the hard wooden stool I'd spent half the morning on. "My biggest concern is that I'll need to find a way to divert our attackers away from Pilk and here to the Wide River's edge." I spoke as I walked up to Ryalgar's wall and pointed to my location on the map. "I have a friend whose brother has recruited Gruenites to help us but I need a new road, one made to look like the old one. And the old one will have to look like a minor trail. It's a big job."

Ryalgar grinned. "Someone has offered his expertise to do that sort of work. I believe you know him."

"I do?"

"You call him Dad."

"You mean our dad ??"

She and a few others laughed at what must have been a horrified expression on my face.

"He's a soil expert and he's amassed volunteers and a lot of shovels. They've already altered the entrance into the realm and now they're working on the path up to Vinx. Your road work will be on his list."

The only hard part of that would be speaking with my father. I didn't look forward to the encounter. Wait. Maybe I could get Idris to deal with him. She'd like that, and he'd probably like it better too.

Later that night Ryalgar and I shared sweet brown after-dinner wine and spoke of more personal things. She shared news about my home and my sisters, and I told her about my life. She found my tale of hiding from my parents in Lev entertaining, especially the part about the ten foreigners who shared my place of lodging.

"You think you slept under the same roof as our enemy?!"

"Think about it. Ten men from another land, only a day's ride away from where these envoys make their demands the next day. What are the odds we've got two such groups running around here at the same time?"

She sat taller, inhaling a long breath of indignation. "So. They thought they'd sample the wares they're about to plunder?"

"Maybe." It hadn't seemed that way. "It's more like they were just thirsty and having a good time."

"In Ilari?"

"I mean, they probably looked around. Wouldn't you do that before you invaded someone?"

"Of course I would." She tapped a finger hard against the wooden armrest of her chair, lost in thought. Finally she said, "Remind me to stop underestimating you."

I don't think my sister could have said anything nicer.

I'll never know if Ryalgar set it up or not, but the next morning when I left her room I passed an older woman in the hall. I looked at her. She looked at me. She had pretty features and a slender yet strong build like my father's. And she had his eyes.

"You're Gypsum," she said.

"You're my dead grandmother?"

"Yes. I suppose I am."

"Good. You can stay that way." I resumed walking. I'd already been far nicer to many more people than I'd intended.

"That dying thing wasn't my idea," she called out to the back of my head.

I stopped walking but didn't turn around. "I know. I've heard the whole story, thank you."

"Really? Including how I dreamed of joining the Velka my entire life? How my best friend Kalina and I used to pretend we were Velka witches when we were little girls? Because whoever told you that must be dead too. No one alive knows that story."

I looked at her over my shoulder. "So you finally got to be a Velka. Wonderful. Was it worth abandoning the kin who loved you?"

She stood a bit taller. I'd offended her.

"What do you think?" she said. "Was it worth abandoning yours to join the reczavy?"

At those words, I turned to face her squarely. "Don't you dare, don't you dare question *my* choices, not after you bowed out of my life and left me to the mercy of others."

"I left you to people who loved you."

"People who struggled to raise me."

"Everyone struggles to raise a child."

I had nothing to say to that.

"I also joined the reczavy because I love a man, and it was the only way to be with him." I don't know why I told her this, it was only part of the truth but I guess I wanted her to know I'd been guided by affection for another while she'd only been guided by selfishness.

She looked at me and a slow smile spread across her face.

"Well now. We have something in common. I too had to choose between people I cared about."

"What?? Who??"

"Kalina and I remained close friends throughout our lives. We joined the Velka together, happy as two little girls who'd gotten their childhood dream to come true. But we weren't here long before a slow disease began to consume her. She'd had no time to make other close friends and though everyone helped nursed her, I became the one she relied on."

"This was before I was born?"

"It started before you were born but Kalina took a turn for the worse about the time you arrived, which is why I wasn't there for my daughter then. Kalina was so sick and I thought my daughter was fine, surrounded by family. When, when word came that Liya had died, I was shocked. But Kalina begged me not to leave her. We both knew if I left I wouldn't be back. I decided to remain by her side and then Markita took you in and issued her edict about my being dead. Although your dad knew I had a sick friend, I doubt he or anyone else suspected what a difficult a choice I had to make."

I softened and started to reply but Grandma interrupted.

"Do understand. I don't regret coming here on any level. I love this home and what I've become. I'm grateful that I could be by Kalina's side when she left this world. And I'm not apologizing to you, a granddaughter I never met. But I don't like having you hate me. So I'm asking you. What you would have done in my shoes?"

The softness left as fast as it came. "I'll think about the question."

I walked away, but I knew the answer. So did she. The remaining question was how long I'd keep hating a woman who'd done what I'd probably have done, too.

Both Idris and our trusty Velka guide accompanied me home and this gave Idris and me a chance to get more acquainted. Idris was talkative and happy as we rode.

"Ryalgar says you don't like to talk about your childhood," I said.

That took the smile off her face.

"Nope. Don't and won't."

"Okay. I respect that. If I told you my plans required a better general knowledge of Eds, and nothing specific about you, would you talk to me about your nichna?"

"Maybe. What sorts of things do you want to know?"

I ducked to avoid a low branch. The donkeys moved well along the narrow paths, stepping over the thick roots and strong vines that I struggled with, but they had a poor sense of the height of their human riders, forcing us to duck often as we rode.

"I need to know about the Eds Royals."

"Why?"

"I'll have to deal with them." I intended to fill Idris in on our troubles with Eds, but not now.

"That's unfortunate."

"Because?"

"Because they're some of the worst rantillions in Eds and that's saying something."

"Really? You've met them?"

She hesitated. "I'll answer that but no further questions. Okay?"

"Okay."

"So. The dad still rules. He's mean but he's smart and he does a decent job for the Edsers. His wife grew up in Eds and she hardly says a word."

I waited for more.

"They have three kids, two grown. I heard that Crown Prince Lufo got married a couple of years ago. Eds rules say he needs to sire a son to take the throne from his dad but so far he only has a baby daughter."

"I assume he's not happy about that."

She ignored me. "Prince Lufo's wife is pregnant again so he may rule soon enough. He has a younger sister and a much younger brother. The sister is my age and to answer your question, Nan and I played together as children. That's how I know what I know."

Snake scump, I shouldn't have promised not to ask more questions.

"The last thing I'll tell you," she added "is that the Crown Prince is meaner than his dad, and stupider, too.

"You're not a fan of this guy?"

Her glare reminded me that was a question.

"When people are mean, I like to be able to outwit them," she said. "So I liked his being stupid. Now, you tell me about the reczavy."

It was a fair request, and for the rest of our journey, I did. But sooner or later I intended to learn more of Idris' story.

When we emerged from the last of the trees, I hoped to see Galen there with his arms outstretched waiting for me. It was a ridiculous hope as no one knew we were arriving then. But perhaps he was in the tent, or near the campfire. I didn't care where he was, just so he was home.

~ 12 ~

A Rescue Operation

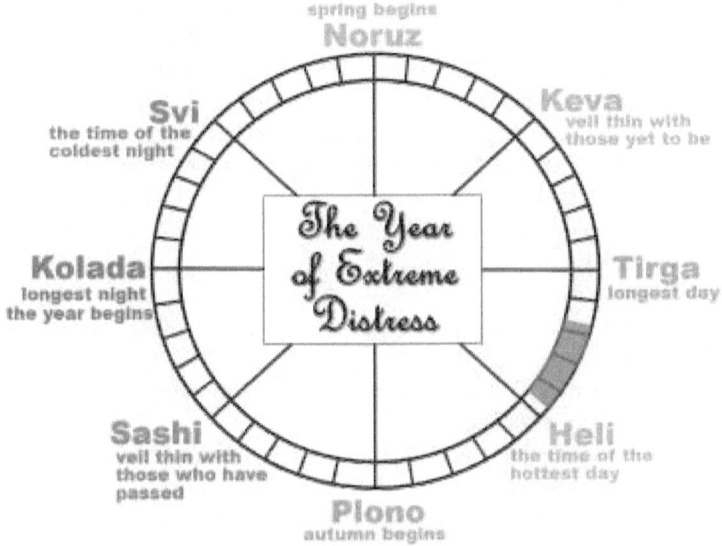

spring begins
Noruz

Svi
the time of the
coldest night

Keva
veil thin with
those yet to be

Kolada
longest night
the year begins

The Year of Extreme Distress

Tirga
longest day

Sashi
veil thin with
those who have
passed

Heli
the time of the
hottest day

Piono
autumn begins

On the day Idris and I walked out of the forest, the camp simmered in the sun. I suppose the heat didn't help when I discovered Galen hadn't returned or sent word while I was gone.

My tentmates' faces told me they feared for his safety and that the smallest niggle of doubt had crept in about whether he wanted to be part of our tent. After so much time, how could they *not* wonder if his rush into Eds had been a clever way to leave without a confrontation?

I faced my own version of that dilemma. I desperately hoped he wasn't dead or injured so badly that he couldn't contact us, but if not, then his leaving by choice was the most probable alternative. Would he have abandoned me? And did I prefer *that* to his death? I never let myself answer the question.

I got through Idris' visit, doing my best to take her around, and give her a feel for the talents and personalities involved. She asked lots of good questions, and I appreciated her enthusiasm, particularly as mine was at an all-time low.

Our best discovery was two thread workers, improbably named Pie and Guy, so I assumed both were shortened names for something. They'd joined us from the southern riverbanks of Faroo but, unlike many new reczavy, both men stayed in contact with those back home. Pie clapped his hands when we spoke of the plan to recruit Faroojers to lay in wait in the river and capture Mongols. Guy started reeling off names they both knew.

"Please," I said. "Get them involved. Figure out how you could do this. It's all yours." My failure to get over to Faroo or to find a Faroojer had nagged at me every day until then.

Idris and I parted by agreeing that we'd relay messages often and she'd return soon.

Two days after she left, I woke in the middle of the night knowing I'd leave for Eds in the morning. Suloom slept near me and heard me stir.

He reached over and touched my arm. "You okay?" he whispered.

"Yeah. I'm going to Eds tomorrow," I whispered back.

"I'm going with you."

"I appreciate that, but I'll draw less attention if I'm alone."

"Yeah but two people invite less trouble."

"I know, but I'm going for information from a particular contact. If it goes beyond that, I'll come back and get you. I promise."

It had been nearly a year since the barkeep along the Little River fed me her surprisingly tasty turnip and goat stew and gave me a student discount on a room. I hoped she still ran the bar.

I saw her as I walked in, a stout woman with nondescript brown hair wiping off tables on the far side of the room. I didn't expect her to remember me, but she yelled out. "The student looking for her boyfriend! What are you doing back here? You didn't lose him again, did you?"

She laughed like she'd made the best joke in the world, but actually, I had.

"Funny you should ask," I said.

"Oh no. Listen, honey. Maybe this one doesn't want to be found. That's usually the case when they disappear twice, you know. You seem like a nice girl, so stop chasing him. There's more boys out there."

"Yes. I know. I just need to make sure he isn't in trouble first." I paused. "How'd you remember me?"

"We don't get so many strangers here. I told your story to plenty of bored customers after you left. Pretty girl from Vinx trying to find some Edser boy out in the wilderness …"

Her last word trailed off. She stopped wiping the table, laid down the wet rag, and looked at me.

"Did you come here from the reczavy?"

Oh dear. Should I lie?

"I did. He and I both ended up there after I found him."

She looked around the tavern, examining her customers. "Come back to the kitchen with me. I need to show you something."

The kitchen was empty except for the two of us. For a heartbeat I wondered if she hated the reczavy so much she'd brought me back here to attack me with one of her knives. Then she motioned to a broom closet. My heart pounded as I followed her in.

"You never heard this from me. You promise?" she said in a loud whisper.

"Of course. You know something that can help me?"

"I know one of those families out by the Canyon River had a boy who ran away and joined the reczavy. Broke his parents' hearts. They'd already lost one to the Svadlu, and they thought that was bad enough."

"That could be my boyfriend."

"Well if it is, he's in deep trouble. Our Royals, they got this thing where they just hate the reczavy. I don't get it. I say let people do what they want but they cooked up this whole plot to get rid of you all. Then your boyfriend shows up here asking about what the Royals are up to."

"So he made it here. That's good. And he asked questions."

"Yeah. Too many of them. If he'd been in my bar I'd have had a talk with him about discretion. Next thing you know, our ruling prince sends a fancy herald to invite him up to the palace. Your man rides up to the castle like he owns the world, and that's the last time anyone has seen him."

I felt as if I'd drunk a jug of water from a freezing mountain stream.

"Pruck. Do you think they killed him?"

"Oh, I know they didn't. What can I say? People talk in a tavern." She threw her arms out, palms up, as though saying *it's not my fault*. "The young man is now a *guest* of our nichna and will be staying in the castle as long as our Ruling Prince wishes."

"Why didn't he send word back to us?"

"I've heard he's kept in a small attic room. Most think if the Ruling Prince got the information he wanted, he'd have let the young man leave anks ago, but it's not entirely up to him. Power shifts amongst our Royals."

"Are you talking about Crown Prince Lufo and his pregnant wife?"

"Oh, she's more than pregnant. She's due to pop that little Royal out in an ank or two, and if it has a pizzle, his daddy gets to take the throne."

"I mean no disrespect, but I've heard bad things about this Crown Prince of yours."

"I'd have been surprised if you'd heard anything but," she said. "He doesn't win popularity contests, except with those few who agree with him. They love him because he'll do things other rulers won't, like what he plans to do with your boyfriend."

"Things like what?"

"Oh, he'll probably put him in a cage and let an angry crowd yell insults, and maybe spit and piss on him, while he riles them up about how awful the reczavy are. He loves to get a group of Edsers provoked."

I had to get Galen out of there. I didn't have time to keep my promise to Suloom and ride back and get him, either. Babies came early, and Galen couldn't be a prisoner when that woman gave birth. With one outcome, Galen became the property of a deranged monster. With the other outcome, the monster was denied the throne, at least for now, but would likely hit new lows of bad behavior in his frustration. Galen would make an easy target for his wrath.

"Do you still have that student rate for lodgers?" I asked.

She laughed. "You still a student?"

"I'm still learning a lot."

"Works for me," she said. "Let me take you around the back way. The fewer who know you're here, the better."

By the next morning I had some ideas. I could use the one thing I did that no one would suspect, except it presented a new challenge. I'd always sewed intentions into my thread work. No one taught me to, I just did it. But I'd also always cared about those I sewed for, so my intentions were good. Okay, maybe sometimes a little self-serving too, but nothing worse.

No matter how much a sister, parent, or friend annoyed me, I didn't sew while angry. Old lore said those who harmed others brought three times more trouble upon themselves. True? Who knew. All I knew was that any ill intentions I felt toward family and friends didn't last long, so I'd never been tempted to test the consequences.

For the first time, circumstances warranted an unpleasant, unwanted, and strong effect on several people at once. I considered trying to make them ill, or angry at each other, or all so unreasonably frightened that they'd hide in a closet while I rescued Galen. Could I do any of those? I didn't think so. The best I could probably do was make them queasy, petulant, or nervous, and what good would that do?

Furthermore, how would I get a castle full of Royals and their servants to all put on something I sewed? It had to be little, too, because I had to sew a prucking lot of them before another day passed.

Once I settled on the best idea I could come up with, the barkeeper helped. I think she kind of liked me, and I know she disliked Prince Lufo. Whatever her motivation, she got me parchment and threads and provided me with fancy clothes like someone official from Pilk might wear.

Days were long in Tirga, and before the sun set that day I rode to the Eds castle to give the Royals the awful news about the deadly flock of birds heading towards them.

"No madam, I cannot let you in, no matter who in Pilk has sent you. The Ruling Prince meets with subjects by appointment only."

I'd expected this.

"As you wish sir. If your Royals won't accept our help, then do make sure you tend well to their empty eye sockets once the birds have plucked them, as infections tend to develop."

"Eye sockets?" the man said.

"Yes, sir. Was I not clear? These birds attack human faces and cause all sorts of disfigurement, but blindness is the worst of what they do. Of course, it is easy to protect you all from this, if you prefer."

"What group did you say you were from?"

I held out the parchment. The barkeep had helped me fill it with official looking signatures and seals.

"I represent a joint effort between the Ilarian Institute for the Study of Malicious Animals and the Royal Pilkese Society for the Prevention of Disfigurement. These small poultices, when worn around the neck, have been shown to eliminate one hundred percent of attacks by this small but vicious flock of birds. We delivered a handful to the Royals of Zur two days ago, and every member of their family was spared as the flock flew over."

"What about the other Zurians?" He looked genuinely horrified.

"Strange birds, these are. They almost always attack Royals only. Perhaps it is their better blood, we're not sure, but the Ilarian Institute for the Study of Malicious Animals is working hard to determine why."

"Let me see if the family would like to see you."

And I was in.

"This is a highly dubious claim," the Ruler glared at his butler, then glared at me. "I've never heard of such nonsense before."

"Oh we keep these attacks well hidden, your Highness. Can't have people panicking. With your permission we'd like to provide your staff with the poultices too as we have had the rare case of a bird who got confused."

"I want one," the man who had let me in said.

"I want mine first," Prince Lufo demanded.

"These horrible birds can't hurt my baby can they?" the pregnant wife asked, her hands held protectively over her stomach. I felt sorry enough for her to reply, "No, madam. Your baby is safe."

I handed out poultices as fast as I could, fastening each around the neck with all the intention I could muster.

"It's important I put one on absolutely everyone in the building," I added. "For, you know, full protection for you all."

"Do what you must." The Ruling Prince had already gone from skeptical to looking a bit dazed. He picked at some lint on his sleeve as if he wondered what it was. His wife sat down, and she stared at a lamp as if she needed to remember something about the lamp but wasn't sure what.

"Is everyone in the household here in this room?" I asked.

"No, there's the young man in the attic," one of the younger maids said.

The Crown Prince turned towards her. "You're not supposed to mention him, remember?"

"Oh, oops," she giggled. "I forgot."

"I'll just slip upstairs and give him one too. Better safe than sorry."

"There's no need ..." the Ruling Prince said but I left the room before he finished.

Luckily the door bolted from the outside because if it had needed a key I don't know what I'd have done. I pushed it open and in the growing dusk Galen and I stared at each other. I put my fingers to my lips as I entered. then pulled an extra-large woman's dress and veil out of my bag.

"Get these on quick and follow me. Don't say a word."

He ignored my instructions, grabbed me, and kissed me.

"Duck Piss," he whispered. "I've never been so happy to see anyone in my life." Then he pulled on the dress, threw the veil over his head, and followed me down the stairs.

"We'll be going now," I called out to the room of confused Royals and their servants as we walked past them. Most of them were staring at each other with puzzled looks.

"You two ladies have a safe journey home," the wife of the Ruling Prince called back.

"I thought I only let one of you in," the butler said, shaking his head as if to clear it.

"Oh no. She was behind me. You probably didn't see her."

"She" gave the butler a little wave of her gloved hand. He shrugged and waved back, and Galen and I stepped out into the night.

~ 13 ~

Cool Water on a Hot Day

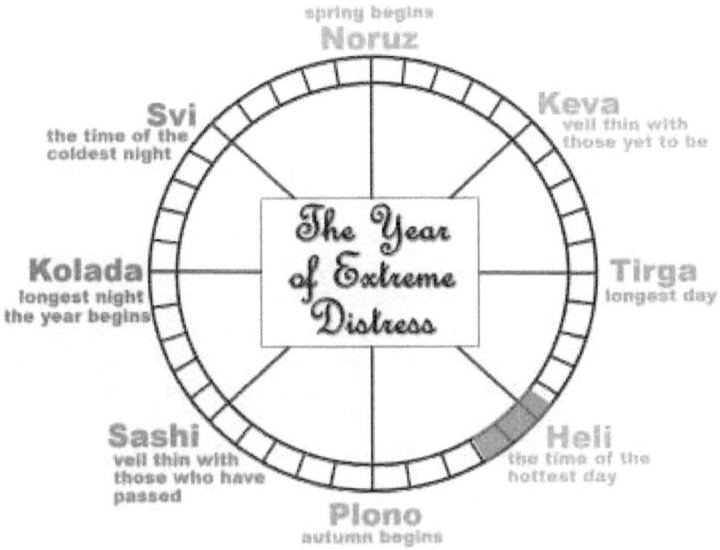

I assumed the Royals would emerge from their dazed state soon and send people to find us. I'll always be grateful to the barkeep who persuaded someone to hide us along the river's banks until dawn, and to all the Edsers who left us alone as we rode past Mount Eds and home. Did they know we were the couple their Ruler demanded to be turned over to him? Maybe not.

I learned of Galen's ordeal as we rode. Yes, the Ruling Prince had brought him to the castle hoping for dirt on the reczavy that would make more people support his attacks on us.

"Did he hit you? Hurt you?" I asked.

99

"No, but only because I wouldn't play along. I answered his questions and did my best to win him over. You know, find common ground. But this man hadn't a morsel of sympathy for me."

"Do you think it was wise to tell him more about us?"

"Of course. The things they say are worse than anything we do. He must have thought so too because he kept asking me to share more. When I couldn't produce stories that would arouse the outrage he wanted, I asked why he didn't just make stuff up."

"Yeah. Who would know the difference?"

"My question pissed him off."

"Oh, okay. So he wanted you to justify his hatred of you."

"I guess. When I didn't, he left me locked in that room for anks with bread and water. I tried to find a way out but that place is built solid."

I felt awful knowing Galen had been going through this while my tentmates and I questioned his loyalty.

"Then he came back and we had this really weird conversation. He told me some of his subjects wanted him to eliminate the entertainment in K'ba, too. I couldn't imagine the realm allowing such a thing, and he agreed with me. Said a helpful advisor suggested all the anger in Eds could be pacified with enough coin and, if he taxed the K'basta heavily enough, Eds would become a nichna of unusually wealthy goat herders."

"Talk about corrupt."

"It gets better. Daddy Prince realized that if the entertainers could provide ample coins, then why not the reczavy? He wanted details about how we support ourselves."

"The Edsers already know about our little enterprises. We have one of the most, uh, unregulated market stalls along the Little River in Eds. They let us sell anything, and I mean anything, there."

"Edsers enjoy our products, and their Ruler knows it," Galen said. "He told me he rather liked the idea of getting rich off of us, but his son has no interest in the idea. Once Lufo takes the throne, we can count on the destruction of the reczavy."

"I heard about this guy's son. A real charmer. So that's the last time you spoke with, what did you call him? Daddy Prince?"

"Yup. He said he'd be back when his grandson was born and he had a better feel for how I could be useful. That was about two anks ago."

"Why would Ilarians bring this kind of conflict upon our realm now, of all times?" I meant it rhetorically, but Galen answered.

"The times *are* why they're doing it. The distraction of a coming invasion gives them a window to make Ilari more to their liking."

"Did you learn anything about the deal with K'ba?"

Galen shook his head. "Not a thing. I tried to get him talking but he wouldn't. Whatever deal he made, he's keeping it to himself."

"I learned something last night," I said.

"About Eds?"

"No. About me. I thought I had this sort of subtle magic I could use. No big deal."

"You mean the way you put good intentions into your thread work? I always thought that was kind of cool."

"So did I. But it looks like I can put less benign intentions in as well."

"Really? Is that a good idea?"

"No, but it sure helped us out last night. What I learned is that if I'm desperate, I can do something stronger than normal. Maybe a lot stronger."

"Wow, Gypsum. You're more than a thread worker."

"Yeah. I'm kind of a weapon maker. And I've just added me to my plan to stop the Mongols."

Over the next few days, Celestine contacted me to see if she and her lover could celebrate Heli in one of our guest tents. Olivine showed up unannounced to tell me all about her new boyfriend and seek my help in finding a place where they could secretly meet. Idris and the scout arrived to exchange information. And Galen got cherished for the first time since I'd joined the tent.

It was a lot.

My sisters were the easiest to handle. I managed to arrange romantic getaways for each, one with us and another along the Canyon River. How convenient to have a sibling like me living outside the confines of society who could do such things, right? Hey, ladies, glad to help.

Idris managed to both frustrate and assist me during her visit. She frustrated me because, despite her enthusiasm and eagerness, she hadn't done a thing to move our plan along. She waited for me to come up with ideas and make them happen. Then she told me they were great. She excelled at encouraging and communicating with the Velka, but I needed to change my expectations of her.

Her knowledge about Eds remained useful though. Now that she understood the threat the Edsers posed to us, she spoke more of her childhood friendship with Princess Nan and her time spent playing at the Eds castle.

"Where is your friend these days?" I asked.

We sat in the shade of the trees, enjoying a slight breeze as the sun neared the horizon.

"I've no idea. Nan and I lost touch when, when I left there. I always assumed she'd married someone suitable. A princess in Eds can't produce heirs to the throne, even male ones, so as long as they stay out of trouble no one much cares what they do."

"Could you find out where she is? Visit her? See what she knows?"

Idris's eyes widened as she sucked in her breath. "How many Svadlu would you send with me if I did?"

"You'd want Svadlu to escort you to visit a friend?"

"You bet I do. Her, um, Nan's family has a quarrel with me. If others got word I was there … I won't go without guards. A lot of guards."

"Um, okay. Let's find out where she is first and I'll see if I can find guards to go with you.

So, I might have to ask a favor of a sister, too. Would Sulphur the Svadlu get a few friends to join her for some extraneous guard duty?

"You knew this would happen," Galen said. He was right. My tentmates had tactfully waited until my visitors left but he was overdue for a cherish ceremony, and it was my tentmates' usual way of welcoming one back and showing support for one who'd experienced trauma.

"You have lots of choices," Ksenia told me, her arm around my shoulders in her best this-will-be-okay fashion. "You don't have to be present at all. Or you can watch from a distance or close up. Or you can participate a little. Or a lot. This is about Galen, and we want him to be comfortable, but we recognize he won't be if you're not."

She was right. I'd enjoyed my own ceremony and was probably due for another as well. I looked forward to mine and I wanted him to enjoy his.

I didn't doubt Galen's affection for me or his attraction to me. I understood that this ritual wasn't about the kind of romance he and I shared. It was about something else. Celebrating sexuality. Healthy bodies. The life force within us and our lust and freedom as it mixed with our affection for each other and our joy in having found a pleasant, easy way to experience something other than just the bonds a couple shared.

I could do this.

"I'd like to watch, close enough to see his pleasure. Touch him along with the others, maybe, but not sexually. I'll save what's between us for private."

She nodded. "Good choices. Many couples have found those work for them. If you do have issues during it, motion to me. But I don't think you will."

And I didn't. I found it oddly joyful to watch nine other people drive Galen wild with pleasure, and the grins he and I exchanged while they did so became treasures in my mind. I know that may be hard to believe without experiencing it, but it was true. When every tentmate had a piece of him, I accepted the partner's ritual role of covering him with a blanket at the end and curling up next to him. Yes, I could have used a little satisfaction myself by then, but I waited. He was exhausted, and I'd get plenty of that from him soon enough.

Three days later I left for Faroo with the two Faroojer thread workers who'd taken over the water part of our plan. A few of their friends joined us, as did Varla and Jofim, both tentmates who'd expressed interest in helping me. After spending nearly an eighth locked in a castle attic, Galen didn't want to go anywhere, and I didn't blame him.

We avoided Eds and circled the forest to the east traveling through Scrud, Vinx, Gruen, and Pilk on our two-day journey. The heat never lifted as we rode, and we arrived at the small fishing village along the Wide River drenched in sweat. We had all worn enough clothes to not offend others, but I'm sure each of us considered stripping down to almost nothing more than once.

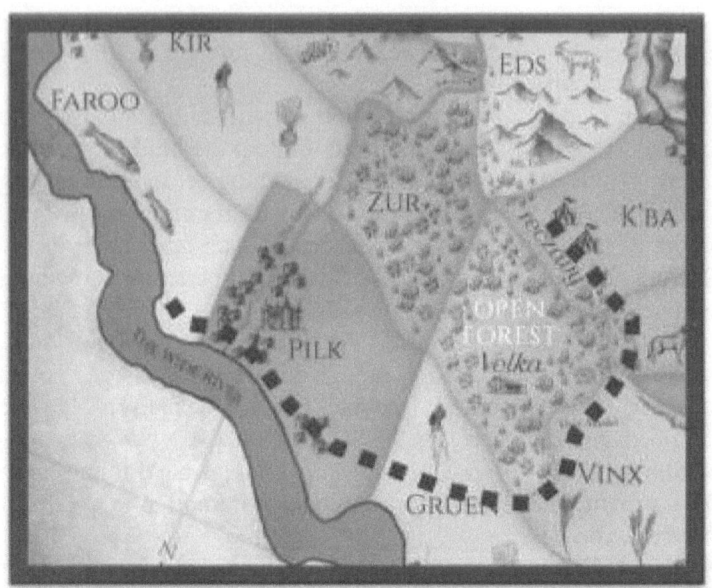

My two new allies, Pie and Guy, looked so much alike that I struggled to tell them apart from a distance. Slender men, they both had the coppery complexion Faroojers were known for and wore their straight shiny black hair in identical long ponytails.

They exceeded my hopes in recruiting Faroojers. Thirty or forty young men and women greeted us at the river's edge, anxious to show me the small rafts they used and how well they maneuvered in the water. Someone somewhere had decided their fishing nets could hold the fiercest of people and, after their demonstration, I had to agree. We planned to meet in Gruen, soon, to get them familiar with the river there and assess how many people, boats, and nets we'd need in the water. Finally something in my plans had come together.

Then we all got into the water to wash away the heat. Guy splashed me hard in the face. I laughed and responded with as hard a splash as I could manage and then water flew everywhere as

Faroojers and reczavy played together like small children. Who'd have guessed that would happen?

It gave me hope. If cool water on a hot day could unite us, maybe we could come together to do something important, too.

I returned to camp ready to charge ahead, but as my sheaf of notes grew thicker I knew what I needed next. Too many caring people surrounded me and told me I was wonderful. I liked hearing it, of course, but I needed someone who'd tell me if my ideas were stupid or too implausible to pull off. I needed someone who wouldn't hesitate to criticize me.

My mother would have done nicely, but this wasn't her area of expertise.

So. I needed Ryalgar, back here in my camp, telling me the truth.

She came when I sent a message and she sat with me in the lean-to where I'd first been entertained. Others brought us fruit and wine while she studied my notes carefully, just as I'd hoped, asking questions as she read. Unlike my new family, she gave little in the way of encouragement.

After she looked at all of it, she said "This is excellent."

I felt relief move from the top of my head down to my toes.

"Great. Then tricks, illusions, and eggs filled with itching powder it is."

~ 14 ~

Hiding a Wall

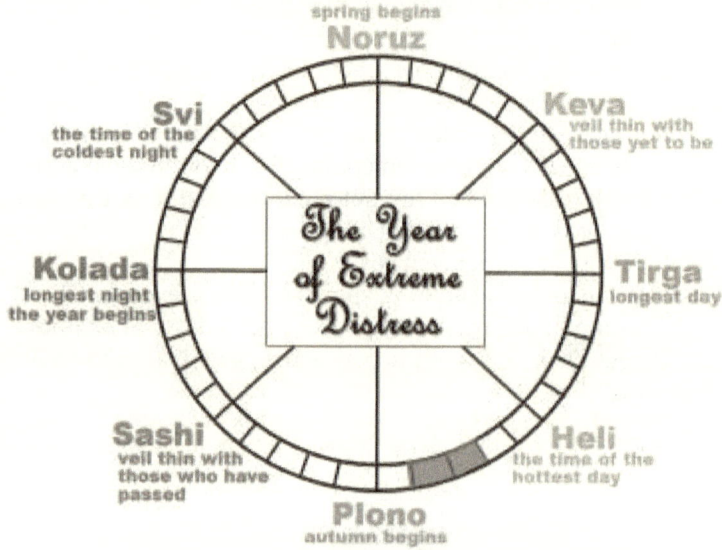

Ksenia rode back from an all-tent meeting held at the other edge of the reczavy land. I'd learned that, as a new tent, we'd had been given space along one edge and often had to travel far on foot to reach the others. It wasn't uncommon to see a tentmate on one of our shared horses, but it was uncommon to see Ksenia ambling as she rode, slumped back in her seat.

"Everything okay?" I called out to her as I walked over. I looked closer. She had tears on her face.

Oh dear.

"Can I help?"

"Not unless you can change the way power is distributed in Ilari," she said. She slid off her horse, always graceful for a woman her size, and handed me the reigns with a long sigh. "I suppose you could put my horse up while I wipe my face and compose myself before I tell the others."

"Glad to. Something special fueling your frustration?"

She glanced up at the sky. Whether she silently begged her ancestors for strength or merely stalled while she composed herself I could not tell.

"We learned this morning that Prince Lufo's wife bore him a legitimate heir last night."

"You mean she had a boy.

"Yes. That *is* what 'legitimate heir' means."

I understood her anger. "It's ridiculous, isn't it? A capable female Royal could do a fine job of ruling Eds, and she might calm everyone down a little, too. Has any nichna ever tried to crown a female?"

"Not that I've ever heard about," she answered. "So the bad news is that Crown Prince Lufo takes the throne. As is their custom, they've scheduled his coronation for the next holiday."

"Oh no." Raheem had joined us, and he took the reins of Ksenia's horse from me so I could stay with her. "That would be Plono, in less than an ank."

Two more women walked toward us.

"She had a varmin boy," Raheem call out to them.

"Toad scump." One of them spat.

"Should we pack up our stuff and hide in the forest?" the other asked. "How fast do you think he'll come after us?"

"Do you think he plans to kill us, imprison us, or drive us away?" the first said.

Ksenia held up her hand.

"Slow down. Nothing will happen that soon. Yes, Prince Lufo will rule Eds but he won't rule K'ba yet. The two nichnas have an agreement that hasn't taken effect, and we don't know when it does. Until then, no one expects the Edsers to engage in outright aggression against their neighbors. Nor does anyone think the Svadlu would stand for such, no matter how busy they are. So hiding in the bushes is premature."

"Maybe," Raheem muttered. "Have you followed the other political news in K'ba?"

"You mean the K'basta who want to surrender to the Mongols? Sure."

"They call themselves the Sage Coalition," he said. "Bunch of scared people, if you ask me."

Suloom had come out of the tent, seen us, and walked over. We'd all been slowly making our way to the campfire area where chairs awaited. Ksenia plopped onto one first.

"They have a point," Suloom said. "They've looked into what happens to those who resist the Mongols and those who surrender. I think Ilari would be well served to listen."

"Perhaps, but I think Raheem worries that if most of this nichna won't fight for their own lives, that sends the wrong message to the Edsers," Ksenia said. "Or least to someone like Prince Lufo."

"We need to pay more attention to what's going on elsewhere," Varla said as she joined us. "We haven't seen Idris for days. Where's she been? She promised to find her childhood chum Nan and learn more."

"She did," I said. "She should be back any day. Now that Prince Lufo's taking over, she knows how urgent this is."

The conversation went on far longer, but no one had anything new to say. It didn't stop us from talking though. I guess we all took some comfort from stating our worries out loud, over and over.

We sought distractions while we waited for Idris, waited for Plono, and waited to find out what would happen. I sewed little poultices like the ones I'd given the Eds Royals. I figured Idris could ask the Velka for herbs to fill them with. Maybe they had something to encourage foggy confusion.

After I'd made ten of them I asked my tentmates to try them on. They laughed and agreed, wearing them tight against their skin. By the time we finished eating, each one felt disorientated.

"It's like having too much wine without the wine," one tentmate explained.

"I couldn't wait for dinner to be over so I could lay down and take a nap," another said.

"Got a question," Varla said. 'How will you get the Mongols to wear these? I mean, we're your friends. They're, like, charging in on horses trying to kill us."

I couldn't help but laugh at the image of handing these poultices out to mounted warriors. *Hey gentlemen. Before you start all that pillaging would you mind putting these on?*

"I thought we could shoot them with slingshots," I said.

"They'd have to be heavier ..."

"I don't think we can aim that well ..."

"They'd just bounce off and fall to the ground ..."

I answered the last objection.

"*Not* if I coat one side with pine resin. That will make them heavier too."

"But they'll pull them off even if they stick ..." Jofim said.

"Not if we shoot them at the middle of their backs they won't," I answered.

My tentmates looked at each other.

"You're serious?" four of them said.

Galen laughed. "She is. I think we ought to learn more about pine resin. And slingshots."

"I thought other people were going to do *those* parts of it," Esteri said, pulling her robe tighter around her body. "We're just supposed to think up the plan."

"No. The Velka agreed to prepare the eggs because they have ways to inject our itching powder into them. We still have to make the powder. And, after they've done the preparing, *we* have to throw the eggs. This is our show."

"Then we ought to be throwing things every day and practicing with slingshots," Galen said.

"We need more tents involved, too," Ksenia added.

"I've tried." This had been my biggest source of frustration. "Some people don't know if they want to be involved. A few tell me they'll side with the Sage Coalition and not resist. Most say I'm worrying about this way too soon and to come get them a couple of anks ahead of time and they'll help. In the past four days, I've been told twenty-two times to relax."

"Ouch," Varla said.

"To be fair, some of our fire performers are working hard on this. And two thread workers from Faroo have organized a whole group of Faroojers to find ways to capture Mongols who run into the river because they itch so bad. But the rest of this – it's up to us to get it done."

"That's a lot to figure out in two eights," Esteri said.

We looked at the ground, realizing the truth of her words.

Finally Ksenia spoke. "Let's hope idiot Prince Lufo gives us the whole two eighths to get this done."

Pie, Guy, and I went to Gruen before the Plono Holiday so they could show me how the Faroojers and reczavy would capture our prisoners. I'd put a lot of faith in my two fellow thread workers, and I felt my trust was well founded. But it was time to go see for myself.

Once we left Vinx and entered Gruen, they showed me the original road and where it joined the new fake road my father and his crew made. The new road still looked new, not well-worn like it needed to, but they assured me it would look like an old road once finished.

Soon after the road narrowed to a trail, showing me how much further they had to go to complete their work. Someone had pounded stakes into the ground to show the proposed path as it skirted established fields and followed trails used by animals and farmers. We rode alongside those stakes towards the river. And then I saw it.

I had *never* seen a structure like it. Made of stone and at least as high as three grown men, it stretched from somewhere inside the Wide River out across … what? Given the sharp bend in the river where it started, I guessed it followed the border of Pilk and Gruen.

"Why would my father's road crew build such a monstrosity?!" I gasped. Pie and Guy both laughed.

"Your father is smart. We like him."

"Yeah. This is *not* his doing."

I looked around and saw saffron-caped officers strutting as they gave instructions to the more junior Svadlu who lifted rocks onto the structure.

"Our army builds this wall?"

"They started it a year ago," Pie said. "All the way up to where the border meets the forest."

"Why?" I asked, then I figured it out. "They want to defend Ilari here."

"That's their plan," Guy said. "Pilk and Kir and Lev are all some of them ever cared about keeping. They'll let everything on the east edge go and all the dry nichnas too. Faroo gets protected only because of where we sit."

"That's horrible."

"That's why we want your sister to succeed. The Velka may be old biddies, but they are old biddies fighting for all of us."

Yeah. I liked that about them, too.

"Wait a minute. We're still far from the river, and that wall couldn't be more obvious."

"Yeah. You can see it a long way off."

"But we want to get these invaders as close to the water's edge as we can. They're not going to ride down to the river once they see *that* thing."

"Probably not," Pie agreed.

"We need to move the road east, further from the wall and closer to Gruen Town. Some fake hills and big shrubs on the west side of the road would help. And maybe the road could come in at more of an angle so the big old trees along the river's edge will help hide it too."

Pie shrugged. "Could work."

"Better than that," Guy said, "if the road intersects the river closer to Gruen Town, we can put the people into the evacuated Gruenite's homes. We'll pretend to be harmless, scared residents until, you know, we start to do stuff."

"Come, we'll take you to the road crew," Pie said. "We know where they're working and it's not far. You need to tell them all this."

"Uh ...."

"It's okay. We talk to your dad a lot. He knows who we are. He knows you're one of us too."

I rode behind them as they led the way, but I wasn't sure this was a good idea.

"Gypsum."

Dad looked at me as I rode up. He said it as a statement, without emotion. The last time I'd spoken with him he'd been determined to undo his mistake of denying me my mother's middle name. A lot had happened since.

"Dad." I dismounted.

Most of his crew watched us. I'm sure they knew my story, or some variation of it.

"Dad, I need to talk to you about the road. You need to modify your plans because of what the Svadlu built."

"Yes, that varmin wall of theirs. I had no idea they'd run the thing all the way down into the river, or I'd have talked to you about it sooner."

"My idea can still work if you can just do this." I picked up a stick and began to draw in the dirt.

I spoke my dad's language now and he followed along with ease.

"Of course. We've got plenty of room to work with. Good thing we caught this as soon as we did."

"Right. Thanks, Dad. Uh, I hear you're doing some pretty amazing things."

"I've heard the same about you. You're, um, you're well?"

"Well enough. And you? And Mom?"

"The same."

"Oh for goddess-sake give the man a hug," Guy hissed at me.

Everyone turned to him because his hiss had not been *that* quiet.

I looked at Dad. He looked at me.

He's the one who held his arms out first and took a step toward me, but at least I responded by doing the same and we exchanged one of the most awkward hugs in our history as everyone looked on.

"See you around," he said as I turned to leave.

"Yeah. Soon." I said it over my shoulder as I walked away.

~ 15 ~

A Royal Connection

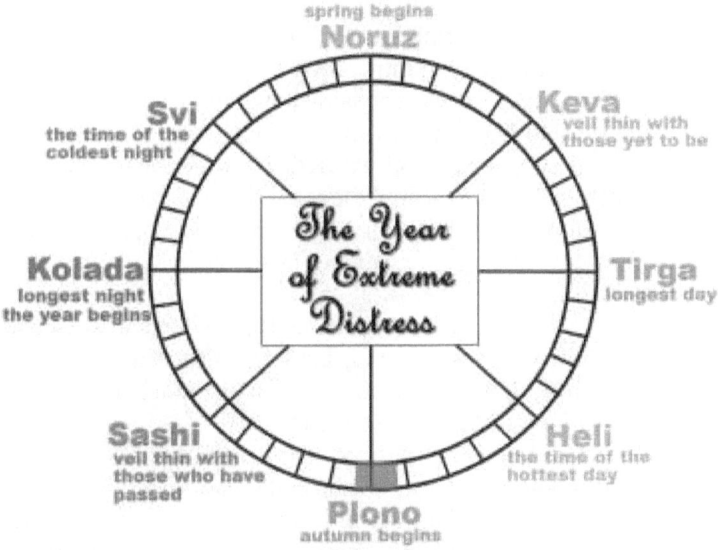

spring begins
Noruz

Svi
the time of the
coldest night

Keva
veil thin with
those yet to be

Kolada
longest night
the year begins

*The Year
of Extreme
Distress*

Tirga
longest day

Sashi
veil thin with
those who have
passed

Heli
the time of the
hottest day

Plono
autumn begins

The guide and Idris stopped and spoke just inside the trees, their faces hidden by the forest's shadows. Then the guide vanished back into the leaves. Idris had never sent send her guide away before.

"Planning to stay longer this time?" I asked, taking unusually big strides towards her so I could reach her before anyone else. I wanted to ease her into the sense of urgency our camp had undergone since her last visit.

"Possibly." She paused to wipe damp strands of her thin dark hair out of her face. "You've heard the news that Prince Lufo takes the throne tomorrow?"

"Of course we have," Galen said. Six of my tentmates followed close on my heels, anxious for any news Idris might bring. So much for speaking with her first.

We got her settled around the campfire with a mug of afternoon wine, and Raheem began giving her a neck massage. We weren't usually this friendly with guests, but Idris was no stranger. As she relaxed into his strong hands I watched the lines on her young face disappear. Perhaps Raheem's greeting was better than mine would have been.

Ksenia finally asked a question.

"Did you locate your childhood friend? Does she know anything?"

Idris set down her drink and leaned forward out of Raheem's reach, but not before giving him a look that said "more later." He gave her a look back that I swear said "much more."

"Yes, I found Nan. Well, I mean I found out what happened to her. She was supposed to get married, and probably to an Edser, but her father and brother scared the local boys. Usually a princess has lots of suitors because, you know, families hope for favors once they've got a Royal connection. I heard she had none."

"So she left Eds?"

"Not by choice. The K'ba and Eds Royals have always been close. Two poor dry nichnas and, both families dealing with an unusually narrow definition of succession in which only a boy sired by the ruling prince can take the throne."

"Why would anyone design such an inflexible system?" Esteri asked, scooting in closer so she could be heard.

"We were taught that when K'ba and Eds were a single nichna, long ago, cousins and uncles kept trying to kill off the ruler so they could take over. It got so bloody everyone tired of it. When a younger brother took the throne by killing the Ruling Prince and his baby son, the murder of a child horrified everyone, so we created these rules to end the discord. The nichnas split apart not long after, and both families have struggled to produce lots of sons since."

Suloom came out of the tent with a plate of small cakes for the group to share. "They're lucky the system hasn't failed them," he said as he set the platter in front of Idris.

"It came close with my generation," Idris answered. "The ruler of Eds only had two boys, Lufo and his little brother. Not much of a safety margin. But the K'basta Royals fared worse. Their Ruler sired three boys, but the first two died. The third son, who's my age, he's had health problems that the family has gone to great lengths to keep quiet. Because of them, he's had difficulty securing a spouse."

"Wait. Let me guess," Jofim said, reaching for a cake. "The Eds Royals have a daughter they can't marry off, and the K'ba Royals need a discreet spouse for their sickly son."

We all nodded along. It hadn't been hard to guess where Idris' story led.

"You're right. Nan got married to K'ba's prince. It solved everyone's problems, except for Nan's."

"What sort of disease does he have?"

Idris shook her head. "That seems to be the most well-guarded secret in K'ba. Nan obviously knows."

Two more people joined us, and one brought a second jug of afternoon wine with her. As she poured, I held my cup out for more.

"You've got to feel sorry for Nan," I said.

"Oh, I do," Idris replied. "Particularly because her ambitious father struck a marvelous bargain in exchange for her."

We'd guessed the nature of the deal, too. Now the annexation of K'ba makes sense.

"That rantallion. He exchanged his daughter for the nichna of K'ba?"

"Not quite," Idris corrected us. "The K'basta Royals would never have made such a daft bargain. Word is the Eds Ruler took a chance. He promised Nan's hand in marriage, along with her frequent dutiful attempts to bear a child, in exchange for a deal. If his fertile daughter, who would have no contact with the Velka and their herbs, didn't become pregnant after two years of, shall we say, serious effort, then the K'basta would accept that their lone son was the end of their line and they were done."

"So then Eds could simply take over K'ba?" Galen said.

"Well, yes, but the Eds Ruler didn't present it like that. He convinced the Ruler of K'ba that letting kindred spirits like the Eds Royals reunite the two nichnas beat the alternative.

"There is an alternative?"

We all scooted in a little closer to hear this news.

"With such a strict definition of succession, there had to be," Nan said. "The ruling documents say if no legal heir exists, a new Royal line must be established, with its leader chosen from the non-Royal population. That means the artists and entertainers who now populate K'ba would get to set up their own royal family!"

"How exactly does this new leader get chosen?" Galen asked.

Idris shrugged. "The documents are rather vague. 'By a method agreeable to all.'"

"I can see how K'ba's Royals would much prefer reuniting the two nichnas over that sort of chaos," Ksenia said. "So now your friend Nan is stuck in K'ba, prucking some sick lad, in the hope that his family will let her father take over the place?"

"Basically, yes."

Galen and I spoke at once.

"That is so pathetic," I said.

"When are the two years up?" he asked.

Idris laughed.

"Pathetic, yes, and the deal ends right when you'd expect. Kolada of this year."

"Prucking pig scump."

"Yeah. It's a mess."

I'd already tucked my sister Olivine and her secret lover in a guest tent as far away as possible, asking her to see herself out. I knew things would get complicated for Plono, and I didn't need my family around. Yet, I hadn't had the heart to turn Olivine away when she had nowhere else to go. Now I and my tentmates let Idris rest after her long recitation as we prepared food and drink for our own celebration of Plono Eve.

On holidays we split into whatever pairs or small groups we preferred or we did whatever else we wanted. Often many of us sought a companion from another camp, someone who'd piqued our interest during the past eighth. The reaching out for variety gave it a holiday feel, and everyone encouraged it as a way for the various tents to maintain a connection to the others.

Ksenia and I talked as we cut up the end of the summer fruits for the group to enjoy.

"So I overheard Idris tell Raheem, 'I just want to celebrate one holiday, one prucking holiday, with a man,'" Ksenia said.

"What did he say back?"

She laughed and clapped her hands together. "He replied. 'I think I can help you.'"

I giggled. "He certainly can do that!"

"She chose well," Ksenia agreed. "I'm glad. She seemed so sad when we first met her, but I think she likes it here."

"I think so too. And a night with Raheem should do wonders for her."

"It does wonders for most women."

Idris stayed for several days, and Raheem gave her his full attention. The attraction between them seemed genuine, though I suspected Raheem also chipped away at the damage some other male had done. I think he knew it too. His playfulness could come on a little strong with the rest of us, but he was gentle with Idris, his very posture conveying that he'd stop if she gave the word.

The two of them snuggled together in front of the fire two nights later, sipping a sweet dinner wine as they talked. We gave them privacy at first, though many of us yearned to sit around the fire too. Then we heard her sobbing. He stroked her hair, muttered sweet things, but looked up hoping for some help. Several of us moved closer.

"I never thought it could be this much fun," she said. It sounded like she'd consumed a bit more wine than was wise. We took a few steps back. Perhaps the call for help had been misread.

"It is fun," he said. "No young girl should ever be given as a toy to some lout of a boy." He pulled her closer; he stroked her hair.

Her sobs started again. "My mother said I had to …. he was a prince … maybe he'd marry me … She beat me when I said I didn't want to …."

We all could fill in the blanks. Talk about pathetic.

"You ran away, to the Velka, to escape from Prince Lufo?" Galen asked it, but we all thought it.

"Yes! After doing what he wanted with me so many times he finally asked my father for my hand. I think his dad told him to. And my dad said yes without even asking me. When I found out I was furious, but Dad yelled at me and told me every girl wants to marry a prince, and I should be thankful I'd been chosen."

She looked at the ground as she talked. "The next morning I told them I needed to go to the market to get some pretty things to make me look more like the betrothed of a prince. My father said he didn't think that nonsense mattered but my mother pressed coins into my hand and told me not to skimp."

She used her sleeve for a long, drawn-out wipe of her nose.

"As soon as I got to the market I looked for someone to help me. I found this farmer from Vinx buying goat cheese, and when I begged her to take me with her and told her why, she agreed to hide me in her wagon when she left. She took me all the way to the market in Vinx where I found the Velka. For the first two years after they took me in I wouldn't leave the forest for fear someone would recognize me and make me go home. And now, and now this horrible man is about to be crowned as the ruler of Eds!"

The tears were back but no one blamed her. I wondered if this was the first time she'd let herself cry, really cry, for what she'd lost.

We sat with her, saying nothing. I don't know about the others, but my thoughts were simple. All these years of being told to marry a prucking prince, and now I'd befriended a woman who'd run away so she wouldn't have to do it.

That night Galen held me close.

"I'm glad nobody prucked up your ability to enjoy sex," he said. "What a horrible thing to do to another."

"Yeah. It goes way past the moment when it happens, doesn't it? And the man doesn't understand that."

"Do you think Idris will …"

"I think she'll always carry some scars, but yes, I think she can discover love, and fun, and her own strength."

"I hope so."

"You know what, Sheep Scump? You're a sweetie under that tough Edser hide of yours."

He chuckled and rolled on top of me to give me a long kiss. "I'm glad you think so because you're probably not going to like what I say next."

"Oh?"

"Soon as Idris leaves for the forest, I'm going to the castle in K'ba."

"Whatever for?"

"Duck Piss. There's another woman, Princess Nan, and she's trapped in a horrible situation there, maybe worse than the one Idris was in. I can't live with that."

"But this has been going on now for almost two years. Be reasonable. You can't just ride in and free her. And who knows how she feels by now?"

"Then I'll go and ask her what she wants."

"It's still ridiculous. I don't want to ride out to the edge of K'ba."

"Who said anything about you going? You have a couple of hundred people you need to get practicing with slingshots."

"They can wait. The last time you rode off to a castle you got trapped there for almost an eighth, and I had to rescue you. You're not going alone."

"Are you ever going to let me live that down? You know, maybe this time I'll have to rescue you."

"Maybe you will. Either way, we're better off going together and you know it."

We stopped talking and moved on to doing what we both wanted to do instead, and for the next bit of time, nothing else in the world mattered.

~ 16 ~

The K'ba Palace

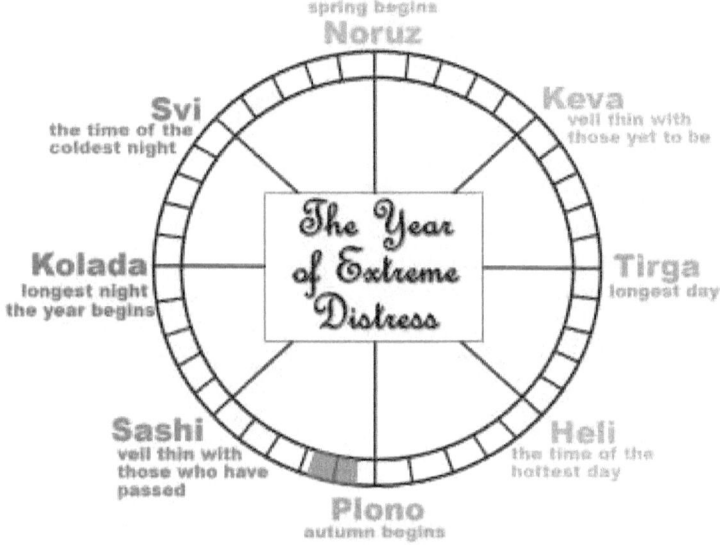

Over many years, K'ba's castle became harder to find. It set west of the settlements, near the Eds border along the Canyon River. I imagined that decades ago a well-maintained road led to it, much-traveled by K'basta who revered their rulers. But as the make-up of the population changed, both the inhabitants of the castle and those of the town had grown less fond of each other, and the road fell into disrepair.

Today, modern K'basta seldom traveled west along the river towards Eds, and Galen and I struggled to stay on the road instead of wandering into the scraggly brush that grew everywhere along the Canyon River.

"Why is this so overgrown? Somebody has to be bringing them food and supplies," Galen complained.

"I bet those come in from Eds, from the other direction."

If the bushes hadn't been so thin and short, we might never have seen it off to our left.

"Could that be a castle?" Galen asked.

The single-story stone home was nothing much, but it occupied the center of a compound, with dilapidated buildings around it and a couple of better cared-for smaller cottages in the back. The wind blew fierce out here, and the home appeared deserted.

"It's the first thing we've seen. Let's see if anyone is there to ask."

Galen and I had already concocted a half-true story about a farm girl from Vinx falling for an Eds herder while at school. We added a bit about traveling from my home to his and becoming hopelessly lost out in the desolation. We hoped our desperation would get us inside so we could learn more.

No, it wasn't much of a plan, but it's what we had.

"Ready?" I asked him, my hand poised to knock on the door.

He never got the chance to answer. The door opened to reveal a tall, thin old man with a long face who eyed us with suspicion.

"His highness is not accepting visitors today."

He began to close the door but I stuck my foot in it.

"We've no desire to see his Highness. Please, sir. Our water jugs are empty as are our stomachs. We've been lost for two days. We beg for kindness."

He paused. It was the rare person who would close the door on another Ilarian who begged for kindness, and whatever this man was, he wasn't that sort.

"Very well. You may step inside but come no further. My wife, I mean our staff, will provide you with provisions before sending you on your way."

He turned his back and walked through the nearest door, leaving us in a hall filled with old tapestries that smelled of dust and led to nothing but more closed doors.

Galen and I looked at each other. We could probably peek into two doors if we each took one and moved fast.

The old man poked his head back in.

"Do remain exactly where you are. Please."

"May I ask you a question?" Galen's voice surprised the old man and me.

"Yes." It was the most cautious yes I'd ever heard.

"I, uh, I had a childhood friend. A girl. Our parents were friends."

The old man gave Galen a baffled look.

"I saw her recently and she told me Nan, the Eds princess, had married into your family and, well, I wondered if it was true."

Direct questions had not been in our plan. What was Galen thinking?

The old man looked surprised.

"I suppose there is no harm in telling you. It is no secret, although the wedding was a subdued affair. Yes, our Royals were delighted when Princess Nan of Eds agreed to wed the son of our Ruling Prince. Now if you'll excuse me, I'll see to your provisions."

"Is Nan here? Now?"

Galen had deviated so far from our original idea that I didn't know what to do. So I tried something too.

"Oh, I'd love to meet a real princess my age. And married to a prince!" I held my folded hands against my heart, doing my best to gush. I wasn't good at it, but I got the idea the old gentleman hadn't heard a lot of fawning in recent years so maybe it wouldn't take much to please him.

"I'm sorry. Princess Nan is quite busy."

"Could I, could I just tell her how proud we Edsers are of her?" Galen asked.

Possum scump. He was better at acting than I was.

The old man gave him a pained look.

"I doubt it, but I will ask the princess if she wishes to speak with you briefly." He gave me a second, stern look. "Stay put."

"Yes, sir."

It took the time it would have taken me to drink a mug of water for Nan to emerge from another of the doors. She wasn't plump, but more well-rounded than most Edsers, with unusually fair skin and soft hair in that rare yellow-orange I'd heard called strawberry blonde. She had freckles, too, which few Ilarians had.

She wore a simple dress with no sign of her royal status. However, she stood tall, as if she'd grown up giving orders.

"Andre. I recognize this boy from my childhood. I will entertain him and his girlfriend in the sitting room. Please have afternoon wine and a tray of snacks brought in."

Andre looked more pained than before. "Are you sure that is wise, madam?"

The undercurrent of insubordination brought a flash of anger to her eyes.

"Quite sure. We've nothing to fear from these two, I assure you."

She smiled at me. "We've not met. You are?"

The truth would work as well as anything.

"Gypsum. From Vinx." I managed a bobble of a curtsey. I guessed Andre and Nan fought for dominance in the household, and Nan held onto it by a thread. I'd do all I could to support her; after all she intended to feed us.

Dust drifted in the air of the sitting room, visible in the sunlight pouring in through the windows. I imagined keeping a home clean in the desolation wasn't easy. I turned to the tray of simple snacks. The fresh bread, soft cheese, and late summer melons, both green and orange, enticed me but I knew most Royals dined on better fare.

Nan watched me eying the dust and judging the food.

"We've only two servants these days," she said. "Andre and his wife, Melda, and they're both getting on in years."

"No disrespect meant, but isn't that a rather small staff for a castle?" I said.

She laughed. "I'm not so royal that I feel disrespected that easily. It's exceedingly small. But we are an exceedingly small group of Royals."

Galen and I both said nothing. We knew this already, but we hoped she'd say more.

"You've no doubt heard of the misfortunes that have befallen this family," she added in a soft voice.

"No, not really. Edsers aren't much for gossip."

I could have kissed Galen.

"Well, my father-in-law sired a son early in life then took the throne as one does here, but his young prince died soon after. It took years for his grief-stricken wife to bear another, and he died from a disease when he was four. The family says she succumbed to sorrow after illness took her second child. But by then she'd given birth to, to the man who is my husband. That left only two Royals to be cared for, so Andre and his wife sent the others packing."

A well-practiced smile emerged on her face.

"Now there are three of us Royals here, of course, and we do fine."

"Do you really?" I asked the question in my softest tones.

"I see," she said. "You wish to know if I need help."

"It crossed our minds," Galen said. "No one in Eds has heard from you in a long time. Only a few days ago, your brother took the throne and word is you and the K'basta Royals didn't attend his coronation."

"By custom, we seldom leave our castle."

Galen didn't take his eyes off of her face. "Are you okay?"

I watched the tiny movements around her mouth as she composed herself.

"It's true that I have little contact with the family I was born into. We've … grown apart. Given that, I avoid interaction with those from my past as it keeps things simpler. There is no problem."

"Of course not," I said. "Your father-in-law? He treats you well?"

I caught the look of surprise before she swept it back under the well-practiced smile.

"Old age has overtaken him, but despite that he wishes me success in my marriage. I have no quarrel with him."

Galen nodded. "And your husband?"

"Most of the nichna believes he suffers from a disease and the rumor is close enough to the truth. My husband had an unfortunate accident as a young man and has struggled to recover from his injuries since. I do what I can to help him."

"He doesn't mistreat you?" Galen asked. It was a bold question, and one I expected to offend her. Instead she seemed amused.

"No, he has never mistreated me."

"And the servants are kind to you?"

She hesitated. "The servants do their jobs."

Galen gave me a look. I thought it meant here goes nothing and don't be mad. I braced myself.

"There is one persistent rumor in Eds that baffles me," he said. "Many Edsers believe we will soon reclaim K'ba after centuries of separation and that it has to do with your marriage. Is there any truth to this?"

She winced. "I'd forgotten how bluntly spoken Edsers can be."

Galan said nothing.

"Very well. It will become official knowledge soon though I'd appreciate it if you would refrain from speaking until then."

Galen still said nothing and I made myself swallow the reassuring words that wanted to come out of my mouth. Silence is the best way to keep another talking.

"The intent of my marriage, well of any marriage to any prince, is to produce heirs for the family one has married into. I understand the job. My husband and I wish to do exactly that, but so far, we have not been so blessed. Should an heir not be on the way by this coming Kolada, my father has generously offered to roll K'ba back into Eds and to provide the K'basta with the stable leadership they would otherwise lack."

Now I knew the question I wanted to ask.

"What happens to you if this occurs?"

Finally, a look of distress broke through the smile.

"I'm not sure. I do not wish to live under my brother's rule. I imagine I would go elsewhere."

"You and your husband?" Galen asked.

"Perhaps," she said.

"Maybe at that time you'd like some help?" I offered.

She gave me her first genuine smile.

"We are aware of the dangers posed by a group of outsiders demanding tribute and of the various schemes in Ilari to survive these demands. Perhaps we could speak of my plans a few anks before Kolada?"

"How do you stay in touch with the other nichnas?" Galen asked.

"Oh. Each eighth Andre travels to Pilk, representing our Royals who are unable to travel. He provides an update and brings news back. We remain informed."

Personally I thought the princess ought to be traveling to Pilk, not Andre, but I didn't say so. We'd pushed the limits of politeness far enough.

I stood. "Your Highness. We thank you for the refreshments. We have sufficient daylight left. If you'll have Andre direct us to the settlements we will make our way there to spend the night."

Galen stood, too, though with more reluctance.

"Princess Nan. I give you my word. I will return here a few anks before Kolada to learn if you are with child and to help you plan for your future if you are not." He gave her a low bow.

It was a formal speech, particularly coming from him, and sort of cute.

"I'll help too," I said.

After we found lodging on the cheaper side of the settlements, we went to one of the better taverns for a good meal.

"Don't you think it's odd we never saw the Ruling Prince or the Crown Prince?" he said.

"Not really. We're a couple of commoners the wind blew in. Why would they bother with us?" I chewed on the juicy leg of a well-roasted goose. It's a task that requires attention otherwise half of it lands in your lap.

"Because they've got to be bored out there all alone. Our showing up should have been interesting, at the least."

"Maybe. But they're both not well."

Galen wouldn't let it go.

"I think 'old age has overtaken my father-in-law' means that dad is daft in the head. What do you think?"

"You could be right," I caught a loose morsel with my tongue before it fell. "Maybe he's so crazy that Andre has locked him in the attic." I laughed. "You know, your favorite place in a castle."

I meant it to be funny but he glared at me. "I wish you'd take this seriously," he said.

"Why?"

"Because it is. The K'basta have a rare, like once-in-centuries opportunity here. They could choose their own leader. Thanks to a brilliant system whereby no other Royal can claim the throne, they could pick the most qualified person they have to run things. Doesn't that excite you?"

I gave up and put down the rest of the goose leg.

"Not particularly. Why would it?"

He put his head in his hands.

"I'm happy with the reczavy," I said. "As long as everyone else leaves us alone, I don't care who runs what."

He peeked at me between his fingers.

"That's my point, Gypsum. Who-runs-what determines if the reczavy get left alone. I think it's time K'ba got a competent and big-hearted leader. We'd all benefit."

"Okay. Fine. That only happens if Nan doesn't fulfill her part of the arrangement, and she seems happy to do what she was sent to do."

He put his hands back in his lap. "Not necessarily. I don't think she wants to see her brother run a nichna twice as big as the one he's got. When we go back to check on her, I intend to talk her into refusing to finish her two years, so her brother will have no clear claim."

"It's only a matter of anks. Who will care about that?"

"A deal's a deal. It is supposed to be a full two years, and if she stops the bargain, he shouldn't get to take over."

"Even if you could get people to care about a few measly anks, I don't think she'd defy her family that way."

"I think she'd love to. We have to be prepared to offer a good alternative, though. We need a leader we can put in place immediately. Maybe once we do, the idea will spread. Imagine every nichna eventually choosing the best leader, not settling for the children of the one they've got. This could change the face of Ilari!"

I wasn't sure I wanted the face of Ilari to change, and I felt certain changing it anks before an invasion was a bad idea. But sometimes you have to let a person run with a plan until they figure out how bad it is.

I picked up the rest of my goose leg. "Hrphhm Ummmm," I said.

"Exactly!" Galen agreed.

~ 17 ~

Black Mustard Seed, Grains of Paradise, and Valerian Root

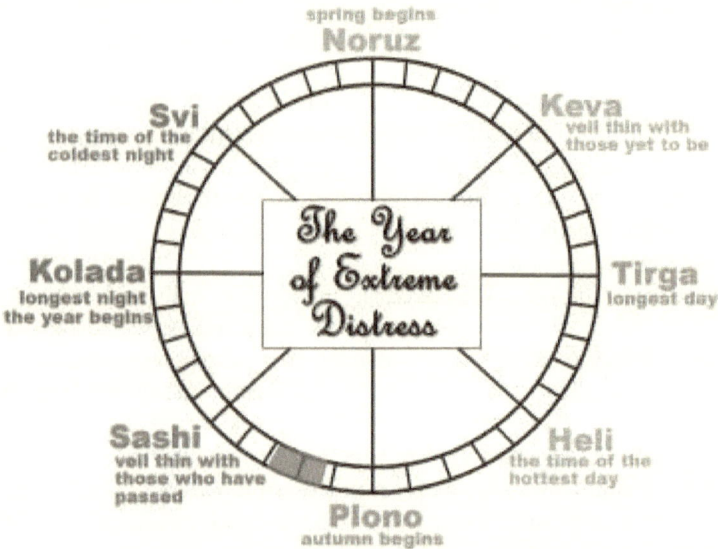

Two anks into Plono our weather finally cooled. Pie walked over to my tent to tell me that future practices in the river would be rare and short as winter neared. He felt confident the Faroojers, reczavy, and Gruenites who had joined in had prepared well enough to perform honorably when the time came.

"Your sister Sulphur came to watch us," he said. "I think she was impressed."

"I doubt it. Perhaps she was polite."

"She seemed genuine ..." His voice trailed off as he reconsidered.

"She has no respect for us, and now probably has no respect for me." Of all the disdain my decision to join the reczavy could bring, Sulphur's potential contempt stung the worst. "She thinks we're useless."

Pie's fidgeting told me he wanted to change the subject, but he picked poorly.

"You know they refer to us as the goat?" he said.

"You mean the Svadlu call the reczavy that?" I was pissed. Goats were known to pruck anything. Well, they were known to eat anything, too but I knew which behavior had earned us the nickname.

"No," he laughed. "Ryalgar named her efforts after some old civilization's mythical beast. It's called the Chimera."

"Why would she pick something so stupid? She and her intellectual friends prize esoteric knowledge from outside our borders because other Ilarians don't know about it or care. What a random dumb-arse choice."

"It has three parts," he said. "A snake, a lion, and a goat so ..." He looked into my eyes. "Everything okay?" He looked harder. "I can tell it's not."

Varla had walked over to join us. Perhaps she'd heard me ranting about being called the goat. Maybe she'd heard me ranting a lot lately.

"You're still angry?" she said. "What else happened at that castle?"

She was right. I'd been hard to get along with since we returned. Varla understood me better than any tentmate except for Galen, and he of course was part of the problem. She'd figured that much out, but Pie deserved an explanation.

"It's you and the Faroojers," I told him. "You're the problem."

"You don't think we've done enough?" He took a step back, surprised. "We've worked so hard."

"You have. It's varmin impressive. Here it is, the middle of Plono, and you are pretty much ready to do what you can."

Varla understood. "The problem is that no one else has?"

"Yes, including me. I need, what, six hundred poultices? I've made forty. And I haven't stuffed any of them because the Velka

S. R. Cronin

haven't gotten back to me about herbs to stuff them with. I've been told I should have collected pine resin in the spring and it's a little late for that, don't you think, but fall will be better than summer so everyone is waiting till autumn to collect pine resin for me."

"They'll get it done," Varla said.

"Even if they do. I need a hundred slingshots. Who's going to make those? Then I need a hundred people who are really good with them. Look at Pie here and the Faroojers. They know you can't just show up and hope for the best. I need a hundred people practicing with slingshots every single day!"

My voice rose at the end, but Varla only nodded. "You do. You've tried?"

"Pruck yes, I've tried. I've talked to all thirty-two tents and every one of them has assured me they will help. In a few days. When things cool off. Come back later."

I sat in the dirt like a child and looked up at the two of them. My legs were tired from the walking I'd already done that day.

"You need people who can impart a sense of urgency," Ksenia said. She joined us, probably because of my yelling, and she plopped down in the dirt beside me, a show of comradery. "I'll get the leader of every tent involved. We'll make this happen. Slingshots made. Practice begun. It's going to be okay."

"Thank you. But it's so much worse. I've got to collect at least five hundred eggs. From where? And enough itching powder for them. How the pruck am I going to transport all that powder and five hundred eggs into the forest and then transport it all to Gruen?"

"Let me guess. Everyone has said they'll help. Get back with them when this gets closer." Raheem laughed as he sat in the dirt with us, but his eyes were sympathetic. "I'll work on your transportation problems."

"Thank you. But it's worse. The people throwing those eggs have to have strong arms and good aim. But, get this, they've got to be within ten, at most twenty paces of people armed with swords and bows. They have to hit them in the face before they get shot. No one, not a single person, has volunteered for this."

"I'm not surprised. They need to know you've got ideas to make this safer," Varla said. "You do, don't you?"

"Sort of. But the first involves construction, building something at the end of the road to split their riders apart. My dad could help but the last thing I want to do is talk to him."

"Why not call in a favor from a sister then? How about one of them that's been using us for a discreet place to pruck on the holidays?"

Raheem's succinct description made me chuckle.

"I could probably do that. The second idea involves costumes to make the egg throwers appear less threatening, at least long enough to get an attacker to pause. I'm not sure what would work, but it is going to involve more sewing."

"Plenty of us thread workers could help you with those costumes," Pie offered. "And we could make little bags the size, shape, and weight of eggs for people to practice with. You know. Less messy." He raised a hand to stop my objection. "I'll talk to Guy. We'll get it started."

"Ok. But then I need people to make a lot of smoke. I've talked to the entertainers, but they're consumed with the part they're playing with the bucking horses."

"You need to find another group of entertainers. There's more than one," Ksenia said. "I'll get you a contact."

"So why are we all sitting out here in the dirt?" Raheem said. "I don't see any problems." He gave me a wink.

"The problem is that I went over this with Ryalgar an eighth ago. And we've done nothing since."

"Where's Galen in all this?" Ksenia kept her voice gentle, but I heard her frustration with him. She knew where he was but she wanted to give me the chance to say it.

"He's developed another priority. One he believes is more urgent."

"More urgent than preventing the complete destruction of Ilari?" Pie asked. The others said nothing, They'd already heard Galen's many rants since our return from the castle.

"Gypsum's boyfriend has decided this is the perfect time for Ilari to develop a more sensible type of government," Varla explained.

"The man wants to get rid of all royalty," I added.

"Why?" Pie said. "Then who would run things?"

I sighed. "Galen thinks we can use the threat of Eds annexing K'ba to promote a better system of rule in K'ba. He dreams of revamping the realm."

"He's got Suloom and Esteri convinced, and he's working his way through the surrounding tents, drumming up support," Ksenia said.

"He doesn't care about what you're doing?" Pie asked.

"Oh no, he cares a lot. He thinks it's wonderful. You know. Design a new political system that rewards competence not parentage and, once that's done, we repel an army." I pulled at my hair in frustration. "He thinks we should concentrate on the governing part now and in mid-Sashi or so we'll switch to focusing on these pesky invaders."

They all four stared at me.

"I've no quarrel with his ideas," I added. "They're brilliant. I just think Galen picked a varmin bad time to make the realm better."

"I'll recruit egg throwers," Varla said as she stood. The others stood with her.

Well, at least my tantrum had gained me help. Now if I could keep my boyfriend from occupying everyone else with his ideas, maybe I could get some of this done.

Idris arrived the next day and again sent her scout back into the forest.

"Can I talk to you alone?" Idris asked me.

I scrubbed the large pots we used to cook most meals, working alongside Jofim. In between drying and stacking them, he looked at me and raised an eyebrow.

"It's a message from the Velka regarding her poultices," Idris said.

"I'll take a break." He hung his towel over the top pot and headed towards the tent.

"The Velka want you to know they are sorry to have delayed for so long, but what you asked of them caused great controversy," Idris said.

"I ask them for ideas of what to put into my poultices to give them some weight." What the Heli was controversial …

"You ask for more than that. You ask them to name herbs that would harm another, and everything in their beliefs prohibits them from doing such."

"Confusion isn't ..."

"Confusion is usually harmful, and you intend it to be."

"But these confused people are planning to ..."

"Yes, that was the counterargument. What is one allowed to do in self-defense? The final decision came down to Ryalgar's extraordinary efforts to prevent loss of life on both sides, a condition hardly guaranteed if she does not prevail. It also came down to every Velka agreeing to accept her share of the consequences – presumably a period of confusion in her own life at a difficult time. We all signed something saying so. Every one of us."

"I didn't think the Velka would be subject to consequences for aiding me ... but I guess it makes sense that they would. I should have thought this through better."

"Before I say more, I'm to ask if you understand the consequences of this to yourself. Do you?"

"I do. I've never harmed another before with my threads, I swear, not until I needed to rescue Galen in Eds. Then I did the least harmful thing I could think of. Yes. I am prepared to pay for my actions. Three times over."

Idris didn't need to know I'd been looking over my shoulder every day since I'd rescued Galen, expecting to wake in a fog.

"Then if you accept the potential cost of these poultices, I'm to tell you to use something plentiful like millet and add black mustard seed, grains of paradise, and chopped roots from the valerian plant."

"Where would I find these things?"

"You wouldn't find the first two, both come from far away and cost a fortune. The Velka have sent you all they have of both, to divide between the poultices. Valerian grows in several places in the realm, and I've been instructed on where to find it. If you'll give me a few helpers and horses I'll gather it for you and chop up the roots and dry them."

"Idris, that would be wonderful!"

She walked over to the rucksack she'd brought and pulled out two bags, both larger than my foot, both sewn shut. She reached in deeper and laughed.

"Well, I'd have remembered this heavy thing soon enough."

She put a clay pot, tightly sealed with wax, on the ground.

"And this is?"

"Bdellion. It comes from afar also, and it's a resin with powerful properties. It may do more for your poultices than the other ingredients combined. The Velka say to mix a little in with the pine resin on each one."

She squinted at me in the bright sun.

"Gypsum. Be careful with all this, okay? The Velka have good reasons for keeping these things locked away."

"I understand."

"I'm to tell you to use every bit of all of them, and then to burn the bags and break the crock into pieces and bury it. You won't forget, will you?"

"That's a great question." She'd gotten me to laugh. "If I'm not too confused at the time, I won't."

I wanted to tell Idris about our visit with Nan, but it seemed only fair to let Galen be part of the conversation despite his obsession with K'ba's leadership. Idris and I walked into the tent together.

"Look who dropped by," I said with a fake cheer meant to cover my current frustration with him.

"Idris, This is great! We could use your help, couldn't we, Gypsum?" As she sunk into one of our soft chairs, he poured out his version of our visit to the castle in K'ba. It didn't differ much from my own, except in his telling of it, Princess Nan felt considerably more inclined to help us destroy her father's agreement than I remembered.

I hardly got the chance to say a word before Idris prodded Galen for more reassurance that her old friend was safe and then gave Galen advice on how to best secure her friend's cooperation.

Well, so much for keeping Idris focused on the task at hand. I had to hand it to Galen, though, he had a charming way of winning people over that I seemed to lack.

"You two go ahead; I've got some sewing to do," I said as I picked up my basket of needlework and headed out into the sunlight. Perhaps sunshine would melt away the edges of this sour mood that hounded me day and night.

~ 18 ~

Eggs

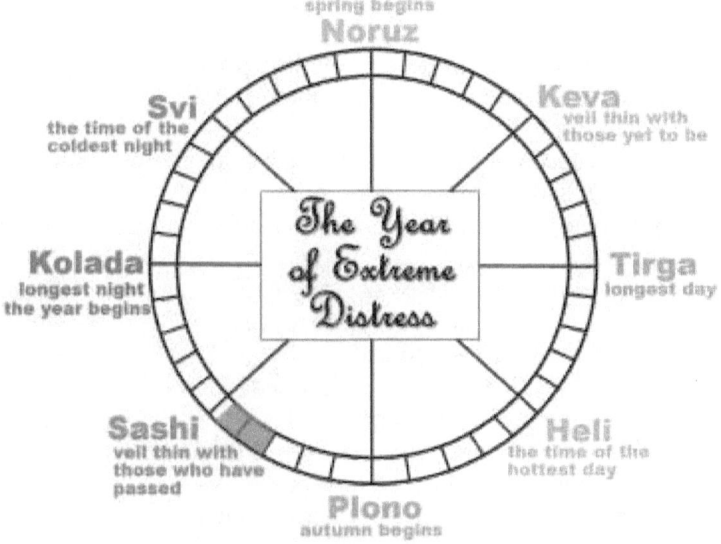

After all my nagging paranoia about the consequences of causing confusion, I woke up the next morning with an unusual sense of clarity. Go figure.

I knew I had to give Idris a message to get to Olivine. She and Dad had always been close and Olivine could tell him that as his road approached the river it needed shrubs and boulders to spilt the horses apart and it had to have thin uneven paths to slow them down, so two hundred sling shooters could arise out of nowhere behind them.

If they were fast, my slingshot people could shoot twice and vanish into the earth before the riders could turn and shoot back.

Once our attackers recognized no harm had come to them, they'd pause in confusion. I hoped.

I could hide my two hundred people with slingshots in camouflaged trenches in green clothing painted like leaves. And we'd use smoke. Lots of smoke. Plenty of attackers wouldn't end up with a poultice attached because some of my shooters would miss, and some of my creations wouldn't stick. But if a hundred of them ended up in a daze, it would affect them all.

Only we didn't have two hundred shooters. Maybe some Gruenites would help? We could ask ones who couldn't swim and hadn't already offered to help the Faroojers. Celestine owed me a favor, too. She could recruit a hundred Gruenites who would shoot poultices.

Maybe Ksenia could get me another group of entertainers to hide my slingshot wielders, to keep them from being slaughtered after they finished their work.

So. I reached over. Galen's spot was cold. The others had all left the tent. It had to be late morning.

I sat up, my mind whirling with plans for practices, as Jofim walked into the tent with a plate of eggs and warm bread.

"Even the commander of an army needs breakfast," he said, motioning for me to move over to where we ate.

"I don't command anything."

"Better decide you do," he replied. "Ksenia's made the rounds this morning, and every tent leader is about to have a serious conversation with their tentmates. I think the message will go something like 'help Gypsum now or die.'"

He smiled at me, and I realized how seldom Jofim smiled.

"You find this funny?"

"No. I find you an unlikely commander, and I find us an implausible army, but by this afternoon you'll have your hands full. So eat up. I want you to succeed because the alternative sucks."

What does one say to that?

"Thanks for the eggs."

"You're welcome.

I didn't have much appetite, so I played with my food, staring at the eggs.

Eggs.

How many egg throwers could I hope to recruit? Fifty? With ten eggs each? Five hundred throws and hopefully a hundred hits. How would they hold the eggs while they threw? They needed vests with padded pockets to hold their eggs. I had to get Pie and Guy started on modifying old vests.

Raheem said he'd handle transportation. Could he take on egg collection from the farmers as well? Younger chickens made stronger shells so I'd get him to request those. Could we do anything else to make the eggs less likely to crack? I needed to find a poultry farmer and ask.

And where would my egg throwers be? The river was straight ahead of my targets. The slingshot people hid behind them. Egg throwers on both sides wouldn't work because those eggs had to crack against faces, not the backs of heads. I needed every Mongol facing my eggs throwers. How could I manage that?

We had that fancy exploding powder. I'd planned to use it at the end, but if I staged an explosion, off to the left towards the Gruen Town, then everyone would turn that way. And, all my egg throwers could wait, hidden in the town's edges, and emerge from the flames. That would make some sense. Now, what would keep six hundred trained fighters from simply shooting these fifty people as they walked out?

They could hold their hands up in surrender. It might help.

We could dress them all as women. Did the Mongols have women warriors? I didn't know.

I thought of the ten men I'd watched enjoying wine in Lev. They hadn't struck me as cruel. Who would they hesitate to kill? Small children, of course, but I could hardly disguise my people as such, and using real small children was out of the question, even for me.

Who else does a normal, healthy human hesitate to attack? Anyone who is helpless, right? How about disguising them all as old people? Grey wigs, canes. Would that work?

Maybe. Or perhaps a bunch of elderly-appearing people walking into an invasion would raise suspicions. Our attackers weren't stupid. Surely others had tried to trick them before.

How about injured people? It would make more sense, as they'd be fleeing an explosion and it would allow my people to get close enough to throw the eggs. My pitiful group of wounded people would hit those closest to them, obviously, and once the itching powder got on the faces of those in front, they'd provide protection from the wrath of those behind them.

This placement left the path to the river open, too. Hopefully, as they struggled to clean their faces, they'd see the water as their best option and would wade out into the arms of the Faroojers.

Meanwhile, the back of the hoard would be filled with the hundred or so riders mired in confusion, making retreat difficult. Then I'd need one more good explosion off to the left to give my egg throwers a chance to disappear and to drive the remaining four hundred or so healthy and alert ones towards the wall where the Svadlu waited to finish the job.

This could work.

But it probably wouldn't. It was way too complicated and filled with guesses. Yet it was a better plan than it had been yesterday.

I left the tent that morning, a plate of half-eaten eggs in hand, as the commander of an army. A pathetically inexperienced one stuck with unwilling and untrained soldiers, but I knew our complete lack of preconceptions remained our biggest asset. Unlike real soldiers, we'd do anything we thought might work, and no invader expected that.

Travel and activity blurred together over the next two anks as we went from doing almost nothing to doing it all. Threads flew, as did poultices and egg-sized bags. Tens of us rode to Gruen and joined ranks with Gruenites who were surprisingly eager to help us. They began digging trenches and tunnels to hide us, blending their work into the changes the road crew had started at Olivine's request. Entertainers perfected thicker smoke. Others collaborated with thread workers and artists to produce bloody costumes exceeding my expectations.

"These make the people appear nearly dead," I said.

"I know. Aren't they great?"

Twenty smiling faces awaited my approval.

A good commander works with the army she's got, right?

"They're wonderful. See if you can make them worse."

The entertainers who'd been helping to get the Mongols' horses to buck had worked independently, but smoke-making had common problems and I wanted to know their solutions. They invited me to a practice.

I knew Coral worked with these people, yet it surprised me to see her bright orange hair peeking out from the mask luskies typically wore. Of course she was one of them, and of course they would be here.

I gave her a small wave, and she waved back. We walked toward each other as the group dispersed. She hugged me and gestured towards the other reczavy.

"I heard about you. Are you happy with them?" she whispered.

"Very." As I said it I realized it was true.

"Then I'm glad for you. Let's get together and visit soon."

We said no more, but all the way home I wished I'd stayed and talked to her more.

I didn't want to fight with Galen. Not now. Fighting with Galen used up all the oomph I had. So I avoided him when I could, spoke pleasantly when I could not, and either fell asleep before he came to bed or crawled in next to him long after he started to snore.

I thought maybe he did the same, for much the same reason, until I accidentally glanced up and saw him watching me one morning.

This was not the look of an angry man. Not of a resentful one either, silently seething because his girlfriend worked on her own project instead of helping him design a better system for governing Ilarians.

No, this was a man who undressed me with his eyes and a man who couldn't have been happier with me.

"How's my favorite military commander this morning," he said, all smiles A lot of the reczavy, especially the guys, called me their commander. I knew they found it amusing, but the undercurrent of admiration made it hard for me to take offense.

"She misses your help." There. I said it. I sucked in my breath, ready for the argument I knew would ensue.

"Of course she does," he said "and I don't blame her. She'll be glad to know I and others have decided how to best shepherd in a new era in K'ba. We need the cooperation of Princess Nan, and a few others, and then Ilari will face a bright new future."

I wore a short skirt, as I found them easier to move in. His gaze moved up and down my legs. I felt the familiar tingle inside. Varmin bat scump. I didn't have time for this now.

"Got a few minutes to celebrate how well we're both doing?"

"I suppose I ..."

I never got that last word out ... he was on top of me before I could.

Okay, I hadn't planned on this with him, but it was much better than arguing.

A few days before Sashi, Suloom called out to me as I sat in the tent stitching poultices.

"Your sister's here."

Did one of the twins need a romantic holiday hideaway again?

"Which one?"

"Tall and blonde," Varla said.

Oh no. The only tall blonde sister was Sulphur, and right now she and I had one thing in common. This was the last place she'd want to be, and she was the last person I wanted here.

To make matters worse, it was a warm sunny day and I was fairly certain Suloom and Varla were outside getting sun all over while they did the dishes.

"Send her in here," I called back. It seemed less awkward than joining them outside.

She pulled back the flap of the tent and entered, carrying a small black cat.

"You're the last visitor I expected," I said. "Have a seat. And why are you carrying a cat?"

Sulphur looked around for something familiar, grabbed a wooden stool from the eating area, and sat. She put the cat on the floor next to her. It sat, tilted its head, and gave me a questioning look.

"This little thing is always hanging around. Cute, but I found her in my saddle bag when I got here. No idea how she managed to crawl in." She gestured to it. "Do you mind?"

"No, of course not." The cat lifted her head and graciously accepted my scratch behind her ears.

"I've been ordered to get more information about what you're planning." Sulphur said, looking at me as she avoided eying the rest of the tent. "The Svadlu are concerned about the handoff of the battle."

I laughed. "It's not much of a handoff. I mean, we've been told to drive as many Mongols as we can into the river and that's what we'll do."

"I saw a practice with the Faroojers," she said. "Looks like they'll be able to capture fighters. Do they have any plans past that?"

This demand for specifics annoyed me.

"Why would they? Ryalgar told us to make a lot of our attackers gone. A lot of them will be."

"I see. So I tell the Svadlu to expect somewhere between one and a thousand Mongols to ride up to the wall and demand tribute? And at that point, it's the Svadlu's show?"

"Pretty much."

"Gypsum, I need more details."

I couldn't miss her frustration, yet, I hesitated to share specifics. Despite all our differences, I trusted Sulphur, but I didn't trust the company she kept. At a minimum, the Svadlu would laugh at our plans. Worst case they'd boot us out of this horribly named Chimera and that would be bad for everyone.

So I said, "I don't know much more. I mean there will be a lot of illusions and weirdness but it's a free-form performance. You have to trust us."

I saw the struggle on her face. My new friends didn't inspire her trust either.

"Look, just give me an example of what you might do, something so I can get other Svadlu off my back."

"Okay." I gave her an overview of the egg throwing, keeping it vague. She seemed satisfied. She reached down with one hand to pick up the cat, then paused. "Do you want me to leave her here with you?"

"Oh no. She belongs back at her home."

I needn't have spoken. As soon as Sulphur asked, the little thing scampered out of the tent and ran to Sulphur's horse, waiting to be put back into the saddlebag.

~ 19 ~

Not That Door

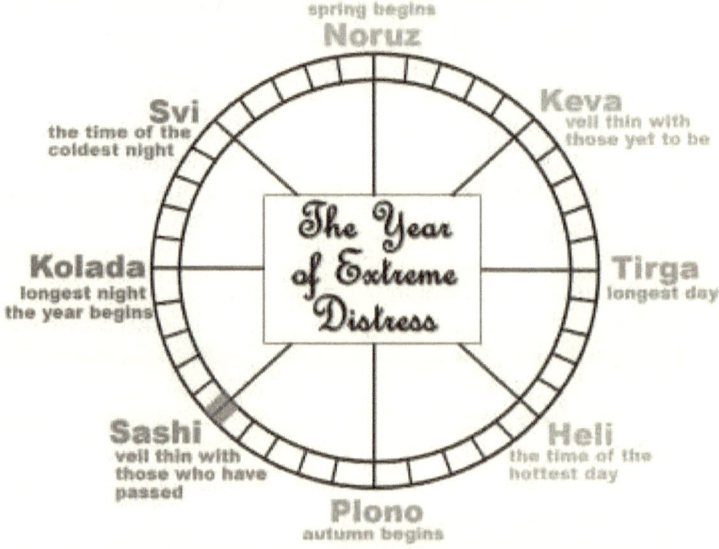

By the time the eve of Sashi arrived, three hundred plus people had accepted the reality of our situation. I supposed I had Ksenia to thank.

A small group of them sided philosophically with the Sage Coalition, preferring to take no chances and surrender to our would-be overlords. Most of them left for the K'ba settlements before Sashi, preferring to be with like-minded others as the rest of us prepared.

Some decided that while being a reczavy had been fun, they wished to be with family or other loved ones when Kolada came.

These set off for their original nichnas, planning to fight or hide alongside those they'd grown up with.

No one faulted anyone for their decision. How to face impending doom turns out to be a highly personal choice. We all had to do it in our own way.

Of the two-hundred and fifty or so of us who remained, everyone committed to doing something when the day arrived. I had a hundred reczavy sling shooters and Ksenia and her brother had found me a hundred more in Gruen. I had fifty brave egg throwers willing to get close enough to our invaders to look them in the eye. Another fifty worked with smoke and explosions while the remainder handled costumes and props, much like a stage crew for a performance.

But this was no performance. This was real. And it would happen after we celebrated a holiday dedicated to honoring the dead. And the dying. And the going to die someday but didn't want it to be anytime soon and that last group included us.

I'm sure other Sashi Eve celebrations in Ilari got out of hand that year, but I take odd satisfaction in thinking ours was the most outrageous. Honestly, there's no point in chronicling the particulars. Most of us were drunk and many of us were extremely so. People prucked anyone they felt like, sometimes in public and occasionally while both screamed obscenities at the universe. There was a lot of bad singing and clumsy dancing and a few rather impressive spontaneous strip performances mixed in with angry outbursts and occasional tears.

That night, all the next day, and the following night, we behaved like the rest of Ilari thought we did every day. Great Goddess. If we acted that way normally, it would kill us.

But, for one bright lightning flash, we reveled in all the unrestrained debauchery we could manage. I won't lie. It felt good. And it probably brought us all together in a way nothing else could have.

Galen and I found each other the morning after the Sashi. We stood outside our tent, blinking in the bright morning sun. He had bruises on his face and a swollen lower lip.

"You okay?"

"Yeah." He laughed. "Got in a dumb-arse fight with Jofim. Have no idea what it was about but there are no hard feelings either way." He shrugged. "Must have done us some good."

He squinted at me and held up his hand to shade his eyes.

"How about you? You okay? Are we okay?"

"Yeah." I wrapped my arms around his bare chest and nuzzled my aching head against it. "We're fine. I like how this can happen and somehow we both understand."

"Me too. I want to make sure you know something, Gypsum." His face scrunched as if he'd taken a bite of lemon. "I love you. Like, really love you."

"I know."

I gave him a light kiss on his bruised cheek and said something I'd never said before.

"I love you too."

We stood together in the sun, our arms wrapped around each other's bodies, not saying a word.

Finally he stepped away from me.

"I have to go back to the castle in K'ba. Talk to Princess Nan, find out what's happening. I worry her idiot brother might plan some last-minute surprise raid and pruck things up."

"If he had any sense, he'd have done that last night."

Galen had to laugh at the truth of it. "Yeah."

"You told the princess we'd give her to mid-Sashi to think about her choices. You don't think she needs more time?"

"I think waiting is a bad idea. I might go tomorrow," he said.

"Okay then. I'll go with you."

"Aren't you too busy doing commander things to take days off?"

I gave him my best smile. Well, my best, considering my pounding head and the aches and pains from disregarding most of my body's needs for the past day and a half.

"This is important, too, Sheep Scump. Let's go get the future of K'ba straightened out, then we'll come back and worry about saving the realm."

We held each other that night while we slept, neither one of us wanting to let go.

When we woke to an overcast sky, we knew the soft clouds would ease our ride through the desolation and decided to make the trip. This time we found the place with no effort. It could be seen from far off if one knew what to look for.

We could be seen from far off as well. Andre greeted us at the door.

"The Royals are not seeing anyone at this time without a prior appointment."

"Andre, it's us. Princess Nan's friends."

"I know who you are."

"Then step aside. We've business to conduct with her," I replied. My thirst and lingering headache did nothing to enhance my patience.

"She has no business with you."

Galen ignored Andre's comment and pushed past him.

"Stop," he yelled. "Or I'll consider this an invasion of our castle!"

Unfortunately for Andre, we both know the castle's entire defense consisted of Andre, his wife Melda, an elderly ruling prince we'd never met, and the ruler's sickly son. Oh, and former Edser Nan who held mixed loyalties at best.

"You go right ahead and do that," Galen said as he broke free from Andre's arm and headed down the hallway trying to decide which door would most likely lead to Nan.

He picked one of the two at the far end. Seemed reasonable to me as the princess would probably wish for her room to be as far from the others as possible. But as Galen reached for the latch, Andre's eyes widened.

"Please. Good Sir. I beg you. Not that door."

I thought he couldn't have said anything more likely to make Galen flip the latch, but Galen surprised me by pausing, giving the man a chance to explain.

"Why? Where does this door lead?"

Andre looked at the ground as he answered. "It is the Crown Prince's room, sir. He, he is not well today."

"I'm sorry to hear it," Galen said. "But I came here intending to meet him and will not leave until I do. If he is feeling poorly, I shan't keep him long."

A woman gasped as he pushed the heavy wood door open. I thought it was Nan, but as our eyes adjusted to the dim light we could see a plump older woman in a plain dress spooning a liquid into the barely parted lips of a frail young man lying on the bed.

S. R. Cronin

"My wife feeds the prince now," Andre said.

"Oh, he is in bad shape," I studied the pale face. The eyes were closed and no flicker of expression indicated he knew we were there.

"He sleeps," Melda said. She stroked the young man's hand with a mother's affection.

"Why do you feed him while he sleeps?" Galen asked.

"Sometimes he sleeps a lot."

I suspected something worse.

"Does he ever wake?" I asked her. She looked to her husband for guidance. He shook his head, but Nan pushed in through the doorway behind him, her strawberry blonde curls in wild and uncombed disarray.

"What in Heli's name are you two doing in here?"

We did expect her to be somewhat happier to see us.

"We told you we'd come back," Galen answered. "To check on you. See if you needed help." I knew he wanted to add "and learn your answer about thwarting your family in Eds," but he didn't.

"You've no business intruding into one of the Royal chambers." Anger flashed in her face, along with something else. Something more important. Embarrassment. It humiliated her to have us see what her father had done to her.

"Your father didn't marry you off to a sickly man," I said. "He forced you wed a prince who is unconscious!"

I turned to the older woman for more answers.

"Did he ever regain consciousness after his accident?"

She shook her head.

"A few times, he's squeezed my hand, maybe, but never anything more."

"How??" Galen waved both hands in the air in every direction, his gesture mirroring his many questions.

"My wife has cared for the boy since they pulled him from the river six years ago," Andre said, standing taller as he said it. "She loves him like her own infant. She feeds him, keeps him clean, and even sings to him on occasion to keep his mind alert."

"I was his nanny, right up to that horrible day when he hit his head on a rock and nearly drowned," Melda added. "Showing off in the fast water with the other boys. They never should have let him go down there."

Andre raised his hand to stop her. "Please, dear. All have paid for that horrible decision many times over."

I turned to Nan, who had busied herself tucking the most offending pieces of hair back into her disheveled braid.

Her self-described job was to get pregnant by this man. How could …? Was it …?

She saw my questioning look. "If you must know more, join me in the sitting room. Andre? Refreshments please."

"Your Highness …"

Her voice turned gentle. "We've nothing else to hide. These two know our worst secret now, so let me speak with them in private. He is from my homeland and only wishes to check on my wellbeing."

"Very well." Andre stood and a look of understanding passed between them. "I'll bring food and drink."

"Spare me the questions." She sat with her back straight, her chin raised, and her hands folded in her lap. "I'll tell you what you need to know. Yes, I have done my best to fulfill my duties and have reported my efforts to my husband's family and my own." She smiled slightly. "Awkward as that has been."

We sat on ornate little chairs covered in a soft green brocade as we sipped green fizzy afternoon wine in small fancy cups. I probably looked at Nan in disbelief because she directed her next comment to me.

"Even a man who isn't awake responds to a woman's touch," she said. "He and I have succeeded in doing what must be done. Many times."

Galen seemed less surprised by this, but then again he was a guy. I grimaced at what she described.

"Yet no child?" I said. It was the most tactful response I could think of.

She swallowed and held her eyes closed for a heartbeat, composing herself.

"While we are, um, able to begin, so far we have not managed to conclude in the way that produces a baby."

Galen responded. "He doesn't …"

"Exactly," she said. "If sophisticated techniques exist to produce this result, I am unaware of them. And it's not like I can ask anyone for help." Her voice rose on the last several words.

"I don't think there are such ways," Galen assured her.

"My newly-crowned brother wrote me three days ago demanding to know if I might be pregnant. I told him my husband's injuries made it unlikely and he responded by graciously permitting me to cease trying."

Galen set his cup down. We'd gotten to the part of the conversation he cared most about.

"What does your brother plan to do?"

"He wrote me yesterday that two anks after Sashi, he intends to declare the agreement fulfilled, and claim K'ba as his own."

"That's in seventeen days. And it's three anks before the Mongols appear," I said. "Why? Why not wait until after?"

She shrugged. "I suspect my father encourages him, hoping Eds will emerge advantageous for acting swiftly. As to my brother, I don't know what he thinks, or even if he does, but patience is not his strength."

"Do you think he'll bother the reczavy before the invasion?"

"I said that I don't know my brother's mind."

She glared at Galen. He stared back. He won.

"Okay. He probably will send palace guards to ride in and scatter you all, just for the pleasure of hearing people cheer him the way they cheer my father. He wants the same adulation."

"Does he know that we're part of the larger plan to defend Ilari?"

"I'm sure he's heard and he's probably claimed he'll do Ilari a favor by eliminating you because you'll pruck up your part and make things worse. Dad thinks your kind always does."

Ouch.

"Nan, would you listen to me if I explained what the reczavy will do?" I said. "It's important somebody understands what your brother would destroy. Please?"

For all the bizarre things fate had brought Nan's way, she remained reasonable. She tucked in a few last strands of hair and nodded. "I'll listen."

She raised her voice enough to be heard outside of our room.

"Andre. We'll need more wine, and prepare food as well. My guests will dine with us and require accommodation for the night."

Andre didn't respond, but I heard the clanking of pottery in the kitchen. When his silence had lasted long enough to be awkward, Melda appeared at the door with a second jug of wine.

"Of course, Madam," she said, bringing it in and beginning to pour.

Andre followed her, but rather than bring food he came empty handed and sat in one of the fancy chairs with us, allowing his wife to pour him wine as well.

His eyes met Nan's. "Under the circumstances I'd like to join you. Your Highness."

"Of course, Andre," Then to me. "Please. Explain why it is important my brother not attack the reczavy before the Mongols invade."

~ 20 ~

Less of a Big Deal Than Usual

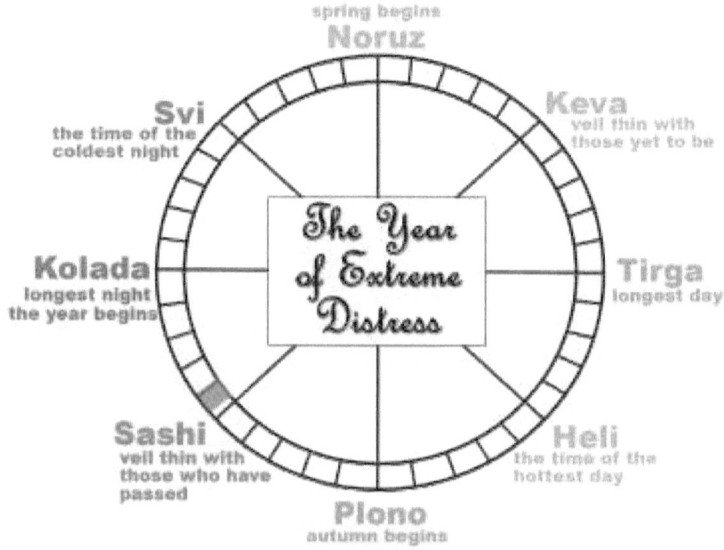

spring begins
Noruz

Svi
the time of the
coldest night

Keva
veil thin with
those yet to be

The Year
of Extreme
Distress

Kolada
longest night
the year begins

Tirga
longest day

Sashi
veil thin with
those who have
passed

Heli
the time of the
hottest day

Plono
autumn begins

I did my best. I covered Ryalgar's three-pronged resistance and our unique role, emphasizing how the plan didn't overlook the oddities of the reczavy but rather relied on them. I provided some specifics but not too many. I didn't want them to critique my plans, just know that no one could replace us.

"This sort of sophisticated thinking may be beyond your brother's capacity to understand," Andre murmured to Nan. He took a small sip of his wine before adding, "If you don't mind my saying so, Your Highness."

She ignored him. "I have to assume my father still advises," she told me. "And he is capable of understanding how we could use the reczavy for something so preposterous, despite his low opinion of them. I'll contact him."

"If I may make a suggestion," Andre said to Galen, "Why not move the reczavy to Gruen now? I'm sure they could find room for you somewhere until Kolada, and you'd be safe and closer to where you're needed." He leaned forward and smiled, a small forced movement of his lips meant to encourage Galen's acceptance of this lovely alternative. "And then we wouldn't have to involve Nan's family at all, would we?"

"Moving our entire camp now would disrupt our preparation and demoralize our group," I said. "No. We need to stop Nan's brother from staging a raid on us to boost his popularity."

"And the best way to do that? It's to make sure K'ba does not become part of Eds," Galen added, right on cue.

"We can't stop that," Nan said. "We made an agreement. Long ago."

Galen and I looked at her.

"Of course you can," I said. "You, and only you, can declare that the terms were never met." At her look of horror, I added, "You don't have to give specifics. Merely announce that the, uh, acts necessary to produce an heir were never fully, uh …"

"I wrote letters to my father stating otherwise."

"A frightened daughter exaggerating the facts," Galen said. "An embarrassed woman reticent to give details. All understandable. All forgivable. But now, given the consequences, you feel compelled to reveal the truth."

"My brother would kill me if I did that." I couldn't tell if she meant he'd be angry or that he'd actually kill her. I supposed either was possible.

"Andre could back up your claims. So could Melda."

"We'd prefer not to reveal the full nature of the Crown Prince's incapacitation, out of respect for his father," Andre said.

"Yes. About his father," I replied. "We need to talk about him, too. Exactly how incapacitated is your Ruling Prince?"

Nan looked at Andre. Andre looked at the floor.

"Come on. If he had half a brain left in his head he'd be leading this conversation and we all know it. Why isn't he here? Where do you keep him?"

Andre probably would have continued to ignore me but Galen spoke up.

"We want to help Nan. And you. And K'ba. We want to do what's best but how can we if we don't know how bad your situation is?"

Andre liked Galen better. I supposed I didn't blame him.

"It's very bad." Andre stood. "You want to know how serious our problems are. Come. I'll show you. Then you tell me about your great solutions."

He led the way out a back door and into the cold windy desolation where a few plants struggled to survive in between the various small buildings making up the compound. Andre strode to the furthest building and we followed. Though only the size of a single small room, this little structure looked better maintained than the others.

The stench when Andre opened the door told me all I needed to know.

"How long has he been dead?" I asked.

Andre wouldn't meet my gaze. "Nearly half a year now. This summer. A head cold overtook him, and we nursed him as best we could, but we hated to send to Pilk for a physician and we had no idea ... he went so fast." Andre wiped at a small tear. "I couldn't believe it. At first I couldn't bear to bury him. Then, well, when it became clear we must, my wife and I tried to dig a grave in this rocky soil, but we couldn't manage it and I dared not ask outsiders for help and..." His words trailed off.

"What was your plan?" I asked.

"I promised myself I'd find a way to bury him once winter came."

"What was your plan for K'ba?"

"Oh. Of course," Andre said. "I still hoped the young woman might succeed against all odds. Unsuitable as it would be, she could rule secretly after I died, until her son was of age of course. Then he could make many sons and get things back to normal. It was a hope ..."

"What was your plan if Nan didn't produce a child?" I asked. *Or if she had a girl?*

He finally looked me in the eye. "When we made the agreement with her family and took her in, our Ruling Prince and I thought rejoining Eds wasn't a bad option. The Eds Royals had always been basically good and we thought they could shepherd the K'basta away from these new ways and back to the values the Ruling Prince and I held dear."

"So you've been running this nichna for several eighths now?" I replied.

He shrugged and gave me a bit of a look down his nose. "I haven't done anything above my station. I've simply allowed K'ba to run itself. I mean, the reczavy and those who live near them have their own system, and the settlements are basically run by the Sage Coalition these days. The other Ruling Princes already tolerated my presence when we met each eighth, as my Ruler was too frail to travel, and they've continued to believe my stories about ill Royals."

"Not one of them questioned ..." I didn't believe it. I wanted more facts but Galen raised his hand in a gentle gesture to stop me.

"And now you have doubts about whether being annexed by Eds is the best fate for K'ba?" he prodded.

I took the opportunity to take a few steps away from the little mausoleum and breath in fresh air. Andre, Nan, and Galen followed me. Nan hadn't said a word and Andre had barely addressed her. Now he turned to her.

"The young woman impressed me, and my Ruling Prince, with her sincerity. Even my wife has grown fond of her. The degree to which she cowers at the thought of living under her father's rule bothered us, and her barely veiled disdain for her brother has given me greater pause. I've concluded Prince Lufo shouldn't be ruling one nichna, much less two."

I watched Galen's face relax. He'd won the battle he needed to win.

"Andre. Who do you think should rule K'ba?"

The old man gave a rusty cough that almost sounded like a chuckle.

"Not me. You see, I think I know how the K'basta should behave, but the problem is that most of them don't agree with me. Who am I to say otherwise? I've decided the K'basta need a leader who is right for them."

"Would you support Nan in her assertion that the Edsers have no legitimate claim?"

"I would."

Galen turned to Nan.

"Are you strong enough to defy your brother?"

"No," she said. "I'm not. But you happen to have caught me facing an impending invasion from blood-thirsty monsters so, you know, pissing off my brother is less of a big deal than usual."

"I'll take that as a yes," Galen said. He didn't manage to hide the grin on his face. I don't know. Maybe he didn't try.

"You know a way to make this work?" she asked.

"You bet I do."

With that, we walked back to the house to plot the overthrow of the government.

Back at camp, Galen gave my plans all the time I asked for. I needed to run tests to see how well my confusion poultices worked on unwilling wearers? No problem.

Galen found volunteers, recruited poultice shooters, and staged our first-ever shoot-things-at-people-for-fun party. Everyone had a good time and the unexplainable bewilderment experienced by many guests only added to the fun.

The next day, two tents asked if they could use my confusion poultices for parties of their own. I had to explain that these were supposed to be weapons to defend us.

"Oh, okay. Then could we use them for a party after this Mongol thing is over?"

"Sure," I said. I'd decided to join Nan in her current approach to life. For the next few anks, I wasn't going to worry much about the consequences of anything.

Nan had been heavy on my mind since Galen and I left the K'ba's castle. Before our departure, the current K'ba Royal family, or whatever they should be called, had consented to issue a decree three anks and one day before Kolada. It would allegedly be signed by the frail Ruling Prince and read by Andre and would declare that after detailed conversations with the wife of the Crown Prince, the K'basta Royals deemed her to be in violation of the agreement with Eds. Out of respect for the Royal family, no further details would be provided but K'ba would not be willingly annexed by its neighbor.

Galen had written the decree, of course, and he included a tantalizing section about how the lack of a suitable heir would force the Royals to anoint a new leader. The Royals would rely on a panel of local leaders to advise and consent to the selection, with the intention of finding someone who represented the current values and interests of the K'basta. He knew this clause guaranteed that most K'basta in the settlements, and the smaller contingent in and around the reczavy, would wholeheartedly support the decree. Not that many would have objected to it anyway.

I presumed Galen's new-found enthusiasm for aiding my efforts meant he had his plan, whatever it was, worked out and only needed to let events unfold. So I took all the help from him I could get.

I needed to know if there was a way to make eggshells stronger, so Galen and two friends rode to Pilk to interview the top experts on chickens. Suloom returned the next day with the news that chickens with access to more bugs and worms made stronger eggshells. Also those who were fed peas by their farmers, although the experts had no idea what peas and worms had in common.

Where were Galen and Raheem? They'd ridden off to beseech farmers to dig deep into the cold ground for worms and to feed their chickens with the precious dried peas they'd stored for their families' use in the winter. They faced a hard sell, but Galen knew that every egg that survived transport could yield one less man with a sword or bow who could kill us.

"Stronger eggs make for fewer killers," he'd said. "I can sell that concept."

I knew he could.

Idris came and went often, always without her trusty scout.

"You've learned to get here on your own?" I asked one morning as she emerged from the trees with a small donkey, a cute little guy whom many in our tent adopted as a sort of pet when he was around.

"It's not that hard," she said. "And my scout has better things to do. She's widening our paths so relays of Velka guides can run through the forest on the day of, if we need to get messages across Ilari fast."

"That's good thinking."

We talked as we walked to the campfire, she to warm up after her ride, me to offer her some late breakfast.

"Yeah. And she doesn't have many days left to work because the Velka scouts will help get refugees to safety when the time comes. Anybody leaving has been told to start two anks before Kolada."

"Why that far in advance?"

"They'll be a slow group. Tiny kids. Old people. Very pregnant women. They need lots of time, and we're not sure our Kolada will match our invaders' winter solstice. What if the Mongols show up a few days early?"

It made sense.

I'd considered stopping off at the farm on one of my trips to Gruen, to wish my folks well before everything happened. For all the frustration between us, an appearance before Kolada only seemed right. But my mother and little nephew would leave with the evacuees. Looked like I better go soon.

As we settled into chairs, her with a plate of food and me with a second cup of breakfast wine, I said, "Thanks for telling me. Where will most of our refugees go?"

"Zur will take in some. Mostly Royals and important people from Pilk I think. The Velka will accept some women, mostly relatives of those already there. They say they can't do more because so many Velka will be involved when ..."

I shook my head. "I never thought I'd see the day when a bunch of old women picked up arms."

"Don't laugh. Your grandmother will be out there with the archers, you know. Along with Ryalgar and your sister Olivine."

"My grandmother??"

"Yes. She's one of those people who can move things without touching them, and they need as many of those as they can get."

Idris stopped chewing and looked at me, deciding whether to say more. "Did you know you upset her by refusing to keep her name? She said she was surprised to learn that you hated her that much."

"Oh for scump's sake. I don't hate her. I did at first, but that was me thinking of myself. Then I heard how she didn't want to give up what she wanted in life because of her daughter's foolish choices, and I understood that. And I didn't refuse her name, I took the name of the woman who raised me. Why should that bother anyone?"

"It shouldn't. I hope you'll get the chance to tell Aliz why you changed it someday."

I didn't think I owed my grandmother an explanation, but I let the matter drop. Idris obviously felt more loyalty and affection for Aliz than I did.

"Where are most of the evacuees going?"

"Oh, you haven't heard? Tolo has agreed to hide them in the mountains and shelter and care for them as long they need it. It's a big offer."

"I'll say. How are they getting up to Tolo?"

"Well, those on the western side will probably follow the Little River up there, but those from the eastern nichnas will follow the forest's edge through Scrud. They'll pass by here and then go through Eds. That will be something to see, won't it?"

I tried to imagine a few thousand people coming down the road. I couldn't. Instead, I saw thousands of our most vulnerable walking into a bloody and needless fight between K'ba and Eds, and never making it to safety because of it.

Galen and I, we couldn't allow that to happen.

~ 21 ~

Not a Prince

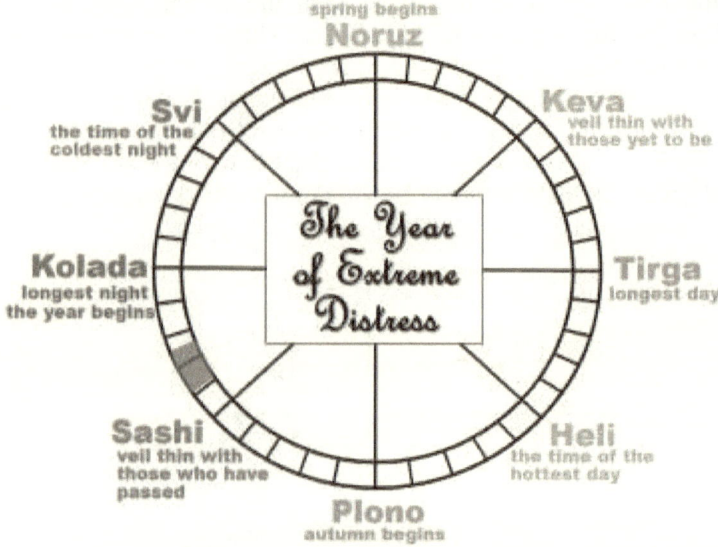

spring begins
Noruz

Svi
the time of the
coldest night

Keva
veil thin with
those yet to be

Kolada
longest night
the year begins

The Year
of Extreme
Distress

Tirga
longest day

Sashi
veil thin with
those who have
passed

Heli
the time of the
hottest day

Plono
autumn begins

That night I dreamt about bunnies. Helpless little bunnies. Cute and cuddly little bunnies that faced slaughter by evil unseen things lurking at the edge of my dream. They were so sweet. How could anyone hurt them?

I woke up knowing what I had to do. No. I woke up knowing one more thing I had to do. I had to sew bunnies.

Unfortunately, my "to sew" list was long. I'd managed to get over three hundred of the confusion poultices made, largely because Esteri and two other women in our tent had stuffed them for me, bravely agreeing to accept responsibility for their parts in using black mustard seed, grains of paradise, and bdellion to cause harm.

Pie and Guy kept all the other thread workers focused on costumes for our egg throwers and on making fake cloth eggs for them to practice with. But I still had eighty-nine more poultices to make. Then I wanted to stitch some small thing for each of my egg throwers to wear, something to impart bravery. I'd wanted to do that for my slingshot shooters, too, but time grew short and my egg throwers needed courage more than the others.

But, someone else needed courage more.

Idris told me that some of the small children would be with grandparents or pregnant mothers, but most would be with distant relatives or even strangers as their parents and older siblings stayed behind to fulfill vital roles in our battle. These little children would face the unknown alone. Unloved and frightened.

Little children should not feel that way.

So I'd make as many tiny soft bunnies as I could and I'd fill them with comfort, the way my skill allowed me to when my passion about something ran high. Maybe I'd get a few hundred of them done, if I worked by firelight into the night, each night. So I began.

Galen joined me two nights later, wrapped in blankets. The nights grew cold, as they do when Kolada nears, but I sat so close to the flames that I didn't notice.

"How are your eyes holding up?" he asked.

"They're tired."

"This is something you have to do?"

"Yes."

"I miss you in bed."

"I miss you too."

Twenty-eight days before Kolada, the ruling prince of K'ba issued a decree. It was quite a feat considering he'd been dead for half a year but only Galen and I knew that. His underling, Andre, hired heralds from the settlements to spend an entire day proclaiming the announcement both there and to all who passed along the roads in K'ba. Andre hired a second group of heralds to ride to the castle in Eds and deliver the same proclamation. He wisely hired a contingent of guards to accompany this group.

Nan, the former princess of Eds, was quoted as vowing that she had failed to fulfill her part of the bargain and regretted misleading her family to believe otherwise. She had been acting out of embarrassment and fear of them. In truth, Eds had no legitimate claim to overtake K'ba.

I'd originally thought this proclamation was a great idea, but I'd been thinking hard about it over the past few nights. I couldn't stop worrying about the safety of the caravan passing through, and I couldn't get Nan's offhand comment out of my head.

"My brother would kill me."

Based on what I'd heard about Ruling Prince Lufo, he might send an assassin after his sister. Perhaps his father could stop him and would. Perhaps he couldn't. Or wouldn't. I hadn't heard many good things about this family.

Lufo's assassin would likely laugh at the lack of protection at the K'ba castle, then get the job done and leave. But if he or she looked around and learned of the true situation regarding the K'basta Royals, then Lufo would learn of it too.

Then the problems would really begin.

I assumed Lufo would declare the K'basta decree invalid as no prince existed to have proclaimed it. I also assumed he'd send people to talk to Andre and Melda to learn how this entire nonsense happened. I hardly expected Andre to withstand threats, much less torture, to protect us.

Galen and I would be named, perhaps immediately, and then I could think of no reason why Prince Lufo wouldn't send his palace guards to scatter the reczavy to the winds and kill me and Galen.

I mean, that's the sort of thing awful people do, right?

And about then we'd have thousands of vulnerable people coming down our road.

So as Galen and I walked back from listening to the heralds do their recitation on the road a few times, I had to say something.

"Well written, Sheep Scump." I gave him a friendly punch on the arm. "But I'm not sure you've thought through the worst of the consequences. What do you expect this Lufo dirt bag to do now? Say 'That's too bad. Guess I don't get to rule K'ba?'"

"I definitely don't expect that!"

"So ...."

"So I think the first thing he'll do is send his personal guards to the K'ba castle under the guise of negotiation. Their real instructions will be to manufacture a confrontation and kill everyone there, including Nan, so Lufo can say and do what he wants."

"Oh." I'd worried that all those midnight hours alone had let my imagination get the better of me. It was oddly comforting to learn my lover's visions were as dark as mine.

"You can't be okay with that?"

"Pruck no. While you've been sewing your little fingers off, dear, I've been getting to know the K'basta better. I've made friends in the Sage Coalition and have good relationships with the movers and shakers of K'ba."

He could make friends anywhere ...

"They don't know the full story, but they now know more details of the agreement that nearly cost them their nichna. They know of Nan's brave stance to save them, and they have a higher opinion of Edsers thanks to Nan."

"You talked them into defending her?"

He rolled his eyes as though that much had been obvious.

"It didn't take persuasion. By midday today hundreds of K'basta will surround that pitiful castle. They may not be the greatest fighters in the world, but Lufo's only got twenty or so palace guards and while your average Edser might be cranky, he's not easily persuaded to go kill a former Edser princess. My contacts in Eds say that at most Lufo could gather another twenty, especially after the work I've done behind his back to ensure Nan is remembered fondly while Lufo's boorish behavior is fresh on everyone's minds."

Galen gave me a smug smile.

"You have been working this, haven't you?" I said.

He squeezed my butt. "Had to do something to keep my mind off of you while you sewed all those varmin bunnies."

"Did it occur to you that Lufo might hear of the role you played and come after you?"

"Sure. And after you too, and we can't have that because you have things to accomplish. So I asked Idris to help us. Well, technically I asked Raheem to ask her. She seems to have a soft spot for him."

"I noticed. What can Idris do?"

"She can talk to the Velka. Turns out they really do not want to see the third prong of Ryalgar's plan demolished by some greedy prince. So, Velka scouts now guard the southern road between Eds and K'ba. Better yet, I sent a message to my brother in the Svadlu yesterday. He's pissed that the Edsers are causing trouble now and replied that Svadlu would arrive soon to patrol the border as well. Nobody will ride in from Eds to bother us."

And no one riding into K'ba would disturb the caravan either. I admit I felt relieved. Very relieved.

"So what do you think? Could you take a day off from your sewing and ride over to Gruen Town with me?"

"Galen, please. I've got so much to do here."

"I know you do, so I've found you some help, but she refuses to come to you. I already tried."

"Okay. Sure I can. Uh … what would you think of stopping at my parents' farm on the way? We could thank my dad in person."

"You want to go to your parents' farm?" He looked like he couldn't decide if I joked or not.

"I do. I want to say goodbye to my mom before she leaves. And I want them to meet you." The last part hadn't occurred to me until the words were out, but soon as they were, I knew they were true.

"Sure, Duck Piss. You want me to meet your parents? I'll meet them."

"Nervous?" I asked as we rode through the early morning cold to the place I'd been raised.

"Sweetheart. I've already taken on an evil ruler and his dastardly plans."

"You did, and you were brilliant."

"Thank you. But to answer your question, yes. I'm scared scumpless."

"So am I."

Galen and I had picked our travel day spontaneously, and there'd been no way to let my parents know. So we just rode up. Mom swept the porch as we arrived. She squinted at us as if she wasn't sure it was me. I'd forgotten that I'd shortened my hair eighths ago and it had only partially grown back.

"Mom? May we get off to say hello?"

We'd had no contact since the messages we exchanged half a year ago. Those messages had been friendly, for us, but much had happened since. To both of us.

"Of course." She gave me a little smile of understanding. "Who is this?"

"My boyfriend. Galen. He's from Eds, and I met him at school."

"Galen? May I offer you something to drink? To eat?"

"That would be wonderful." He was off his horse before she could change her mind.

"Your father is with his road crew. He'll be so sad he missed you."

We all looked at each other. No one knew what to say.

"I came to wish you well, Mom. I heard you're taking Coral's baby into the forest and ..."

"Yes, yes. Everyone can't believe I'd do such a thing. And I of course I've heard you're .. what? Throwing eggs at our invaders?" She tried to add a little laugh but it didn't come off very well.

"It's more complicated but yes."

"I see." She glanced at Galen, she then studied his face more closely. "Well, at least Gypsum found someone attractive. I don't suppose you're a prince, are you?"

"Mom!"

"Don't worry, it's a family joke," she told him, ignoring me. "Gypsum has five older sisters and each one has found a different and creative way not to marry a prince, just to spite me. You should hear some of their schemes. So I thought maybe ..."

"Actually, Madam, your daughter is about to overthrow a prince. Does that count as a creative solution?"

Now she looked at me. "You're about to do what?"

"I'm about to do what?"

We said it at the same time and then stared at each other.

"He's confused," I said. "He's overthrowing a prince. I'm just watching."

"Oh. That's nice. What nichna?" she asked him politely.

"K'ba.

"You picked a good one. I hear the Royals there don't do a thing for their people."

"They've fallen on hard times," he said. "They need to be replaced with a hero. A person everyone looks up to. So after we repel these invaders, if we do, then K'ba's most illustrious architect of our success will step up and take the reins of leadership, much to every K'basta's delight."

Mom looked at me, horrified. "Is he talking about you?"

"I sure as Heli hope not," I answered. "It's the first I've heard of it."

"She and I need to talk more about it," he said to my mom in a loud stage whisper. "I probably shouldn't have sprung it on her here, but I wanted you to be proud of her."

Mom gave me a funny look. "Well, at least he thinks highly of you." She took a sip of her drink. "Please be careful, Gypsum. With all of this. Contrary to what your new friends may think, this is not a game."

"I know, Mom. I'll be careful, I promise."

"Have you heard much about your sisters?" she asked.

When I said no, she filled me in on family news as if the previous conversation had never happened. For once I appreciated Mom's reticence to discuss difficult subjects.

She invited us to stay the night, but I saw her shoulders relax in relief when I told her we had to get over to Gruen before dark. She sent us off with more provisions than we could use, and gave Galen a short hug, and me a longer one.

"I'm glad you stopped by." I thought she meant it.

"I'm glad I did, too."

Galen and I rode off in silence but he knew we had some serious talking ahead of us.

~ 22 ~

More Than Bunnies

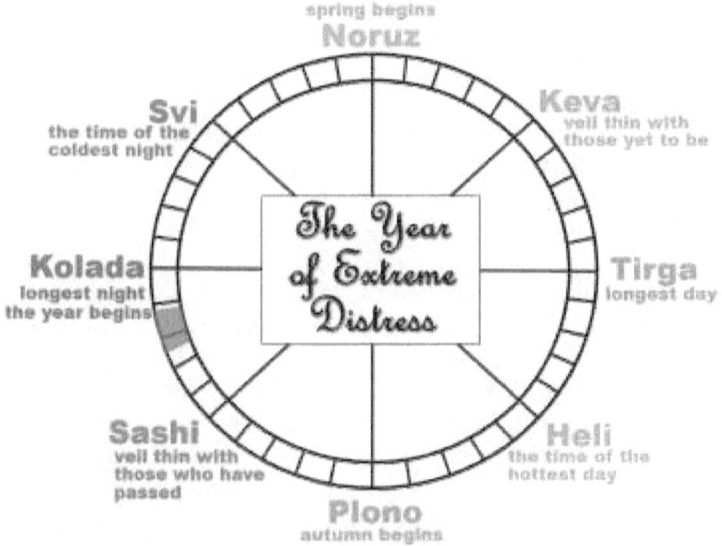

I don't like to talk about something important while I ride," Galen shouted over to me. He'd kept his horse farther from mine than usual, making conversation more difficult as we made our way to Gruen.

"Fine. We'll talk when we get there."

"We're stopping at a farmhouse. The man's a chicken farmer who's supplying us with eggs. He agreed to feed his flock peas and worms because he knows about the stronger shells. That's where I met her."

"Who?"

"His wife. She doesn't help with the chickens because she's got her own business sewing things for half of Gruen. He says people stand in line for her stuff because it makes them feel good."

Now he had my interest.

"What she sews makes them feel good??"

"Yup. He denies there's anything magic about it, says his family doesn't believe in that nonsense. They believe in science, and she's just a good seamstress."

"You can believe in both."

"I know. With him standing there, she said she'd been trying to squelch those silly rumors for years. But after she agreed to make the vests to hold eggs, she took me aside and asked what these egg throwers needed to feel most."

Maybe I didn't have to make some quick half-arsed wristbands for my egg throwers. Maybe this lady handled that problem already. That hope helped me push aside Galen's preposterous plans for me.

I gave my horse a light nudge.

"Can we ride faster?"

He fed the chickens when we arrived, while a younger couple worked to repair one of the pens. Inside, a middle-aged woman sat in front of the fire sewing.

"I'm sorry I couldn't come to you, dear," she greeted me. "I know how busy you are, but I just couldn't. I hope you understand. Can I get you some warmed breakfast wine? I know midday has passed but in winter it always seems like morning to me." She shivered. "I'm cold all day."

"Yes. Please." The ride had chilled us, and we needed fire and a warm drink.

"You're making our vests?" I asked as she gathered up the refreshments.

"Happy to do it. You won't find a seamstress anywhere who knows more about eggs than I do. Will she, dear?"

Her husband had come inside and he chuckled. "She does know eggs, though I can hardly tear her away from her threads. I'm lucky my son and his wife like doing chores." He gave us a good-humored eye roll and headed back out with a pastry in his hand.

"Your husband doesn't care much for the old ways?" I thought my remark was subtle, but Galen narrowed his eyes at me.

"My husband's family has had this farm for generations, priding themselves on using science to increase their yield. Nobody can change who they are. Certainly not me."

"I see. How are the vests coming along?"

"Oh, I'm almost half done with them, dear. Tell me. Is it true these egg throwers will need to get close to our attackers?"

"They will. Even with the smoke and distractions, they'll be in great danger, more so I think than anyone in all of our plans."

"Well then, we do ask a lot of them. I'll make the remaining ones particularly well."

I left satisfied that she would.

Galen led us in a gallop to the edge of town, where so many people waited for us, and so many of them needed questions answered.

Had they dug enough tunnels? With trees losing their leaves, was the river well enough hidden behind the curve in the road? They could still add more evergreens. Should they?

I stared at the amount of foliage that had disappeared since I'd last been here. Why hadn't I paid more attention to which plants lost their leaves?

By the time Galen and I walked into our little room in the inn, a day filled with hard riding, a stressful encounter with my mother, and an overwhelming number of questions from those relying on us left us exhausted. We glared at each other as we undressed for bed.

"I have no intention of ever leading anything again in my life," I said.

"We probably shouldn't talk about this tonight," he answered.

"I hope you have a great backup plan for choosing a leader because you're going to need it."

He laughed. "Several people suggested letting everyone vote on the new ruler. Is that ridiculous or what?"

"It seems sensible enough. And I like it because people would never vote for me as their monarch."

"That's my point. You know how to run something, but it wouldn't matter. People would vote for the last person who bought them an ale. You can't pick a ruler that way."

"It seems better than inheriting the job."

"No, it's worse. The sons of princes are seldom impressive, but they're also seldom inclined to do harm. Well, except for Lufo. So, isn't it better to have a mildly competent helmsman groomed for the job than a clever one who gets elected so he can sink the boat for his own gain?"

That varmin comment sucked me in despite my determination to ignore him.

"Galen! There is no way to select selfless leaders. Or capable ones. None."

"Of course there is," he said. "You find someone who has sacrificed a great deal to do something for the land and its people. Someone who has shown leadership skills in the doing of it. Then you get a committee of important people to appoint him or her as your next ruler."

He stared at me.

I stared back.

"I don't want to talk about it tonight."

"Neither do I."

After that, we managed to sleep together in a tiny bed without once touching each other.

I just wanted a day of peace when we arrived back at our tent. Kolada came in twenty short days, and our evacuees would pass through here in three. I had hopes for making a lot more bunnies.

A coalition of Velka scouts and a few Svadlu now stood guard at the south road connecting Eds and K'ba, providing us as well as the incoming caravan with a measure of safety. Meanwhile, hundreds of Sage Coalition members, whose political philosophies had kept them out of Ryalgar's plans, continued to use their free time to surround the K'ba castle. Their presence protected Nan, Andre, and Melda as they awaited Galen's glorious plan for selecting a new ruler.

His glorious plan gave me a headache every time I thought about it, so I didn't. I had too much else to worry about.

Just when I didn't think I could handle another thing, Ksenia poked her head into the tent.

"Your sister Olivine is here, hoping the two of you can have a nice visit and get caught up." The fake cheer in her tone told me she anticipated my response.

"What? Today? Steaming skunk scump! I don't have time for a chat. What's wrong with her?"

Ksenia touched me lightly on the arm.

"Breath in. Breath out. Then go tell your sister you love her but now is an awful time for you and a worse time for your tentmates. Stick her in the guest tent for the night, and I'll send her provisions. She'll be fine."

"Yes. Thanks." Then as Ksenia turned to go, it occurred to me to ask. "Why is this a worse time for my tentmates?"

"I'll tell you about that after you deal with your sister."

Olivine understood and even apologized, pointing out that while she had plenty of duties too, none of hers involved directing others.

"People wear me out," she confessed. "I don't know how you do it."

I didn't know how I did it either, but I left her with a promise that we'd talk through all of this someday when it had ended well. Neither of us added "if it ends well" but we both knew it belonged there.

"Idris told us about the evacuees who will pass by on our road," Ksenia said. "Why didn't you mention that's why you spent most nights in front of the fire, sewing into the early morning?"

"I .... don't know. I guess I thought it didn't matter. Why would it? I figured if I couldn't do anything else, at least I could give those scared kids some comfort." I felt tears forming in my eyes. The last thing I wanted to do was cry now. About this.

"It's okay. Our tent wants to find ways to help. Other tents, too."

"Oh, no. The last thing I wanted was to cause trouble ..."

"You didn't. You reminded us there's a bigger world and this is about more than planning trickery in Gruen Town. For starters, the tent leaders want to take a head count and see how many will be here instead of Gruen on the day.

"No one, I think."

"I thought so too but we've got twelve who haven't volunteered for anything, for many reasons. We've designated them as our hearth tenders."

"What do we need that for?"

"In case none of the reczavy who go to Gruen come home for a while. If the Mongols don't bother with the desolation, we've still got wild animals and storms. Our hearth tenders will keep fires going and tents safe, so there is a place to straggle back to. They'll provide refuge for other Ilarians too. We need to look at a bigger picture."

She was right. I hadn't let myself think about anything but my part in the plan. That had been plenty. But somebody needed to think beyond those things.

"That made us wonder what we do have here that we don't need. What food, drink, and supplies would be better off in the hands of our evacuees? So everyone is sorting through everything. We'll keep enough for the hearth tenders and store some for those who return, but we want to hand out the rest along with your bunnies. We hope you don't mind.

Varmin bat scump. I *was* going to cry. I turned away from Ksenia before I started.

"It's okay," she said squeezing my shoulder from the back. "Acts of kindness always make me cry too."

Seventeen days before Kolada we spied the start of the caravan coming towards us out of Scrud, and we began to gather along the road.

Soon we could pick out Velka scouts riding at the front, side by side with a few Svadlu. Behind them we saw others on horseback, probably those barely too young or too old to stay and fight but still able to ride. Behind them, we saw what must have been every cart in Ilari that could be hitched to a horse.

When they approached where we stood, the Svadlu in front called for a halt. We looked behind him at the toddlers sitting on the laps of the very elderly and at the pregnant women soothing the babies of others. We saw carts of injured tending to the sick and carts of children tending to the injured.

The Svadlu glared down at me, as I happened to be standing in front.

"How dare you reczavy attempt to impede the progress of your countrymen as they move to safety!"

I couldn't have been more surprised.

"Sir, we are doing nothing of the sort. We stand here because we have extra supplies we'd like to give them."

"Oh." His chin shot up, indicating he did not like being told he was wrong. "Well, you should have cleared that with Svadlu headquarters. I'm not authorized to stop for anything or to take on supplies that haven't been properly inspected."

He turned to the others, motioning them to move. The horses began to shuffle forward.

"I have stuffed toys to give to the small children!" I yelled to the back of his head. "They will provide comfort and make them cry less." Then I added, too quietly for him to hear, "What the pruck is wrong with you?"

The horses stopped. One of the Velka turned back to me and for a heartbeat I feared my words had carried further than I intended.

"Toys would be nice," she called out. Then she said something to the Svadlu I couldn't hear. He turned to look at me.

"Less crying would be nice. You may hand out the toys as we pass through, but nothing else."

"We have extra blankets to better cushion the injured as they ride," Ksenia yelled. "Less groaning and moaning would be better too, would it not?"

He glared at Ksenia. The riders at the front stopped altogether and conferred.

"All cloth items will be accepted," he said. "We'll slow the caravan down so you may hand them out."

Suloom stepped up next to me.

"We've apples left in our cellars. Let us give them to your sick. Fruit helps the ill recover their strength."

More conferring.

"We can accept small food items that don't unduly weigh down the wagons," the Velka who'd already spoken said. "Thank you. Fruit is hard to come by this time of year."

"May we give some watered-down breakfast wine to your adults?" Esteri asked.

"Only small amounts," the Svadlu called out. He looked at us, perhaps seeing us for the first time.

"You're fully clothed," he said.

"It's prucking winter," Galen said back.

The man laughed. "True. What else are you holding?"

"Cooking gear. Extra candles and lamps. Tools. Pens, ink, and paper. Grooming items."

"What did you do, empty your camp?"

"Mostly," Ksenia answered. "We'll be in Gruen and won't need these things."

Another Svadlu, a woman, spoke for the first time. "We've heard of what you're doing there. Dangerous work." She turned to her superior but spoke loud enough for us to hear.

"We'd do a disservice to those we protect if we didn't slow down and let each cart take on a few items."

Before he could respond she looked at me.

"Can you promise to see that no one takes on too much extra weight?"

"Glad to do it."

"Fine." The head Svadlu addressed his compatriots, not us. "Ride back and let every cart know they may accept gifts within reason, and we'll move through this line of people slowly enough to give everyone time."

With that, the caravan started forward.

"Not too much extra weight anywhere," Ksenia yelled to the reczavy as they began to move between the carts offering their items.

"Back here," an old man shouted, "Don't give it all to the people in the front."

"Don't worry, we won't." Raheem laughed as he gathered twenty or so people to bring items to those in the rear.

After that, I only saw small children. Their fingers reached out as I pressed a soft bunny into as many little hands as I could. A few said thank you with their lips, most said it with their eyes. I neared the end of the caravan before I gave away the last one.

In the final cart, a little boy looked up at me with tears in his eyes. He knew I had no more toys. I searched my pockets for anything I could give him when the Svadlu woman rode up behind me.

"You dropped this one. I thought you could probably find a good home for it."

The little boy yelped in delight when I gave him the last bunny.

"This one is extra special," I told him. "Because it jumped out of my hands and hid just so I'd give it to you."

"Special," he repeated as he held it to his heart, and that was worth every varmin cold night I spent sewing the prucking things.

"Yeah. Special."

~ 23 ~

A Well Delivered Message

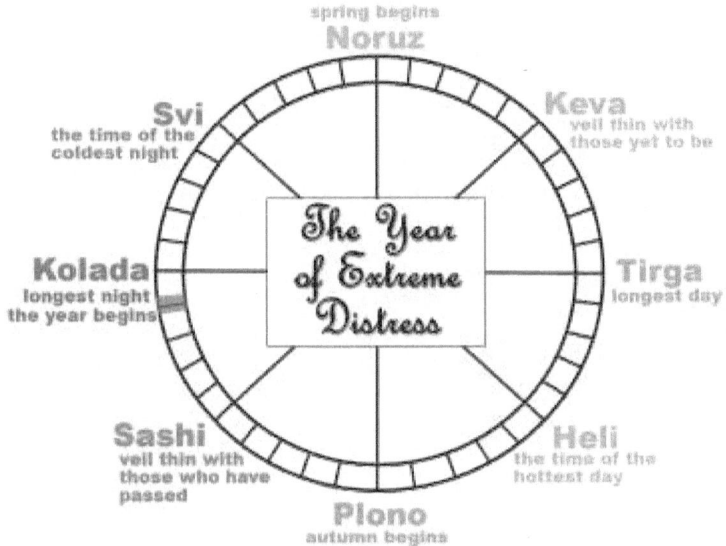

Only flashes of the next ank remain in my mind. I have this clear memory of my secret thread witch seeking us out in Gruen, finding us at the tavern where we stayed. She walked past the rowdy tables to tell me she'd finished all the vests.

"I believe they are everything you hoped for," she said. Her eyes sought my understanding in the light of the flickering lamps, begging me to understand that she'd put all she had into these garments. I don't remember seeing her again.

The group working with the fancy exploding powder needed a lot of guidance. I remember that we spoke of all our plans in certainties as if everything would happen exactly as designed. No one thought that was true. Not really. We just didn't have the capacity to consider more alternatives.

Then, ten days before Kolada, Galen confronted me. "Here's the deal. I have to tell the K'basta something."

"I told you I don't want to discuss politics."

"You don't have to. All I need from you is silent cooperation. Can you manage that?"

I didn't answer. He smiled at me.

"Perhaps we should discuss exactly what you would be agreeing to. If you become the ruler of K'ba, they are going to want you to wear more traditional clothing. Those short skirts probably have to go."

"I'm not dressing differently for anyone."

"After a while, some will expect you to live in a special residence, not here in a tent with the reczavy."

"I like living here in a tent with the reczavy."

"And they'll probably want you to enter into a more traditional relationship. Maybe marry and act like a wife."

"Pruck that. I don't want a traditional relationship. I don't intend to live my life to please anyone, much less please everyone."

His grin got wider. What was so prucking funny about the many ways I was ill-suited to rule a nichna?

"With that kind of attitude, they'll find a gentle way to kick you out in a year, at most two, and replace you with someone more anxious to please. Hopefully, that person will be as competent and kind as you."

"You want me to get ousted?"

"I'm counting on it, Duck Piss. I don't want you to change at all."

I wanted to kiss him when he said that. Almost.

"Then why put me in there to begin with?"

"Because you're an easy solution to a tough problem, and we need that now. Everyone loves a successful commander and I've worked hard behind the scenes to ensure that you'll be wildly popular in K'ba, if all goes well."

"You do remember I'm worse than a commoner, don't you? My father was a foreigner, and I was born to a single mother."

"Oh yes, I know. It's wonderful. If you can rule a nichna, anyone can. Let's see, where was I? Oh yes, without particularly caring about it, you'll dispel the stupid notion that a woman can't run things. The second lady who does this won't face half the opposition. And as a final bonus, you'll actually do a decent job of it before they find some creative way to replace you. By then, you'll have accomplished plenty, and you and I can go live happily ever after. What do you say?"

"That's your plan? You want to put me in there because it's easy, and then you plan to stand by and cheer when I get ousted?"

"Pretty much."

Well, bat scump. I hadn't expected this. "You know, I think I could do that."

"Great. I've gotten consensus from almost everyone who matters in K'ba and I'll keep those wheels turning. When asked, you tell people it's premature to make decisions about leadership until this attack is over."

"It is."

"I know."

I thought it was time for that kiss, then I remembered something else he'd said.

"Wait. You said you and I could make a happy life together?"

"I did. I don't know what our version looks like, Duck Piss, and I bet you don't either. But if we're lucky, we'll have a lot of fun years to find out."

He went for the kiss before I had a chance, so I just kissed him back.

"Gypsum!" Nine days before Kolada, Raheem shouted my name as I walked outside the tent. I heard the laughter in his tone as I turned towards him.

Then I saw it flying towards my face. I didn't get my arm raised in time so it hit me on the right cheek.

"Pruck you, Raheem. What the Heli is wrong with you!"

The shell had splattered against my cheekbone, leaving a mess of yolk running down the side of my face and onto my clothes. Worse yet, the yellow goo stunk and it burned against my skin.

"This varmin stuff itches!" I said.

"It better!" He came closer with a bucket of water. 'Here. Get off what you can and don't get it into your eyes. Idris gave me these test eggs to try. The Velka worried that the seals on the little holes might not hold. I see no problem."

"How many did they give you?"

"Just six."

"You mean you've got five more?" My annoyance gave way to his spirit of fun. "Let's make sure they all work. You know. Just to be safe?"

"You want to go visit our neighbors?"

"Sure. But bring the water."

Raheem and I walked back to our tent still laughing after annoying five other people who had the misfortune to be standing outside as we walked by. Two had reflexes fast enough to block the egg, ending up with a mess on their hands and arms instead of their faces. I hadn't considered that, but eggs on hands caused nearly as many problems.

After we thanked them for participating in our experiment, all five stopped cursing us and three asked if they could throw one. Reczavy .... wonderfully predictable in ways that made me love them.

"Idris will leave the Velka and join us after Kolada," Raheem said as we walked back to our tent. "If ... you know. If it's possible."

"I'm not surprised, but shouldn't Ksenia have talked to us first?"

"Oh, I misspoke. Idris isn't joining our tent." He looked down, hiding his expression from me.

"She didn't want to?"

"She cares for us but, well, she says she never got to be a tidzy like everyone else. I mean she went straight from those horrible experiences with Lufo to hiding with the Velka and she needs time to be unattached and discover things. She said she won't feel that freedom if she's with us. I care for her, so I won't stand in her way."

"But other tents..."

"... all have their own ways. There's more variety than you may know. She's found a group – I think it's the tent Pie and Guy belong to, actually – and their motto is 'maximum freedom.' It's the right place for her, for now, and they've offered her a spot."

"I'm happy for Idris." I wasn't sure what else to say.

"Don't be unhappy for me," he added, grabbing a piece of my half-grown-our hair and giving it a pull. "She's promised to be a frequent visitor, particularly on holidays." He shrugged. "We'll see what happens."

Once again, neither of us added the obvious "if we survive." There just wasn't any point in adding it every time.

Eight days before Kolada a messenger arrived. He was a skinny kid wearing the identifying sash over layers of clothing. He rode towards our tent as if he'd been directed there, keeping his eyes straight ahead, refusing whatever improprieties he might otherwise observe.

"Gypsum Renata Glonti," he sang out in a deeper voice than I expected. "I bring you a message from the castle in K'ba."

"Coming …" I grabbed a robe to cover the legs visible under my short skirt. "Hold your horses."

Through the door of the tent I could see him continuing to stare straight ahead. As I walked out he cleared his throat and raised his hand to don the mask of whomever he spoke for. As soon as he did, he raised his head and stared down his nose at me, giving such a good imitation of Andre that I had to smile.

"We send word that a long-anticipated tragedy has befallen the Royals of K'ba. The Crown Prince took his last breath yesterday. After his long struggle to regain his health, he is finally at peace."

I guessed that was for the best. Interesting timing, though, as it also nullified the agreement with K'ba one more way before the two years ended. Convenient. Had Melda seen fit to ease her beloved ward out of this life before we faced our attackers? It wouldn't have surprised me.

"In addition, we have been informed that a coalition of local leaders met late last night and approved a plan for appointing a new ruler for K'ba."

The chin raised higher.

"We do not approve of rushing into this decision, however, the residents of K'ba have made it clear that they accept Galen's proposal with enthusiasm. Many now know of their current Ruler's previous death, thanks to the large number of them roaming around the premises in recent days. They insist on providing a proper burial for both the Ruling Prince and his newly deceased son, to be held three days hence at the castle. I think," the messenger paused and wiped at his left eye, "I think many of the K'basta will actually mourn their passing."

The messenger cleared his throat and composed himself, much the way I imagined Andre had done. This kid was good.

"The K'basta think it is wise to inaugurate you at the same time, ahead of the battle, so that our nichna is not without a leader. I suggest you attend and do what you can to appear worthy of what is about to befall you."

"Oh for pruck's sake."

"Is that the response you wish for me to deliver?" Although the messenger asked the question, he did it with a perfectly straight face and without giving up Andre's persona.

"No."

I yelled into the tent. "Galen! You persuaded your coalition too well and now they want to coronate me, or whatever, in three days! I have to be in Gruen then to set up. Can you come get me out of this?"

Galen walked out of the tent. "You need to be able to invent this kind of scump yourself," he whispered to me. "But okay. Listen and learn."

He turned to the messenger, swept both of his arms outwards, and declared in a firm, even regal voice.

"Please tell the caretaker of the castle and all the K'basta occupying the grounds that while Gypsum is stunned and unbelievably humbled by this great honor, she asks that the ceremonial transfer of power occur without her being physically present. She understands that we all share a common desire for our bloodless defense to be effective, and she must work tirelessly to that end during these remaining few days. Once the much hoped for peace between us and our would-be invaders is established, she promises to dedicate her every breath to improving the welfare of all K'basta."

He grinned at me. "That *is* what you meant, isn't it?"

"Right. Of course it is."

The messenger looked from my face to Galen's and back, searching for the right etiquette for his quandary. He moved his hand in front of his face to show that he spoke for himself.

"Do you wish for me to deliver his words as if you spoke them?" he asked me.

"I do."

"Very well. If you declined my invitation, I was told to add this." Up went the hand. Up went the chin.

"You may also wish to be present to say farewell to your friend Nan as she will return to Eds after the formalities are over. We received word that her brother Lufo and her father were both killed early this morning as they tried to storm past the Svadlu guarding the entrance into K'ba. They and the small band of Edsers with them wished to make a symbolic last-minute raid on the reczavy but the encounter went poorly for them."

Gasps came from all those within earshot. I felt too numb to make a sound.

"We thought you should know that one of the wounded Svadlu is the brother of Galen. It is a slight injury, and he is expected to recover."

I heard Galen exhale. "I almost got him killed by asking for his help."

The messenger kept talking.

"Nan's mother has declared her youngest son to now be the rightful ruler of Eds, and he will assume the throne. Nan is to act as princess regent until he is of age. Under these rare circumstances, and given Nan's exceptional qualities, we approve. Nan will do a reasonable job as regent. Now, would you like to reconsider whether you can make time to attend?"

The news about Lufo's death, and Nan's new fate, moved me. I wanted to answer in my own words.

"Andre. I'd really, really like to be there, even before learning of this last part and certainly after. But several hundred people who are about to risk their lives expect me to be in Gruen Town with them as we get in position. I have to put them first." I hesitated. I needed a softer ending. "I beg those at the castle of K'ba to understand."

"Very well," the messenger replied. He turned and rode off without bothering to remove his mask.

~ 24 ~

Burying the Crock

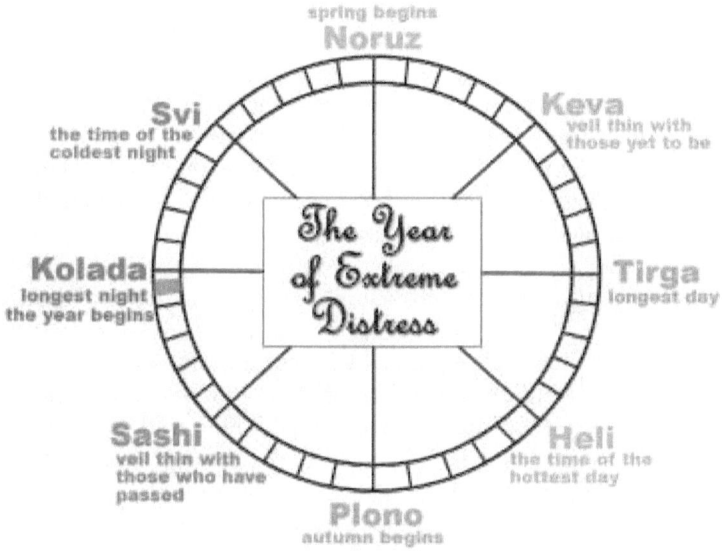

spring begins
Noruz

Svi
the time of the
coldest night

Keva
veil thin with
those yet to be

Kolada
longest night
the year begins

*The Year
of Extreme
Distress*

Tirga
longest day

Sashi
veil thin with
those who have
passed

Heli
the time of the
hottest day

Plono
autumn begins

Seven days before Kolada, a small group of us gathered at the forest's edge. Esteri and the others who'd already helped with the poultice magic sat on the ground with Suloom and Varla. We all shivered in our heaviest cloaks as we held them tight against a cold wind. We stared at the three hundred little bags awaiting the pine resin and a few drops of the mysterious bdellion to seal the deal. Was what we were about to do so awful? Perhaps it was.

We looked at each other.

"If any of you wants to leave now, it's fine. No one has to do this."

They looked at each other. They looked at me. No one got up.

"Okay then. Mostly pine resin, and a bit of bdellion. If we have any left-over we'll add more to each bag at the end."

We made fast work of it, anxious to get on to the part that scared us and be done with this.

As the others finished the last few bags, I brought burning embers from our main fire and started a small fire beside us. I didn't want to use our camp's cooking fire to burn the bags that had held the black mustard seed and grains of paradise, or the larger bag Idris had used to hold the surprisingly smelly chopped-up roots from the valerian plant.

As we worked with the resin and bdellion, I put the bags into the middle of the flames. At first, none caught fire, and I worried they possessed some power that made them inflammable. Then what would I do? I had no feel at all for bad magic.

But the wind kicked up and all three burst into flames, showering sparks on us. We jumped back, and Suloom laughed.

"I think we're spooking ourselves."

"Maybe," Esteri said. She picked up our shovel. "I'm going to start digging. Let's get this scump underground and get back to our tent where it's warm."

I watched her dig, impressed with her technique.

"I grew up in Lev, a daughter of those who worked the fields. Dug a lot of holes for planting grape vines." She said no more but her comments made me realize how little I knew about so many of my companions' pasts.

"You understand there is nothing inherently evil about grains of paradise, don't you?" Varla asked us. "It's what we use it for that's the problem. We can't bury that."

"Can I break apart the crock that held the bdellion?" Suloom asked. He held a small ax.

"Go ahead, although I've no idea why we're supposed to do that."

"It's symbolic," another woman said. "It separates our actions from the spirit of the bdellion plant, severs the connection. Protects us and it."

She looked at us all, frustrated. "Breaking the crock is not a bad thing to do. It's a good thing."

"Whatever. Break the crock and let's get this done."

Suloom raised the ax and smashed the crock into pieces. Several flew off into the trees and we had to go find them. Esteri kicked the pieces into the hole she'd dug while I pushed the remaining embers and ashes in as well.

Everybody helped cover it with dirt.

"We're pretty inept at causing harm," Varla said.

"Yeah. Let's keep it that way."

Six days before Kolada, the first of several caravans to Gruen assembled. I was to lead this one. Many Gruenites had abandoned their homes, either evacuating or leaving for assignments of their own. They'd offered us their empty houses, their remaining food, and the horses left behind. The latter would help transport the rest of the reczavy in stages because unlike others we kept far fewer horses than people.

The remaining Gruenites showed us the tunnels and trenches they'd constructed to protect us, the ways they'd managed to hide the river from the road, and all the obstacles at the end of the road designed to slow down and separate hundreds of men on horseback.

After I'd inspected it all, an older woman looked at me with her eyes full of hope. "Will this work?"

I had no idea.

"We can't imagine how you could have done it better," Galen said. She smiled in relief.

After that, I often let Galen answer for me and, to be honest, I don't know how I'd have gotten through those few days without him.

Five days before Kolada, the Faroojers who'd trained to capture Mongols in the river came to town, with their massive fishing nets in carts behind them. I'd largely stayed out of this part of the operation, but Galen suggested I walk around and say encouraging things.

"Like what?"

"Like you're glad they're here. You *are* glad, aren't you?"

"Pruck yes. What would we do if they hadn't shown up?"

"Exactly. So tell them that."

Then I discovered most of these swimmers didn't care for small talk either.

"So glad you are here," I said.

"Great," they replied.

Yeah, I liked these people fine.

I felt less warm towards the Svadlu I met the next day. The Gruenite farmer, the one who seemed to be in charge of helping us, insisted I ride with him the short distance to the massive wall the Svadlu had built between Gruen and Pilk. It was no secret that Gruenites hated the wall and the way it blocked them off from safety.

It would have its uses, however, and even I understood them. Because of the wall, our army of five hundred would be much closer than they would have been over in Pilk Central. On the day of, they'd be on top of and behind the wall, ready to fight the remaining Mongols as needed, or to begin negotiations with them.

There seemed to be a great deal of confusion about which outcome we preferred. The Sage Coalition, many of them my new subjects although I tried not to think about that, continued to urge all of Ilari's Royals to surrender if negotiations failed. I'd been told that many Royals agreed, at least privately.

Yet the Svadlu never mentioned surrender. They spoke publicly of driving the Mongols back out to Bisu and then perhaps negotiating with them there. If at all.

When I saw the wall, I wondered how either was possible. It approached the height of four men and went on into the distance towards the forest as far as I could see.

"You're wondering how we get to the other side of our wall if we must, aren't you?" a saffron-caped Svadlu officer asked me.

"I am. I see paths up on the inside, but your soldiers can hardly leap off the top."

"Many of us will be up on the wall during the attack. Archers and others. But look." I saw the pride in his eyes. "Open the doors!" he yelled.

Three openings appeared near the bottom of the rocks, each about knee height off the ground, and as tall as a man and not much wider. Horses and humans could get through, separately. The doors were camouflaged with rocks on the outside.

"Special teams can come through these if we want," he said. "Including those authorized to negotiate. How will we know what to do?" He pointed to two flag poles, one nearby and one off in the distance.

"The Svadlu have devised a clever warning system to keep everyone informed. Citizens with strong eyesight help us, and we've designed flags to communicate all sorts of situations."

I had heard of this and been told the meaning of the various flags so my people could prepare. However, I thought the Velka had devised them. Or maybe some professor in Pilk. Certainly not the army.

"So see?" he said to me. "You needn't worry. We've planned for everything. Do what little things to disturb our enemy that you have in mind, then step back."

I guess he wanted to make me feel better, but the visit left me more unsettled than I'd been before.

Three days before Kolada the final members of my group arrived. I, as well as those I'd grown closest to, settled them in and made sure everyone understood where they were to be once the flag said our lookouts had spotted the invaders in the distance.

That night we went to sleep, mostly calm, mostly determined to do what needed to be done.

We lived in the desolation. We'd created a comfortable existence out of nothing. We could handle this.

The next morning we woke to the red flag waving in the breeze.

They'd been sighted on the horizon. Tomorrow they would reach our border. The day after, they would ride into Ilari. That afternoon, they'd reach us.

Every person I saw looked scared scumpless.

We could have hidden in the forest. Why the pruck had we agreed to this?

As the morning passed, I'd never seen the reczavy so serious.

"What can I do to help?" The words hovered on everyone's lips.

And there was plenty to do. By noon Rakeem and his crew arrived with three carts of eggs layered in between soft blankets. These needed to go into the fifty padded vests, sewn by the Gruenite thread witch with courage in every stitch.

"Each egg is precious, so take your time," I told my volunteers. "We expect the Mongols in Bisu tomorrow, so we *do* have all day to do this."

Once I'd have been worried they'd forget themselves and throw the eggs at each other. But not today.

The wagon with the poultices had traveled with me. They had to be kept separated and in a single layer so the resin wouldn't make them stick together, and kept cool in the shade so the resin wouldn't harden. I figured those who handled them innocently needn't fear consequences, but just to be sure I decided to talk to everyone involved.

"Can you get all the sling shooters together for me?" I asked Ksenia. She and her brother had recruited the group, and she'd overseen the slingshot practices.

"How about just before sunset, out on the road where this happens?"

"Perfect. I don't just need the reczavy ones, though. I need the Gruenites too."

"So I figured. I'll have them bring their slingshots so we can make sure everyone has theirs. Any problems I need to know about?"

"No. I'm going to have a little talk with them that I probably should have had sooner."

She smiled. "I think it's good you're having one at all."

My timing wasn't as bad as I thought. Ksenia used the gathering to check everyone's equipment, to hand out spare slingshots to the few who'd lost or broken theirs, and to pass out the last of the green clothing that Pie and Guy had added grey and brown to as the leaves fell. When I arrived, she talked through the hiding places, working to make sure everyone knew where to be.

"You really think the hoard will ride by and not notice us?" a Gruenite asked her.

I answered. "You'll be well concealed but, more importantly, not expected. They'll watch for archers up high, not people in ditches planning to make things stick to their backs."

"About that," a reczavy said. "I hear these things we shoot are magic. True?"

"We hope so," I said. "Look, when we conceived this plan, we sought a way to survive without killing. But ... I've since learned that those who use magic to cause harm, any sort of harm, invite consequences. I don't know if it's true."

"Most of us don't believe in that nonsense," a tall older woman from Gruen shouted to me.

"Yeah. And if this harms those varmin Mongols in any way, I don't care," yelled another Gruenite.

The reczavy looked at each other, many of them less convinced.

"Well, for those of you who do worry about such things, I want you to have the facts. These poultices contain products, magic and otherwise, designed to cause confusion."

"Not death?" a young man asked.

"No. There is no death in our plans."

"Why not?" a Gruenite man asked.

"Yeah!" others echoed him.

"My sister will use our lack of killing as a negotiating point. We take prisoners only. I thought you knew that's why all those people have been practicing in the river."

"So you're warning us we might get confused too? Like at the same time?" a reczavy woman asked.

"I don't know. Maybe then, maybe later. I'm not sure how it works." Pruck I should have asked the Velka more questions.

Their muttering got louder and several asked me things at once. Galen stepped up behind me.

"Given the high stakes and your commitment to this, we assumed you'd risk these consequences," he said in his loudest voice, carrying over the growing noise of the crowd. "Gypsum felt she should tell you about this magic situation, but it is no cause for concern. Right, Gypsum?"

"Right. It's nothing compared to our other risks. Heli, I don't mind if I'm confused for days if we end up with a safe Ilari." There. *That* I could say.

"Yeah." "Me too." "Bring it on."

It looked like I'd managed to get out of this one.

"Thanks," I muttered to Galen and Ksenia as we walked away.

"I think it's nice you told them," Ksenia said.

"Whatever made you do such a boneheaded thing," Galen said at the same time. They looked at each other and laughed.

That night I dreamt about my family celebrating a holiday when I was five and a drunk man calling my mother a pruska. Only this time the dream went further.

After my father offered the man a daughter, because he had so many to spare, the stranger locked eyes with me. His eyes were identical to mine.

"I'll take that one because she *is* my daughter and she's better off with me now that her mother is dead," he said. Then he started to laugh his drunken laugh, and I cringed in terror. This horrible man couldn't be my father.

When I looked up again, he was behind prison bars, and I had no idea how he'd gotten there.

"Don't worry, little one, I never said it. I walked away from you even though I knew who you were. How many families in Ilari had seven little girls with a frundle as the youngest, eh? Yeah, I learned who'd taken you in and my biggest gift to you was to let you be. I hope you appreciated it. Pretty little thing like you -- I sure could have used you in some of my schemes."

I woke up in the small cot belonging to some Gruenite child. It's hard to sleep well when your feet hang off the edge of your bed. I sat up, feeling sick.

Could this be true? Did my sleeping mind understand something my waking mind did not?

Galen lay stretched out across the adult bed in the room, where I'd left him snoring. Suddenly his snoring didn't seem so bad. I crawled back in next to him, wrapped my arms and legs around him, and held on tight.

Who gave a pruck who sired me? It had taken more than a man's seed to produce the woman I was. Jepsa Yemi Glonti had become Gypsum Renata Glonti, a woman who was about to lead an army of misfits with no qualifications. And a woman who was about to rule a nichna with neither pedigree nor training. She had turned into a woman who thought she could do anything, despite plenty of evidence to the contrary.

Maybe she could. Maybe she couldn't. No wonder I was having bad dreams.

~ 25 ~

Dead Fish and Three Riders

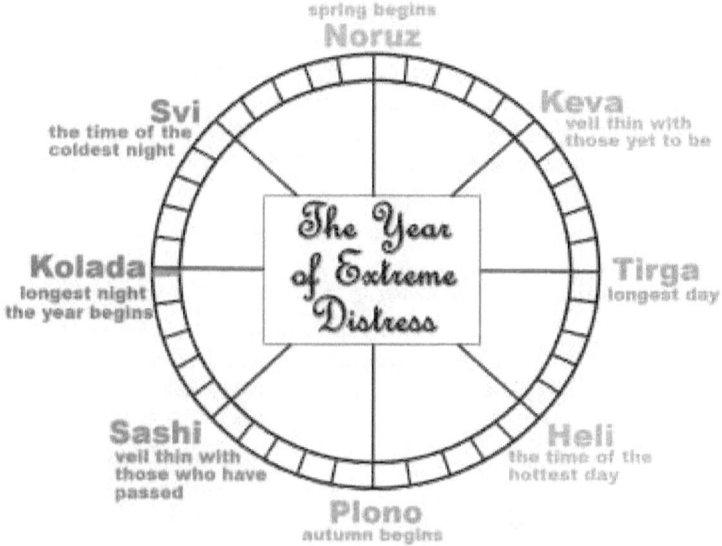

The Year of Extreme Distress

Noruz — spring begins

Keva — veil thin with those yet to be

Svi — the time of the coldest night

Tirga — longest day

Kolada — longest night the year begins

Heli — the time of the hottest day

Sashi — veil thin with those who have passed

Plono — autumn begins

The sun rose on the day before Kolada. Any other year, women would be up baking the last of the sweets while men placed candles and small mirrors around the house to create the sparkly lights required for a proper Kolada Eve.

Today our realm was dark and silent. We expected our attackers at our border in the morning. They'd find fog and an altered landscape, but they wouldn't find the tribute they'd demanded or the entrance to the realm. We'd removed it.

As we looked towards winter's late-rising morning sun, we could pick out fog on the horizon blending into the grey clouds overhead. One thing had gone right. The Velka had made fog.

Not long after, a large yellow triangle replaced the square red flag.

"They've entered Ilari," the Gruenites shouted. Hugs and cheers followed. This wasn't great news, but it meant things went as planned.

The Gruenites showed more enthusiasm for the flagpoles than I'd seen in other nichnas, perhaps because they were the third and last stop on our predesigned route. They knew every flag's meaning and by early afternoon I saw them watching the flagpole with concern.

When a giant purple and white striped semi-circle replaced the yellow triangle, they cheered again. This flag told us that somewhere in Bisu, the combination of the Velka's rich winter grass and the ever-thickening fog had persuaded the horsemen to make camp and hope for a clearer day tomorrow.

Both Ryalgar and the Svadlu worried the Mongols might send lone scouts ahead who would discover the obstacles we'd placed in their path. We hoped the thick fog would discourage this, but were told to remain quiet and without fires once the horde entered our realm.

That night we ate stale bread, raisins, and cheese, foregoing the fires and music that would have brought us solace. Many turned to others for physical comfort but whether we went to bed alone or not, we all retired soon after the early darkness overtook us.

I don't think anyone slept well. I lay awake thinking of soldiers on the night before a battle. All soldiers. All battles throughout time and in all the places in the world. None of them slept well the night before, did they?

At first light I heard the Gruenites gathering outside, discussing the flag pole. Yesterday's giant purple striped semi-circle still flew, indicating the Mongols slept in their camp in Bisu.

I knew two of my sisters and my grandmother waited near them, part of a crew of archers using various magical talents to shoot arrows uncommonly far in the low light. If this opening salvo failed, it boded poorly for those of us further down the path.

I pulled on warm clothes and hurried outside, as anxious as the Gruenites for news. I stomped my feet and shook my arms to stay warm as I waited. And waited. And waited.

We didn't see activity on our flagpole until the sun crept above the horizon. Down came the purple-striped semi-circle. I knew the alternatives and I joined everyone in a deep exhale when the bright green triangle appeared.

We'd shot their horses, the horde had moved on, and they now rode below the cliffs of Vinx. The green triangle meant it had gone as planned and our invaders would enter Vinx through its north corner and meet the next obstacle by mid-morning.

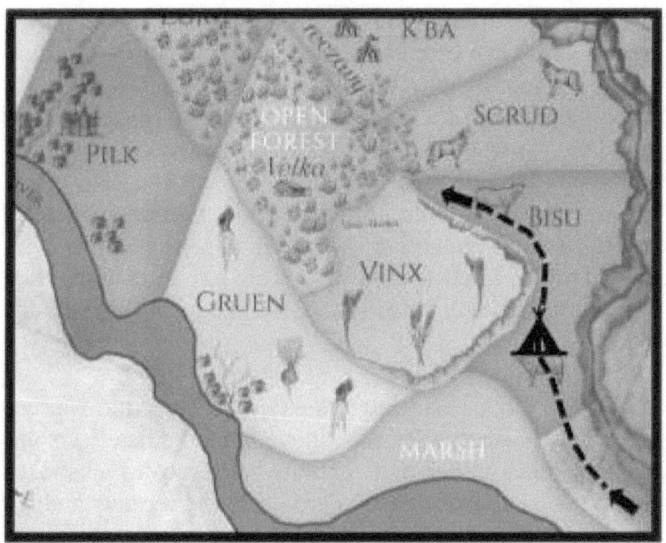

Most people hugged the person nearest to them, sharing silent smiles. Maybe every part *could* work. Perhaps this was possible after all.

By mid-morning most eyes returned to the flagpole. The wait was shorter. Down came the green flag. Then nothing. And more nothing. Had those raising the flags been harmed? Should we send a rider over to the next pole?

Finally, we saw the cause of the delay. Three flags were hoisted.

We understood. The top flag was meant for all and would be hoisted around the realm. At the sight of the small blue square in the large white rectangle, we sucked in our breath. The Mongols had passed through the second obstacle, but it had not gone well.

The flags below added extra information for those further down the path.

Under the blue and white flag sat a solid red semi-circle that meant beware. Danger moves towards you.

The grey triangle below signaled no more messages would come.

Everyone looked at each other. Then many of them looked at me.

Galen stepped forward but I shook my head. I had to speak.

"It's nearly half a day's ride across Vinx and Gruen to get here. Do not hurry. Take care of yourselves. Move into position as you are ready. You know what to do. Stay calm and do it."

"We can prucking do this!" shouted one of the Faroojers who'd joined us.

"We can prucking do this!" Ksenia yelled back.

"We can prucking do this," three Gruenite farmers who stood with their arms around each other shouted in unison.

"Yeah," I yelled to all of them. "We can. Let's get it done!"

It was all the pep talk I had in me, but it was all the pep talk they needed.

By noon the clouds had left the sky, and sunshine warmed our first day of winter. People moved methodically, some mumbling dark jokes under their breath. I noticed the unspoken cooperation between the Gruenites, Faroojers, and reczavy and felt some joy that our common purpose enabled us to rise above our differences.

Then a plethora of rude words broke the near silence we'd maintained all day.

"It wasn't my fault, you varmin bag of scump! You're the one that tripped over it."

"Yeah, well, you're the prucking idiot who set a bunch of fragile eggs in the path of us hauling these heavy nets."

I didn't have to guess. We'd lost eggs. I sprinted to the source of the ruckus.

Our altered eggs had arrived in three carts. Now one cart lay on its side, felled by a massive net. It didn't matter whose fault it was. Nearly every egg lay broken.

"Grab some buckets. Grab some brooms," I yelled to the growing crowd of bystanders, determined to save what mattered most. "Get as much of that yolk and stuff into containers as you can. Quick."

"Are you nuts?" the Faroojer said. "You can't throw egg yolks at them. You'd have to walk up to them and smear them in their faces!"

"I care about the itching powder, not the eggs. Maybe we can still find a way to use it."

I grabbed a broom and helped sweep up the gooey stuff. "Watch your hands. Don't touch it. And don't worry about getting shells and dirt mixed in. It won't matter."

A Faroojer woman came up behind me. "We've half an afternoon yet, don't we?"

"Probably." I recognized a woman with an idea when I saw one. "What do you have in mind"

"Fishing."

Raheem had joined us. He took responsibility for these eggs and for the men and women who'd signed on to throw them.

"If you stuff this goo into fish, I don't think they'll break apart when you throw them," he said.

"They won't," she answered. "But if you cut open the fish and coat everything in the goo, then you can just throw fish instead of eggs."

"You're forgetting about the itching powder," I said.

"No, I'm not. We clean a lot of fish in Faroo, but no one wants her hands to smell that way so we use coated gloves. I've enough with me for twelve women. Or men with small hands."

She turned to Raheem. "Pick the twelve you want to throw fish instead of eggs. It will be better than nothing, and they won't even need to wear those vests."

I had to interrupt. "Trust me. They should wear the vests anyway."

The nice thing about not having much time was that no one argued. Some of our egg throwers became fish throwers and that was that.

Faroojers caught the small fish we needed, and they'd been put into twelve pails of yellow goo when a commotion arose in the direction of the Pilk wall. I saw three people approaching on horseback and guessed the Svadlu came to check on us or worse yet to offer advice.

I did not need interference from them. Not now.

I walked out to intercept the riders, determined to prevent them from demoralizing my people. From a distance, I recognized two men and a woman, none wearing the saffron or crimson capes of the officers. These three slumped as they rode, as if exhausted.

Once they came close enough to recognize, I feared I'd somehow fallen asleep and entered another weird family dream. For while I didn't know the two men, the woman was unmistakable. My sister Ryalgar, the architect of this plan, rode towards me. How was this possible?

Having her show up now was varmin worse than having the entire Svadlu command ride in!

"Gypsum!" Her eyes begged me for information. "Have they been through here yet? Tell me, what has happened?"

"What are you doing here?"

She gave me a puzzled look. "We rode here, from the mid-Gruen forest exit. Had to borrow some horses to get to you in time. We came to help!"

Help? I don't know what kind of help she thought she could provide, but as I opened my mouth to answer, I stopped and put a finger to my lips. I heard it, and I felt it. Others did too. Horse hoofs. Hundreds of them.

"You got here before them," I told her. "But they approach, and we can't talk now."

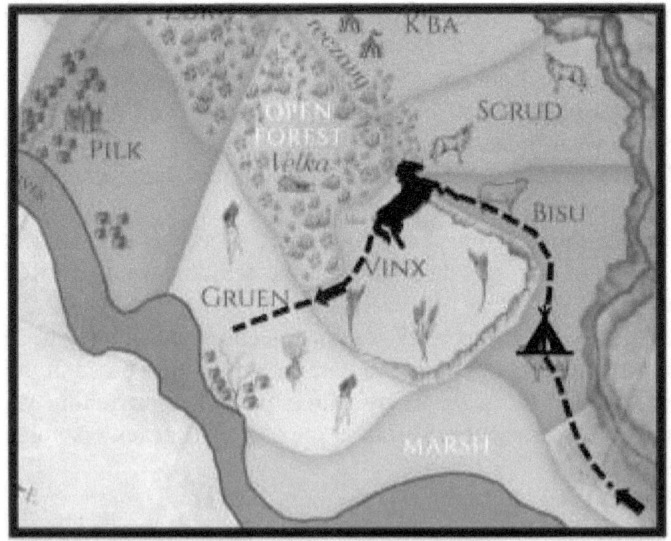

"Get her to safety, back towards the village!" Galen shouted his directions to anyone in earshot. Suloom and Varla both stepped in to guide our unexpected visitors away as I spoke to everyone else.

"Now! Into position, if you're not already. This is happening. Let's prucking do it!"

They all moved. Every one of them went towards where they needed to be. Except for me. My feet felt frozen to the ground.

"Do you need a good push?" Ksenia whispered in my ear.

"Please."

She gave a me playful shove and I stumbled backward, but it worked. Once I got my footing, my feet took me towards the little tree-house command center Galen and I would occupy. Then as I climbed up into it, I wondered why Ksenia was covered from head to foot in purple veils.

The Gruenites had built a perch for Galen and me in an old tree. We sat on a small wooden floor, concealed behind dead leaves and branches. A few well-hidden people stood below us, ready to risk the Mongol's arrows if urgent messages had to be delivered as events unfolded.

I smelled the smoke before I saw it. Dirty feet? Spoilt cheese? My mind flashed back to burning bags at the forest's edge. I knew this odor. My crew was making smoke using valerian root!

Whose idea was this? What were they thinking? The valerian root would confuse anyone who breathed it, not just our enemy, and we could ill afford to befuddle ourselves.

Did I need to put a stop to this? Or did they have a plan to keep the valerian from overpowering us?

I saw the smoke drifting towards me. It was purple. Purple! How does one make smoke purple?

I tried to force my mind to be calm. I'd always known much of today would be spontaneous. I'd asked the reczavy for their best, and that included whatever creative thing occurred to them on the fly. The smoke did move mostly away from them and towards the area the Mongols would occupy. That was good. My group would breathe in little of it. Only Galen and I, out in our strategic perch, would get the full brunt of the fumes.

Then the noise from the hoofs went from loud to deafening. There was no time to correct anything now. Somewhere on the other side of those trees, riders approached.

If the first part of the plan went perfectly, and the second went horribly, then about eight hundred horsemen would come into sight in one ... two ...

At three, I saw them. The man in front, a stout man with no hair on his head, held up a hand to slow down those behind him. For with no warning, the well-maintained road they'd galloped along fingered out into tens of ill-maintained paths filled with brush and bumps. With the horses in the back still moving fast, the men in front slowed but knew better than to stop. They scattered out among the many paths as best they could, moving to make room for those storming in behind them.

Then they looked ahead. All paths led straight into the Wide River.

The man in front screamed a word that needed no translation.

From my well-placed vantage point, I watched the men in front look at each other.

I expected fiercely determined fighters, people who'd respond to our subterfuge by wanting to demolish us. Instead, I saw people overcome with frustration.

Had the apparent death of their horses from unseen arrows in the dawn spooked them? Of course it had. And despite their horses' failure to throw them, the bucking had no doubt shaken them too. Such disobedience from their precious horses may have been more frightening than we knew.

I recognized their expressions.

They weren't *we didn't expect this change in the road.*

They were *prucking horse scump this nonsense has got to stop.*

Then the smoke grew thick again, right on schedule. The valerian smell intensified, and I'm sure the stink added to their misery.

I shook my head to clear it. Was I being affected? Was Galen?

"Pinch me if I act dazed," I whispered to him.

"Can I pinch you if you don't?"

I answered with a glare because saying anything became pointless. Out of nowhere, a chorus of insane laughter drowned out everything else. I recognized Ksenia's beautiful deep voice amidst the many others. The laughter continued, alternating between eerie and maddening but it never paused.

I'm sure it was supposed to be disturbing, but when the men in front picked up their bows, I saw the anger in their faces instead. They thought we laughed *at* them! And this was not a group that appreciated being laughed at, even when exhausted. Now, they *did* want to kill someone.

Bad call on our part.

~ 26 ~

Anyone in Purple
Can Help You

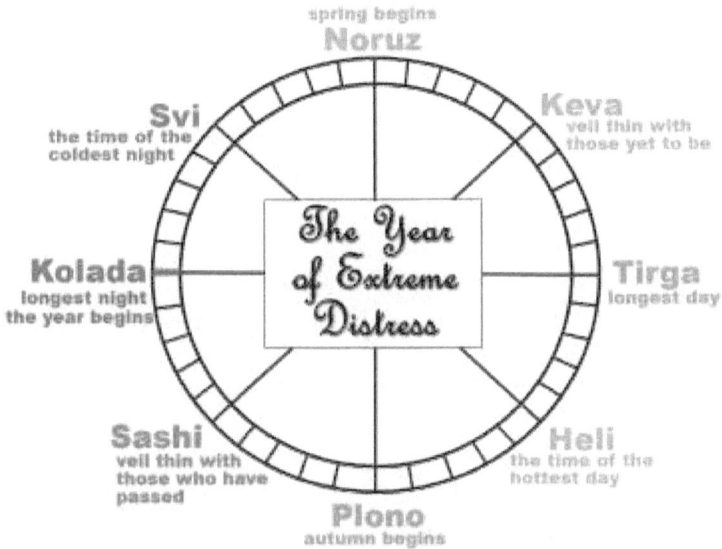

When the horses in front refused to get any closer to the smoke, the men in front dismounted and moved towards the source of the laughter on foot. They crept towards the purple smoke, with bows drawn, and the laughter stopped. My people had figured out the danger. I hoped each of our laughers was as well shrouded in purple as Ksenia, but even if they were, we'd soon have a problem if something else didn't distract our attackers. Lucky for us, something was planned.

Most of the horde watched their leaders seek out the source of the laughter. I thought they acted a little confused, but it was hard to say. Maybe I was too confused to tell.

Then on cue, our two hundred sling shooters rose out of the ditches behind them, their grey and brown cloaks blending them into the background. I watched with my mouth open as each pulled out a slingshot and they aimed as one. I'd never seen so many people do anything in unison. Then … they shot as one. Well, maybe a few were a little off, but it was varmin impressive. A heartbeat later they shot again, then they dropped, vanishing back into the earth, seen by only a few.

I watched the poultices I'd made fly through the air and then I watched so many of them hit the ground! What a waste. A few stuck to the backsides of horses where they'd do little good, as far as I knew. Maybe a third of them hit a Mongol somewhere in the back. I'd hoped for better, but at least most of those that hit stuck.

The impact was soft. The riders who'd been struck reached back in curiosity, not fearing injury. Then one warrior shouted something and threw the poultice he'd managed to grab to the ground, repeating the word over and over.

Everyone near him stopped trying to reach their own backs and yelled the word to others. They pulled out their swords, not an ideal outcome, and they began trying to brush the poultices off each other's backs with their swords.

They didn't want to touch the poultices. Was it the resin? I couldn't imagine such tough guys being afraid of getting sticky stuff on their fingers.

Then I knew what they feared.

They had witches, too. Or something like them. Of course they did.

The entire day had offered evidence that we attacked them with magic, but something about these poultices was familiar and frightening. Perhaps the worst of their witches used something similar.

The leaders emerged from the smoke to check on the commotion. Several of the poultices had now been tossed into a pile on the ground. Once the leaders saw the pile, they stepped back from it, as distressed by the little products of my needlework as the rest of their men.

When they saw none of their group had been injured, they remounted their horses and came together to confer. *What now?*

It was the perfect time for our next step.

"Now!" I said to the runners below me but I needn't have bothered. Before a runner could leave, a massive explosion sent green and gold sparks flying high into the air behind us and off to our right.

"Ahhh," the Mongols said as the sparks flew. "Ohhh," those near the back added. They seemed impressed by the beauty of the sparkles in the late afternoon sky. No one quaked in fear.

Those near the back stared at the sky long after the sparks disappeared. I guessed the poultices contributed to their odd response, but there was no doubt they admired the splendor of our explosion.

Again, not the intended response.

However, there was nothing beautiful about the fifty or so figures that came forward out of the smoke and walked towards the front of the horde.

I looked closer. I expected to see signs of injury, mostly blood, but my group had done better. Our costume makers had faked partially missing limbs in realistic detail. One woman in the middle held on to a bloody left stump with her right hand. A man hopped on one leg with his arms around two comrades. A large headless man carried his head in his hands. How had they managed that?

And we had more than gaping wounds. We had leaking entrails. Lots of them. Pig guts maybe? I didn't want to know. Several horrible burns left the most unfortunate of the lot partially clothed in the winter wind. But the worst were the maimed faces. I fought a desire to retch as I examined the handiwork of my people.

Then the fifty half-dead, or fully dead, stopped and stared at our attackers, only twenty or so paces away from them. As planned.

They began to moan. That was not planned.

I half expected the Mongols to pick up their arrows and shoot, just to quiet our enthused actors, but I supposed any army hesitates to shoot at those they think are already deceased. Our attackers did nothing but stare back, mostly horrified.

When the moaners reached into their pockets and buckets and began hurling eggs and fish at the warriors closest to them, the

Mongols barely responded. I'm sure they recognized that the flying objects posed no real threat, but I also think a certain level of confusion had taken hold. They stared at the horror show, almost as if they watched a performance. As they watched, some got hit in the face. Others deflected the eggs and fish. They all brushed the yellow goo off for the nuisance it was. Then one of them yelled. The substance itched and burned. A few had gotten it into their eyes, and they yelled louder.

This was it. Everything we'd hoped for.

Soon the itching warriors would run to the river for relief. Meanwhile, our finale, the final explosion, would push the healthy and aware on towards the wall and the Svadlu, leaving the most confused in the back to wander around and be captured.

It was perfect. We had done it! It couldn't have gone better.

But their leader had other ideas.

Before the crew could light the second explosives, the hefty man without hair lifted himself high in his saddle and screamed "Cong. All Tie. Cong all tie."

I translated it as "enough of this scump!"

Most of the men, even the itchy ones in front, and the confused ones in the back, yelled their agreement. "Cong all tie." Then they all turned their horses around to face the way they had come.

Wait, I wanted to shout. *We're not done yet. We've worked hard on the next part. And what about all those Faroojers out there in the cold water who practiced for eighths to capture you? They are going to be really pissed if you ride away now!*

But these people didn't care. They'd had enough of our witchcraft and our tricks and they were going home. I would have bet on it.

The reczavy and I had done our job, and we'd done it well. Too well. We'd sealed Ilari's doom with our over-the-top performance. And everyone thought the reczavy were a bunch of underachievers.

I wanted to cry as I watched the backsides of eight hundred horses amble northeast towards Vinx. Scaring off these attackers was no success. These people didn't stay away. No, they'd be back, at a time of their choosing, with more warriors and a better idea of what to expect.

Because they'd yet to encounter the Svadlu, they had every reason to believe they could retreat without a fight. Perhaps they surmised our soldiers were in Pilk. They would have been, too, except for the wall, but the Mongols hadn't stuck around long enough to discover that.

However, evening approached. They couldn't make it to the grasslands of Bisu before dark, not this time of year. They were stuck in our realm for the night.

Given my own experience with fear and darkness, I guessed none of them wanted to camp here. We could use the opportunity to scare them more, but what good would that do?

I had to face the fact that by doing what was asked of us, we'd failed. I'd failed. Sure, we'd get a short reprieve, maybe even until next winter, but we'd spend the whole time knowing they'd come back.

I wasn't surprised when I heard horses approaching our tree, or when I heard Ryalgar's voice shout up to me.

"Gypsum. Get down here. We need to fix this!"

"There is no fixing this!" I shouted back.

She was right about one thing, however. I did need to come down. Not because I could undo our spectacular fiasco, but because the people I'd dared to lead, and who'd risked their lives today, deserved hearing from me. I didn't know what to say to them, and I guessed that for once Galen wouldn't either. None-the-less ....

"Come on, Sheep Scump," I pulled on his arm. "We have to go face people."

Maybe the valerian smoke had gotten to him more than me.

"Sure." He grinned. "Can I pinch you now?"

"Come up with something good to say, and you can do anything you want to me."

"Woo. That's an offer."

I hoped he had enough coordination to get out of this tree house without getting hurt. I hopped down and saw my sister on her horse.

"It never occurred to me we'd scare them too much," I called out to her.

She rode towards me.

"Gypsum, dear sister, most of what just happened never occurred to anyone. Don't blame yourself."

"Yeah. Sure." *Did she just call me "dear sister?"*

The smoke was thicker down here, and I felt woozy.

"I mean it," she said. "All that ever mattered was to get them to negotiate with us, and that can still happen."

Her words made no sense. "You think we need to chase after them and beg them to talk?"

She got off her horse. Her two companions had ridden up behind her and they did the same.

She pointed to one of them. He had short curly brown hair and a nice smile and his clothes, though rumpled, had been sewn by an excellent tailor.

"This is Nevik. He's the crown prince of Pilk. It's not much of a stretch to say he speaks for the realm."

Nevik? The guy who'd jilted her? What was he doing riding around with my sister in the middle of an invasion?

She pointed to the other.

"This is Nikolo. He and I have information no one else knows. So, have a few words with your people. Send them to safety, they've done their jobs." I could have sworn she gave me a conspiratorial grin before she added, "Then you and I need to figure out how to finish saving the realm."

My knees grew weak as she said it, and I landed on the ground with my legs sprawled out in front of me, looking up at her completely confused.

When I opened my eyes, someone covered in purple, probably Ksenia, stood in the middle of everyone waving lavender appendages as she issued orders. After one set of instructions, Galen, who appeared to have made it out of the tree okay, got his face doused in cold water. I giggled. Then two purple apparitions escorted him away towards the water's edge. Pie and Guy waited there with a hundred cold wet swimmers as they emerged from their camouflage in the river. A cart full of wool blankets followed Galen, along with two entertainers with lit torches capable of starting campfires.

So, he got the difficult job. I hoped his golden words were up to it.

Then someone splashed cold water on *my* face, gave both my checks a firm slap, and pulled me to my feet. I stumbled backward again, as various rude responses formed in my mouth.

"Listen to me. You have to come with me to address everyone else. Now." Ksenia looked hard into my eyes as she spoke. "Are you ready?"

I nodded. "I think so. Thanks."

"Good." She helped me up onto a horse and hopped up behind me. We rode out to where we could see the full wide road crossing Gruen, and we watched our enemy's exodus continue. They hadn't picked up their pace, even a little.

Everyone else had begun to gather out there when she pushed me up into a big wagon so I could be seen. Then she climbed up next to me and handed me one of the wooden cones to carry my voice. I looked down at the appalling egg throwers in front of me, and the smoke makers and purple laughers lining up behind them. The smoke makers giggled and leaned on each other. Behind them came the brown- and- grey-cloaked sling shooters, both Gruenites and reczavy.

More rode out to join us, two or three to a horse. Some had done things behind the scenes, others never got the chance to make their appearance. Several wore ghostly costumes adorned with bells. Ten or so made their way taking giant steps on tall wooden sticks that made them appear twice a person's height.

"Why'd we come out here?" I whispered to Ksenia as my mind cleared.

"Less smoke," she said. "And the lovely sight of our enemy retreating. Enjoy it."

Ryalgar stood off to one side, with her two men, but I pretended she wasn't there. Her presence made this all more difficult.

I waited until the crowd stood in place.

"We did it!" I shouted. My mouth was dry and it felt funny. "We couldn't have done it better!" I added. This would not be a long speech.

"But they were supposed to ride to the wall!" several shouted.

"What about the ones we were supposed to capture?" others asked.

"Yes, yes, the end didn't go as planned, but that's because we can't control what *they* do. We did our part perfectly. We lost no lives. Ours or theirs. Yet look at how much we frightened them. Look at them riding away from us." I gestured towards the retreat we could all see. Not one rider had turned around to look at us. "Imagine that?!"

"Now what?" Many yelled it, but they all probably thought it. *Okay, think. What do these people need to hear?*

"The afternoon ends and dark comes. The night will be cold. Everyone should find shelter and food and drink to get them by. You are in no danger, so let's keep things simple tonight, and tomorrow everyone returns home."

"You mean we're done with the likes of them?" a tall Gruenite sling shooter called out.

"Not quite, but the remaining work goes to others, and they'll do their part."

I thought that remark would suffice, but they all stared at me, wanting more. More what? *Bear scump.* I sure could've used Galen.

"Look. Ilari, all of Ilari, came together to do the most amazing thing we've ever done. Later, we'll tell these stories to our children. Sooner, we'll celebrate as we should. But tonight, just tonight, remain quiet and be calm as others finish the work. Do you understand me?"

"You're saying just because they turned and rode away doesn't mean this is over?" The tall man yelled out again. He was starting to annoy me.

"Yeah. I'm saying some negotiations have to happen before we're done with them, but that's not our concern. Everyone here is safe. Okay?" I asked him directly.

"Okay," he said.

"Good. I need to assist my sister now. Uh ... Ksenia will handle any further questions."

I really should have asked Ksenia first, but I needed to get out of there. She took the speaking device from me, and her smile told me it was all right, I should go.

As I climbed out of the wagon I heard Ksenia yelling at the crowd.

"Anyone in purple can help you. We took precautions against the valerian smoke so we're more alert than many of you. Now, who doesn't already have shelter for the night?"

I shut out her voice and walked over to join Ryalgar.

~ 27 ~

A Lot of People, a Lot of Trees, and Not Much Space

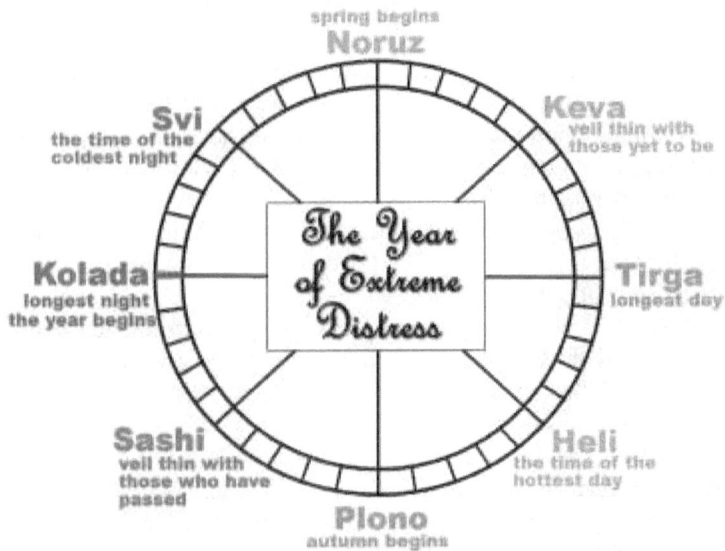

Ryalgar and her men had moved further away from my cart, and they argued in forceful tones.

"What was I supposed to tell him?" the not-the-prince said. "He's a Svadlu officer. He rode over here for a status report. I couldn't not give him one."

"You could have said we didn't know anything. It would have been largely true!" Ryalgar replied.

"No, it wouldn't have been. We just watched from a hundred paces away while these people tapped into deep Mongol fears and sent adept fighters fleeing like scared children." The not-the-prince turned to me. "Heli of a show by the way."

"Thanks."

"Let's address the obvious question first," the prince said. "Are they fleeing, or are they faking a retreat?"

"What? They fake retreats?" I asked. This wasn't good news. "I just told my people that the attackers have left for good, and they believed me. I believed me. Are they going to turn around and come at us again?"

"No," Ryalgar said. "That's not what he means. Some armies pretend to retreat, almost leaving the land they've attacked. Their adversaries think they've won and can't resist chasing them out. And then …."

I understood. "Once they've chased them far enough, the fleeing army turns around and fights. But that won't happen here, because no one is chasing them. We're just, you know, waving goodbye." I gave a wave of my hand to the eight hundred horse rumps ambling off into the distance. "Wait. Is that why they're moving so slowly? They *want* us to follow them?"

"I think so," she said. "They don't understand that you're not associated with our army. They think these tricks and traps are the work of our military, and they've had it with this type of fighting. They want us to come after them with bows and swords and engage in a battle they can win."

"Problem solved," I said. "We won't do that. We'll let them amble all the way home."

They all three looked at me. My thoughts managed to focus.

"Right," I said. "We can't let them do that. We have to negotiate. But chasing after them to talk is a bad idea because they'll turn around and fight us instead."

"Exactly," Nevik said. "They're trying to execute one strategy and, if we pursue them, they won't know we're trying to do something else."

"Then we need to sneak around and get in front of them. Be waiting for them when they try to leave Ilari." I looked at Ryalgar. She and I knew Vinx far better than the other two, and she knew what I had in mind.

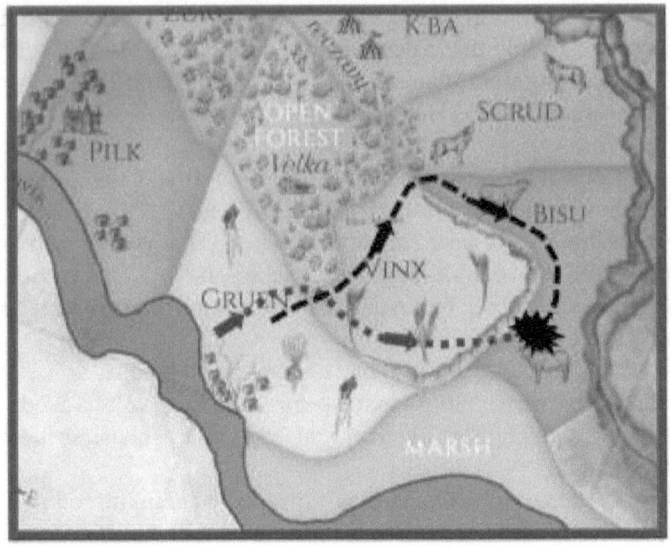

"There are paths down the cliffs of Vinx," she said. "Not good ones, not paths you could take horses down. But people could use them and then maybe find more horses in Bisu. We *could* intercept the Mongols on their way out."

"That might work it if weren't for the Svadlu," Nevik said. "The man Nikolo spoke with is back at the wall by now, and our army's leaders know that our enemy retreats. They won't leave well enough alone."

"I'd think they'd be ecstatic to do nothing," I said.

"Let me guess," Nikolo replied. "You haven't spent a lot of time around Svadlu."

"You think they're gathering up their weapons to chase our attackers out?"

"Not yet," Nevik said. "Night's coming. They know the Mongols will have to stop and camp. But I'm sure they've decided to charge after them in the morning."

He gestured out towards our slowly exiting attackers, and we all noticed a change.

"I think they've stopped."

"I think they're setting up camp! Within sight of us."

"Maybe they feel safer here where they can keep an eye on us."

"Maybe they're hoping to goad us. Give us time to get angry and chase them out in the morning."

"Probably both," Ryalgar said. "And unfortunately, the Svadlu will do the chasing for us."

"Then let's explain it to the Svadlu. Get them to hold back," I said.

They all three looked at me in disbelief.

"I can't imagine them listening," Nevik replied. "All along they wanted to save the realm but lacked the resources to do it. They'd love nothing more than to get the final credit for saving the day."

"Yeah but when the Mongols turn on them, the Svadlu won't have a chance, will they?"

"They'll have a slightly better one than they used to," Nikolo said. "This is what we came here to tell you. The Mongols sent an extra hundred horsemen in through Eds to surround our army at the very end. Ryalgar and I removed those hundred from the fight."

"Yes, but we'd also hoped to have hundreds more from the main horde captured by now," Ryalgar said, "giving our soldiers a chance. Facing eight hundred, they still have none."

"Then let's hope our adversaries don't turn and fight in Vinx," I said. "If they draw the Svadlu through Vinx and out into Bisu, we can be there to intervene."

"They *will* do that!" Ryalgar said, her face brightening. "Because they don't know we took out the hundred extra fighters. How would they? And those guys rode towards Bisu, so that's where the Mongol army expects its reinforcements. It's where they'll turn and fight." Ryalgar's cheeks glowed in the setting sun.

"Perfect. Then the Mongols will find us waiting in their path first, ready to talk before this ever happens." I supposed my cheeks glowed too.

"You're not coming," Nevik said. "It's too risky."

"Yes, I am. Hard as it may be to believe, I have some authority. I, uh, I currently rule K'ba."

"You do what?" Ryalgar said.

"How is that even possible?" Nikolo added.

Nevik stared at me, perhaps worried I'd taken leave of my senses.

"It's been a strange year out in the desolate nichnas," I said.

"Fine," Ryalgar answered. She gave Nevik a look that said *drop it for now*. "We can sort other matters out later, but I could use her help finding our path down the cliffs."

I let her keep talking.

"Tomorrow, we leave once the Mongols are out of sight. If we see the Svadlu coming we'll have to let them pass, but if we can get ahead of them, we will. It will give us more time to cut across Vinx, get down those cliffs, and be in place to intercept the Mongols."

"The four of us need excellent horses and good provisions," Nikolo said. "Can your people help us?"

"Of course."

I turned as Galen rode up. He looked exhausted from his efforts to calm down Faroojers and Gruenites who didn't understand why we hadn't simply forced the Mongols into the water where they belonged. It had taken him this long to get the entire cold, wet and angry river crew around campfires sipping on a strong dessert wine.

He wrapped his arms around me. We held each other, then I looked him in the eye.

"Sheep Scump?" I said.

He winced in anticipation.

"We have one more little problem."

"Who are these people?" he said, suspicion in his voice.

"They showed up right before the attack. Remember?"

He shook his head. "There's still foggy spots."

"Okay." I pointed to Nevik. "This one is the crown prince of Pilk."

Galen stared at him, any sort of bow the furthest thing from his mind, so I moved on.

"This one is, I don't know, a nice archery coach from Gruen. The other is my sister."

"Your sister?" he said.

"Who are you?" Ryalgar asked.

"I'm the man who loves Gypsum. Unless she asks me to do one more thing today, then maybe not."

"It's not today, it's tomorrow," I said. "Do you want to ride with us to Bisu in the morning to negotiate with the Mongols?"

His fatigue dissolved into a grin. "Does a racing horse want to run?"

He shone his smile at the other three. "I've got a bit of a flair for talking myself out of sticky situations."

Then to me. "One good night's sleep, Duck Piss, and I'm ready to go."

"What did he call you?" Ryalgar whispered as we rode back towards the settlement.

I laughed. "You heard him."

She had the wisdom to let it go along with her other questions.

I wouldn't have thought any of us could have slept with the campfires of the Mongols flickering through the trees, but I was wrong. After the day we had, we slept. And after the day they had, I guessed they slept too.

I woke the next morning filled with relief.

It was the day after Kolada. The. Day. After. And we were alive to see it.

Galen lay next to me. Beside him was my bag, filled with as many poultices as people had been able to gather. Someone must have decided I'd want them back.

My sister had likely risen early to prepare for our ride. Today I'd help her find the best path down the cliffs, and my boyfriend would help her convince the Mongols to leave us in peace.

Wait. How the pruck could he do that?

I saw her on the way to the outhouse.

"Ryalgar? Do you speak Mongolian?"

"Of course not," she said, laughing. "But they have a translator, we saw him when the envoys came to Pilk. And the Svadlu have one too, now, and I'm sure they'll bring him. Don't worry about it."

Early in the morning, the Mongol horde left, heading into Vinx in no particular hurry. We hadn't seen or heard anything from the Svadlu yet, but Ryalgar and Nevik remained positive they wouldn't be far behind.

"Now's the time to leave," she said. "We'll start on the main road, match the Mongols' pace, and hope to get to Vinx before the Svadlu overtake us, so we can hide in the forest as they ride by."

"You sure you don't want to explain our plan to them?" I asked.

S. R. Cronin

Ryalgar shook her head. "No one explains to the Svadlu. As far as they're concerned, they gave me my chance and now it's their show. I don't want to give them the opportunity to order me to stay away."

I understood. I'd operated on similar principles many a time.

She looked each of us in the face. "If they do pass us before we can hide, they'll inquire about our destination. The rest of you are escorting me up to the forest so I can return to the Velka. Nothing more."

Everyone nodded. We gathered our things, got on the finest horses that could be found, and kept a lookout in front of us and in back as we rode.

As we approached the forest where it met the border of Gruen and Vinx, we heard the hoofs behind us.

"Run," Ryalgar called out. She meant our horses, of course, and we urged our mounts on to the nearest trees and then pulled them into the brush behind us as the Svadlu come into view.

I had to admit, they looked fierce. There probably were four hundred of them, all armed and moving with the glee of an expected victory. We watched them ride by, the yellow and red capes of their leaders unfurling behind them. They'd have to slow soon to let their horses rest, but they'd have no trouble catching up with the hoard in Bisu.

After the Svadlu passed, I moved away from the others to relieve myself. I'd finished when I heard a noise and froze.

"Well, that was quite a sight!" a deep male voice said. I dropped my skirts and turned to berate the depraved man who'd watched me pee.

He wore Scrudite clothes and stood at the forest's edge, looking out to the road as the Svadlu vanished into the dust. He resembled the man who showed up with Olivine to celebrate a holiday, but perhaps my mind played tricks on me. How long did it take for this varmin valerian root to wear off?

"Sorry to disturb you, I didn't realize…" he said as he turned and figured out what I had been doing. "I think we've met," he added, giving an embarrassed shrug as he offered his hand to help me up.

So he was Olivine's boyfriend. I struggled to recall his name.

"Bohdan," he said

"What are you doing here?" I admit the circumstances made me less polite.

"I'm our lookout. We've been hiding in here since late yesterday afternoon."

"Hiding? From who?"

"From the Mongols of course. We were on our way to help you. Yesterday afternoon, after we couldn't get the Mongols' horses to throw them. We were just inside of Gruen when we saw the whole varmin hoard coming back towards us. The last thing we wanted was to run into them again, so we hightailed it into the trees here. Pretty much like you just did. Planned to come out after they rode past, but they camped for the night and came through here earlier this morning."

"Yes, we know. We're following them."

"And avoiding the Svadlu too, I see." He smiled. "Smart. So where are you off to?"

The others must have heard me talking because Ryalgar came looking for me.

"Are you okay, Gypsum?" she asked.

"I'm fine. Olivine's boyfriend is here in the forest, hiding with some others."

Ryalgar pushed her way through a couple of fronds to see us both.

"Exactly who is hiding in here with you?" she demanded.

Bohdan looked at her but didn't answer.

"I'm sorry," she said. "But I don't trust all the Velka at the moment."

"Oh." He laughed. "Don't worry. Your sisters don't either."

"And how would you know what my sisters think?"

If her words or tone offended him, he didn't show it.

"Because last night I camped with Coral," he said. "And Sulphur. And Olivine. And Celestine. That is most of them, right?

By then we'd made enough noise that Nevik and Nikolo found us, as did all the sisters Bohdan named plus two women I recognized and two men I'd never seen before. And a Mongol captive the two men kept between them.

It was a lot of people, a lot of trees and not much space.

"Let's get out of here and back on the road," I said. "Do you all have horses?"

They did. Ryalgar explained our need for speed, and we held off on greetings and conversation until we were underway.

She intended to send the others home after we exchanged news, to no one's surprise, once my four other sisters heard of Ryalgar's plan, they insisted they could help us find the best path down the cliffs. Ryalgar acquiesced. This wouldn't work unless we found that path fast.

As we rode I learned that one of the unknown men, a Faroojer, was Coral's new boyfriend. The other was a Svadlu friend of Sulphur's. I recognized one of the women as Ryalgar's Velka friend who I'd met in the early stages of planning. The other woman was easy to remember. She had come to the reczavy camp with Celestine.

Ryalgar wanted to send them all back, but each argued that they could be of help. Finally she threw out her arms in surrender. Our stealth party of five had become a band of fourteen, plus a captive.

~ 28 ~

Down the Cliff

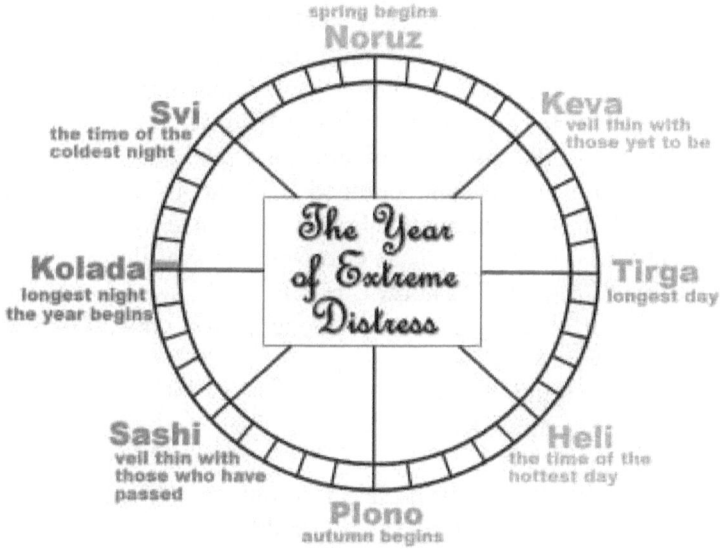

The Year of Extreme Distress

spring begins
Noruz

Svi
the time of the
coldest night

Keva
veil thin with
those yet to be

Kolada
longest night
the year begins

Tirga
longest day

Sashi
veil thin with
those who have
passed

Heli
the time of the
hottest day

Plono
autumn begins

We left the road and headed east. The cliffs of Vinx began to drop off to our right and the precipice grew larger as we traveled. We followed them as they turned and as the marsh below the cliffs changed into Bisu's grasslands. Somewhere nearby our path down waited for us.

The cliffs were the most exciting thing in Vinx, and every adolescent I knew tried to climb down them, despite every adult in the nichna warning them not to. Most gave up before they got hurt, and most shared their route with their younger siblings, swearing them to secrecy.

Ryalgar had made it an impressive third of the way down before she decided she'd gone far enough. Coral had followed Ryalgar's path but found a little cave that opened onto a better route and got further. Sulphur had taken Coral's path all the way to the bottom, but only someone with Sulphur's physical prowess could manage the lower part.

Olivine had talked Dad into taking her to Bisu with him, then used her long eyes to study the cliffs and find a better alternative to Sulphur's lower route. She and Celestine had taken it together only to discover that the climb up was more frightening. So my twin sisters had persuaded a young farmhand to give them a discreet ride home by bribing him with a song Celestine wrote for him to sing to his girlfriend.

I hated to do only what others had already done, so I took the family route down and climbed back up as well. I never wanted to do that again, but this time we only had to go down.

The others let us argue as we made our way along.

"No." "Maybe?" "I know this is it!" "I know it is not!"

"If four of us agree, we send one person down. Gypsum, what's your vote?"

"I don't think this is it."

"Three to three. Keep moving."

And we did.

"Here it is!" Five of us said it at once as we looked at the smooth dirt curving down to a small boulder.

"Sulphur, you go first," Ryalgar said, but she needn't have bothered. Sulphur was halfway to Coral's cave before Ryalgar finished speaking.

We went in an order Ryalgar devised. One more physically capable followed by one less so. Two before the captive to watch him, two above while Celestine's girlfriend Firuza kept watch with her moon glass. Sulphur's Svadlu friend went last in case of trouble.

Only one small part of the path had washed out, and Sulphur found a way around it. We hit the grasslands of Bisu and looked around, thinking it seemed easier than when we'd done it years ago. Then again, maybe we'd done so many more difficult things since.

The cliffs now loomed above us. We heard one horse neigh, then others, and walked faster towards the sounds, anxious to be mounted again.

I hung back, and Nevik slowed his steps to walk with me.

"You know, they made all the Crown Princes, or recently crowned Ruling Princes, hide together in the forest in Zur," he said as pleasantly as if he were commenting on the weather.

"Then why aren't you there?"

"I was but I snuck away with your sister and Nikolo yesterday morning. We wanted to help."

My curiosity got the better of me. "Okay. Who was there for Eds?"

"We expected Prince Lufo, but they sent his twelve-year-old brother instead. The boy told us his father and older brother died in a skirmish with K'ba so he would assume the throne. Why in Heli's name did Eds and K'ba skirmish at a time like this?"

"It's ... complicated. Did the boy tell you more?"

Nevik hesitated. "Only that against all precedent, his older sister will be his regent until he turns eighteen. Under the circumstances, we showed him all the kindness we could. I admit that Prince Lufo wasn't particularly well liked, but this kid seems decent enough."

"I hear he is."

We looked at each other, both unsure of whether we wanted to discuss K'ba.

Nevik went for it.

"We didn't know who to expect from K'ba. For the longest time, some administrator named Andre traveled to Pilk to convey the K'basta Royals' wishes, claiming poor health on everyone's part. But even Andre sent someone in his place this time."

"Who?"

Nevik laughed. "At first we thought he was Andre's son, which would have been odd enough, but eventually we learned he was a messenger whom Andre hired. Uncanny likeness between the two. When pressed for information, the messenger said K'ba was in flux, and he had been sent to hold the place on K'ba's behalf."

"The K'basta have chosen a new Royal of their own," I said.

"People can do that?" He searched my face for confirmation of what he suspected. I guess he found it. "You mean you? A reczavy? A woman? A ..."

"Yes, the list of ways I'm not qualified goes on. Don't bother reciting it. For the moment, I'm their hero, and Galen has convinced them that a hero should lead them."

"I see."

We looked at each other again.

"I'll give you all the support I can."

"Thank you. I don't intend to be in the job for long."

"That may be best," he said.

"I couldn't agree more."

We left it at that.

We took twelve riding horses from the abandoned ranch and crept along the bottom of the cliffs in silence. What awaited us? We didn't know, but advertising our presence wouldn't help.

We heard a rustle in the bushes then Coral's boyfriend yelled. She rode in front of him, and her gasp followed. We turned to see an arrow in his bleeding shoulder as two men on horseback shot out of the bushes and sped off to the west.

"I think they're the last of the ones we took out," Nikolo said.

"Probably. Heli, these people are persistent," Nevik agreed.

Rooslin and Sulfur moved in to tend the wound and Coral fashioned a sling to hold his arm close to his chest.

"Are those two going to keep shooting at us?" Celestine demanded to know. She pointed. Their horses were now visible in the bushes further along our path.

"No, they're not." Olivine answered. "Joli? Want to do this?"

"How about you get one, and we'll get the other," Ryalgar said gesturing to Nikolo.

"Won't a couple of dead bodies sabotage our negotiations?" I asked.

"Oh they won't be dead," Olivine said. "This poison only makes them look dead for a while and we've got poison arrows meant for people." She turned to Nikolo. "Here. Have two."

He rolled his eyes at the implied insult but took them both.

Although the others had seen it often, I'd never seen the oomrushers and long eyes work together to shoot arrows impossibly long distances. I watched in wonder. Olivine assured me both would be unconscious for a while.

We rode on, reverting to silence. Then we heard them. Hoofs, moving at a fast pace towards us. As soon as we recognized the sound, we galloped away from the cliff face, the better to see and be seen as they rounded the cliff's bend.

Once we came within view of each other, we knew they saw us. We knew it because the wall of horses coming at us split effortlessly into two streams. One would pass us on the left, the other on the right. They had no intention of slowing down because we were in the middle of their path.

Perhaps they'd given up on the Svadlu chasing them. Maybe they wanted to make it to where they expected a hundred more reinforcements. Whatever their reasoning, fourteen of us couldn't stop them.

I saw the look of panic on our prisoner's face. He did not wish to be left behind.

He held his wrists out to Sulphur in a universal plea to cut his bonds. She hesitated, but she did it. He responded by leaping into a standing position on the horse they shared. As if that wasn't enough of an acrobatic feat, he then began waving his arms and shouting.

It was hard to miss a man standing on a horse yelling, and his choice of hairstyle, two ponytails on top of his head, made him easy to recognize. The front of the stream on the left began to slow down, preparing to stop. The right one kept moving until they passed us. Then they came to a stop as well.

We were fourteen people surrounded by eight hundred angry warriors and armed only with our wits and good intentions. Our inability to speak Mongolian rendered those assets useless.

They were going to kill us, rescue our captive, and leave. I couldn't think of a single reason why they'd do anything else.

"Send the prisoner out to them," I begged Sulphur.

"Why? He's our only hope," she said.

"No he isn't. I've got an idea but we can't give them a good reason to think too hard about it. Please. Trust me."

I know only a few heartbeats passed, but it felt like many more as a lot of emotions crossed my sister's face. Then she dismounted, pulled Two Ponytails off their shared horse, and pushed him towards his army.

He gave her a questioning look. Was shooting prisoners in the back our way? She smiled and motioned for him to go. That was good enough. He broke into a sprint and ran to his people.

I dismounted and removed my pouch. Of course, I'd brought the bag of poultices they'd picked up off the ground yesterday, knowing the fear my little creations invoked in our attackers. Many of them were stuck together in the bag, but I pulled enough free to form a large circle around the fourteen of us and then began filling it in with stuck-together extras.

"What are you doing?" Joli asked.

"Using the one thing we have that they're scared of. I don't know why they are, and I don't care."

No one else said a word. By the time I'd finished making a pretty impressive ring of the little bags, our attackers had ridden close enough for the leader, the big man with no hair, to look me in the eye.

He stared down at the poultices from his horse, considering.

I crossed my arms defiantly and stared back. *Oh yes, I'm a very bad witch.*

Then he saw something behind me and his eyes widened.

"Bowl. Chi," he yelled, pointing at Celestine.

"You two have met?" I asked her over my shoulder.

"Yeah. It didn't go so well. I don't think he likes me."

"Wonderful. Come stand next to me. Maybe he'll dislike the two of us together even more."

But my other sisters couldn't let well enough alone. The other four hopped off their horses and joined Celestine and me, forming a line of narrowed eyes and crossed arms as each of us tried to look as dangerous as possible.

The funny thing was, a year earlier I'd have said you couldn't find six less dangerous women. But it wasn't true. Not anymore. Each of us had dug deep into dark places over the past year, and the looks we gave were backed by actions we might never wish to discuss. I think the message came through. He stared back, hesitating, wondering what he faced.

I knew the stand-off wouldn't last long, and it wouldn't end well for us when it failed.

But it did buy us time, and time was what we needed most.

I heard the hoofs. We all heard them.

Our Svadlu, who I'd characterized as woefully inept and insufferably pompous, rode to our rescue. Well, not exactly to our rescue because they didn't know we were here or that we needed help, but their appearance on the horizon changed everything.

The Mongols turned towards the incoming arrivals, who were a far more formidable force than the fourteen of us, and left us in our circle. I turned to the others, afraid we'd run out of tricks.

"You should consider heading for cover while you can," Sulphur said to us. "Perhaps you can continue to shoot at them from a safe distance," she added to Olivine.

"What about you?" Coral asked.

"Rooslin and I fight with the Svadlu, of course" she answered. Rooslin didn't look quite as sure.

"No!" Ryalgar barked it out as an order. "I need you, all of you, here with me to make this negotiation take place."

"It's not going to occur," Nevik said gently.

"I don't believe that," Ryalgar said. "Stay here, I beg you. We don't know what will happen when the Svadlu get closer."

She was right. We looked at her, we looked at each other, and none of us moved. Instead, we watched the saffron and crimson capes at the front of our army grow more visible. Then Olivine began to jump up and down.

"Look! Iolite! She rides with the Svadlu! I can see her. She's near the front."

We all squinted into the distance but none of us could distinguish any of the riders.

"Are you sure?" Ryalgar asked.

"Positive."

A smile spread across Ryalgar's face. "I knew it would somehow take all seven of us to get this done." She turned to the others with us. "Be patient. I promise you, this isn't over yet."

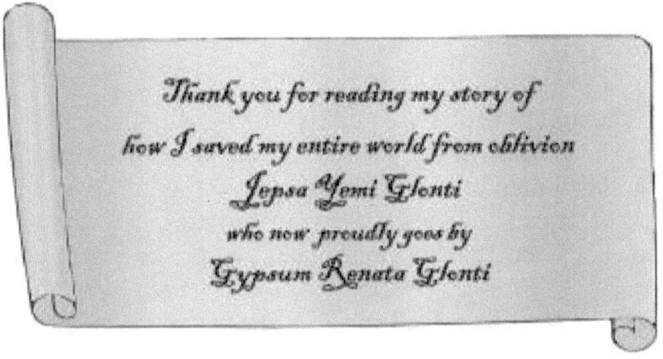

Thank you for reading my story of

how I saved my entire world from oblivion

Jepsa Yemi Glonti

who now proudly goes by

Gypsum Renata Glonti

About These Books

The War Stories of the Seven Troublesome Sisters consists of seven short companion novels. Each tells the personal story and perspective of one of seven radically different sisters in the 1200s as they prepare for an invasion of their realm. While each of these historical fantasy/alternate history books can be enjoyed as stand-alone novels, together they tell the full story of how Ilari survived

Which sister do you think saves Ilari? That will depend on whose story you are reading. How do they save it? Each sister will offer you surprising information on why this didn't go as planned.

Want to make sure you don't miss a release? Go to my landing page at https://mailchi.mp/11db23804c68/tell-me-about-new-books to be notified when each book is ready for purchase. I promise you'll only get notifications about the release of these books.

If you enjoyed this story, please leave a review somewhere. If you enjoyed it a lot, please leave a review in several places.☺

About the Author

Sherrie Cronin is the author of a collection of six speculative fiction novels known as 46. Ascending and is now publishing a historical fantasy series called The War Stories of the Seven Troublesome Sisters. A quick look at the synopses of her books makes it obvious she is fascinated by people achieving the astonishing by developing abilities they barely knew they had.

She's made a lot of stops along the way to writing these novels. She's lived in seven cities, visited forty-six countries, and worked as a waitress, technical writer, and geophysicist. Now she answers a hot-line. Along the way, she's lost several cats but acquired a husband who still loves her and three kids who've grown up fine, both despite how eccentric she is.

All her life she has wanted to either tell these kinds of stories or be Chief Science Officer on the Starship Enterprise. She now lives and writes in the mountains of Western North Carolina, where she admits to occasionally checking her phone for a message from Captain Picard, just in case.

Find her at:
Facebook: facebook.com/46Ascending
Goodreads: goodreads.com/author/show/5805814.Sherrie_Cronin
Amazon: amazon.com/Sherrie-Cronin/e/B007FRMO9Q
Twitter: twitter.com/cinnabar01
Book Series Blog: troublesome7sisters.xyz/

About Ilari

Words Used by Ilarians

Ank: Nine days. Business is conducted during the first six days while the last three are intended for family life and leisure.

Heli: The hottest time of the year, but sometimes used as a cussword.

Frundle: A person born with a condition that mildly alters their appearance, causes some health problems, and leaves them prone to visions of the future and other psychic experiences.

Luski: A feared, possibly imaginary person who can control others with her voice.

Mozdol: A member of the Svadlu who has been made into an honorary prince due to brave actions defending the realm.

Nichna: One of the twelve principalities of Ilari. Each has its own royal family and is ruled by a prince. All twelve coordinate as regards the Svadlu and other matters of the common good. There is no king, therefore Ilari is not a kingdom.

Oomrush: telekinesis.

Pruck: An extremely rude word sometimes referring to copulation and other times merely expressing disgust or dismay.

Pruska: An extremely rude word referring to a female having any number of undesirable qualities.

Rantallion: A man who is being disagreeable, dishonest, or disgusting.

Reczavy: a group of free-spirited people living in the open forest who choose to continue and extend the sexual freedom allowed to tidzys.

Scump: a rude word referring to excrement.

Svadlu: The Ilarian army and police force. A member of the Svadlu is called a Svadlu.

Tidzy: A young adult who is searching for a mate and is allowed a great deal of sexual freedom around holidays.

Velka: A group of women who live in the open forest, possibly performing magic. A member of the Velka is called a Velka.

The Ilarian Calendar

A year in Ilari is divided into eight parts based on the seasons. Each eighth lasts for 45 days and is named for the holiday at its start.

Each eighth is subdivided into five anks. An ank is nine days long. Businesses and schools are open during the first six days of an ank while the last three, called the ank-break, are intended for family life and relaxation.

Every year astronomers consult the stars to decide which of the holidays will be inside their eighth and which will be treated as extra days. Most years, five or six are ruled to be extra days.

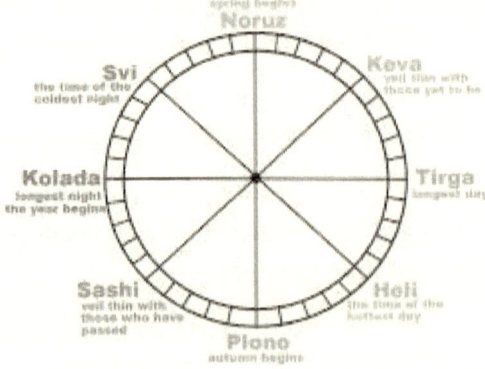

Holidays Marking the Beginning of Each Eighth

Kolada: The winter solstice, the shortest day of the year, and the start of a new year.

Svi: The coldest time of the year, halfway between the winter solstice and the spring equinox.

Noruz: The spring equinox, the start of spring.

Keva: A celebration of those yet to be, held halfway between the spring equinox and the summer solstice. More babies are conceived at Keva than at any other time of the year.

Tirga: The summer solstice, the longest day of the year, the halfway point of a year.

Heli: The hottest time of the year, halfway between the summer solstice and the autumn equinox. Ilarians are not fond of the heat and sometimes use "Heli" as a cussword.

Plono: The autumn equinox, the start of autumn.

Sashi: A celebration of those who have passed, held halfway between the fall equinox and the winter solstice.

The Twelve Nichnas

Ilari is a small hidden land consisting of twelve principalities.

The Entrance
Bisu: These low grasslands at the eastern edge of Ilari supply coveted beef and cows' milk to Ilarians.

The Dry Lands
Scrud: Rain-deprived Scrud is the poorest and least populated of the nichnas and the most lacking in natural resources. Most Scrudites survive by taking menial jobs in adjoining Bisu or K'ba.
K'ba: This drought-stricken nichna has survived by becoming home to artists, entertainers, and those seeking more freedom of choice. It is also a playground for the richest Ilarians and boasts a densely populated area known for its spectacular food and lodging.
Eds: These dry hills leading up to the mountains are sparsely populated with independent-minded goat herders.

The Mountains
Tolo: Home to the highest mountains in Ilari, independent Tolovians mine for ore, produce lumber, and serve as a gateway to the even higher mountains to the north.

The Farmlands
Lev: This nichna is home to the realm's famed vineyards and supplies Ilarians with wine, their most important beverage. It also leads the fashion scene and sparks trends within the realm.
Kir: Ilari's oldest farming region nestles between Pilk and Lev and grows specialty items for the connoisseurs in both of its neighboring nichnas.
Gruen: The fertile soil along the river makes for easy farming of fruits and vegetables and makes Gruen home to one of the two more densely populated areas outside of Pilk.
Vinx: With incredibly flat land sitting above cliffs, the high plains of Vinx provide the wheat, oats, rye, and barley that are the staples of an Ilarian's diet.

The Wet Lands

Faroo: This flood-prone nichna in the rivers bend struggles during heavy rains, but is known for fishing and the boating prowess of its residents.

Pilk: As the informal capital of Ilari, Pilk is home to the Svadlu headquarters, most of the institutes of higher learning, and much of the commerce in the realm. The ruling prince of Pilk coordinates cooperation among the twelve ruling princes. The Pilk Palace outshines any other building in Ilari.

The Forest

Zur: As the only nichna inside of Ilari's large central forest, Zur shares the woods with occupants of the Open Forest including the Velka, the reczavy, and scrounger Scrudites.

Map of Ilari

Meet the Ilarians in this Book

Aliz: Gypsum's grandmother
Andre: caretaker of the K'ba castle
Celestine: Gypsum's older sister, a musician
Coral: Gypsum's older sister, a luski
Esteri: Gypsum's tentmate
Galen: Gypsum's boyfriend from Eds (also called Sheep Scump)
Guy: one of 2 reczavy thread-worker Faroojers helping Gypsum
Gypsum: sixth of the seven sisters
Idris: Velka from Eds who wants to be a reczavy
Iolite: Gypsum's younger sister, a frundle
Jepsa: Gypsum's original name, given to her by her birth mother
Jofim: Gypsum's tentmate
Ksenia: leader of Gypsum's tent
Lufo: crown prince of Eds
Liya: Gypsum's birth mother's name
Markita: Gypsum's mother
Melda: caretaker of the K'ba prince
Nan: Idris's childhood friend, princess of Eds
Olivine: Gypsum's older sister, an artist and a long eye
Pie: one of 2 reczavy thread-worker Faroojers helping Gypsum
Raheem: Gypsum's tentmate
Renata: family middle name of Markita and her six daughters
Ryalgar: Gypsum's oldest sister, a member of the Velka
Suloom: Gypsum's tentmate and Galen's close friend
Sulphur: Gypsum's older sister, a member of the Svadlu
Varla: Gypsum's tentmate and close friend
Yasen: Gypsum's father
Yemi: Aliz and Gypsum's mother's middle name, Gypsum's original middle name

www.ingramcontent.com/pod-product-compliance
Lightning Source LLC
Chambersburg PA
CBHW022009170626
46808CB00001B/343